Praise for *The Art of Being Normal*

Winner of the Waterstones Children's Book Prize
Sunday Times Children's Book of the Week
Shortlisted for the YA Book Prize

'A life-changing and life-saving book' *Philip Pullman*

'A sensational, heart-warming and life-affirming debut'
Juno Dawson

'The sort of book I hope will change lives. Amazing'
Non Pratt

'Please, please, please read *The Art of Being Normal*!
I want to scream from the rooftops about it!' *Lucy Powrie*

'Impressive and affecting' *Guardian*

'Passionate and gripping . . . a powerful tale of a
teenager's struggle with identity' *Telegraph*

'Heart-warming, and ground-breaking' *Independent*

'Life-affirming' *Marie Claire*

'A compelling story with a ton of heart' *BuzzFeed*

'Incredible and heartbreaking' *Express*

'Life-affirming, powerful and heart-warming' *BookTrust*

'A revelation' *Books for Keeps*

'Wow' *Fiona Noble, The Bookseller*

Praise for *Paper Avalanche*

One of *The Times'* Biggest Children's Books of 2019

'Pacy, instantly absorbing' *Guardian*

'Relatable characters and well-crafted dialogue make this a thoroughly engaging read' *Financial Times*

'Poignant, thought-provoking and intensely readable, this is UK YA writing at its best' *The Bookseller*

Praise for *All About Mia*

'Absorbing, hilarious . . . witty and touching' *Guardian*

'This zingy rites of passage novel is filled with warmth and insight' *Financial Times*

'Mia is a chaotic, charming character and one of the most irresistible teenage voices I've read in a long time' *Fiona Noble, The Bookseller*

'A tumultuous but poignant tale about family, friendship and being a sister' *Sun*

FIRST DAY OF MY LIFE

www.davidficklingbooks.com

Also by Lisa Williamson:

The Art of Being Normal
All About Mia
Paper Avalanche
Malala (Yousafzai) – First Names Series

Co-written:

Floored

LISA WILLIAMSON

FIRST DAY OF MY LIFE

David Fickling Books

31 Beaumont Street
Oxford OX1 2NP, UK

First Day of My Life
is a
DAVID FICKLING BOOK

First published in Great Britain in 2021 by
David Fickling Books,
31 Beaumont Street,
Oxford, OX1 2NP

Text © Lisa Williamson, 2021

978-1-78845-153-6

1 3 5 7 9 10 8 6 4 2

Papers used by David Fickling Books are from well-
managed forests and other responsible sources.

MIX
Paper from
responsible sources
FSC® C018072

DAVID FICKLING BOOKS Reg. No. 8340307

A CIP catalogue record for this book is available from the British Library.

Typeset by Falcon Oast Graphic Art Ltd, www.falcon.uk.com
Printed and bound in Great Britain by Clays Ltd, Elcograf S.p.A.

For Mum, Dad and Helen

Prologue

OPERATOR: Emergency. Which service? Fire, police or ambulance?

CALLER: (*breathless*) Police!

OPERATOR: Connecting you now.

POLICE CALL HANDLER: You're through to the police. What is the address or location of your emergency?

CALLER: (*hysterical*) Someone's taken her! Someone's taken my baby!

POLICE CALL HANDLER: Can you repeat that please?

CALLER: My baby! She's gone! Please, you need to help me!

Caller breaks down in tears.

POLICE CALL HANDLER: OK, I need you to listen to me. Can you tell me your exact location?

CALLER: (*inaudible – voice muffled*)

POLICE CALL HANDLER: I'm sorry, I didn't quite catch that. Can you say that again, please?

CALLER: I'm in Newfield. Newfield, Nottingham. The BP garage on Larwood Avenue. Please, you need to do something. They've got my baby.

POLICE CALL HANDLER: A unit is on their way. Can I get some more details from you? What's your name?

CALLER: It's Caroline, Caroline Sinclair.

POLICE CALL HANDLER: OK, Caroline. When did you realize your baby was missing?

CALLER: Just now. I came back to the car and she was gone. I was only inside for a few minutes. Oh God . . .

Caller starts crying again.

POLICE CALL HANDLER: How old is the baby?

CALLER: (*inaudible*)

POLICE CALL HANDLER: Caroline, how old is the baby?

CALLER: She's twelve weeks.

POLICE CALL HANDLER: And what's her name?

CALLER: It's Olivia.

Caller becomes hysterical again.

POLICE CALL HANDLER: Try not to panic, Caroline. A unit will be with you very soon.

CALLER: Tell them to hurry, please! I just want my baby back. I just want my baby.

PART ONE

FRANKIE

Chapter 1

'Jojo, it's me. Where the flip are you? I've got to be at the salon by midday, remember? If you're not here by eleven, I'm going without you, OK?'

I hang up and place my phone face down on the table.

'Still here?' my eighteen-year-old brother Luca asks, making me jump.

'It's not polite to sneak up on people,' I tell him as he lumbers into the kitchen, wearing nothing but a pair of grimy-looking boxer shorts.

'As if I'd waste my time,' he retorts, opening the fridge, then letting out a lingering belch as he peruses the contents.

'You could at least put a T-shirt on,' I say, scrunching up my nose in disgust.

'Are you joking? It's thirty-three degrees already,' he replies, shutting the fridge and opening the freezer below. He sticks his hand into the almost-empty bag of ice cubes and pulls out a fistful, stuffing them into his mouth.

'I hope you washed your hands.'

'Maybe. Maybe not,' he says, grinning as he crunches down on the ice.

'You're disgusting.'

'Why, thank you,' he says, performing a little bow.

I drag one of Mum's rubbish magazines across the table towards me and pretend to concentrate on an article about a woman who's convinced her goldfish is actually her dead husband, while Luca bangs about making toast.

Mum and Dad purposefully had Luca and me close together (there's just eighteen months between us), in the hope we'd get on. Their plan backfired spectacularly. In fact, Mum reckons if bickering were an Olympic sport, the two of us would have a clutch of gold medals by now.

I didn't think it was possible, but just lately Luca's been even more of a pain than usual. He picked up his A level results last week, and despite barely revising got more than enough points to secure his place at Bristol. He's been lording it about ever since, making out he's God's gift to academia.

'You know what your problem is, Frankie?' he says, leaning against the sink while he waits for his toast to pop up.

'Enlighten me,' I say, rolling my eyes.

'You've got no tolerance.'

'Now that's where you're wrong. I've got no tolerance for you, Luca Ricci.'

'Nah, you're the same with everyone. No wonder Jojo's ditched you.'

'Erm, excuse me?'

'I heard you leaving that arsey voicemail just now.'

I close the magazine. 'So you *were* eavesdropping on me?'

'Don't flatter yourself, Frankie, you're not that interesting. I had no choice. You've got a voice like a foghorn.'

'It's called projection,' I snap. 'And for your information, I wasn't being arsey, Luca, I was being direct. Jojo's nearly an hour late.'

I gesture at the oven clock. 10:59.

'Maybe she went to school without you,' Luca suggests, slathering butter on his toast.

'And why would she do that? We had an arrangement.'

Jojo was due to call for me at 10 a.m. From here, we were going to walk to school together, pick up our GCSE results, then celebrate/commiserate* (*delete as appropriate) over a McDonald's breakfast before my shift at the hair salon, reconvening in the early evening for a party at our classmate Theo's house.

'*We had an arrangement*,' Luca repeats in a high-pitched voice.

I chuck the magazine at him. He dodges out of the way just in time, leaving it to land in the sink.

'When are you going to uni again?' I ask, standing up.

'You'll miss me when I'm gone.'

'Yeah, right,' I mutter, hoisting the slightly soggy magazine out of the washing-up bowl.

I deposit it on the table and glance back at the oven. 11:00.

'Looks like you're on your own,' Luca says, wiping his buttery fingers on his boxer shorts.

'Oh, piss off,' I reply, picking up my phone and marching out of the kitchen.

'Good luck!' he yells after me. 'Something tells me you're gonna need it!'

Swearing under my breath, I slam the front door behind me and set out across the green that separates our row of houses from the main road. Not that it's especially green right now. We're in the midst of a massive heatwave, and every patch of publicly owned grass in Newfield, the town where I live, has been bleached a dirty shade of yellow.

I thought it was amazing at first. After a damp, miserable start to the summer, I rejoiced at the rocketing temperatures and record hours of sunshine. Fast-forward seventeen days and I'm well and truly over it. I'm over waking up every morning covered in a sticky layer of sweat. I'm over the constant noisy whir of the fan next to my bed. I'm over wearing the same shorts and vest-top combinations. But most of all, I'm over feeling knackered all the time. I've only been walking for a few minutes and already my breathing is heavy and laboured, sweat trickling down the back of my neck. I stop walking and remove a bobble from around my wrist, sweeping my already damp long dark-brown hair into a messy topknot.

Today must be one of the hottest days so far. The air is thick and syrupy and the tarmac so hot it shines like liquid. I squint up at the sky, an ominous shade of dull blue dotted with sickly yellow clouds, and wonder if today might be the day when it finally breaks and we get the thunderstorm the weather forecasters keep promising is just around the corner.

I cross the road, and then take a left down Temple Street, before turning onto Larwood Avenue.

Only it's blocked off by a length of police cordon tape.

I frown. If I don't go down Larwood, I'll have to go the long way round, and I'm cutting it fine as it is.

I glance behind me to check no one is looking before diving under the cordon.

I've walked maybe two house lengths when I hear footsteps behind me.

'Oi! Where do you think you're going?' a voice calls.

Reluctantly, I turn round.

A police officer is striding towards me wearing a deep frown. 'And what do you think you're playing at?' he asks.

'I'm going to school,' I reply with a shrug.

'In August?'

'It's GCSE results day.'

'I don't care what day it is. Did you not see the cordon?'

'The cordon?'

'Yes, the cordon.'

He points. I turn around and pretend to notice the cordon tape for the first time.

'Oh my God, I totally didn't see it there,' I say, shaking my head in wonderment.

The police officer folds his arms across his chest and sighs. 'Funny that, considering I watched you duck right under it less than thirty seconds ago.'

'Did you really?' I say, blinking in confusion. 'Wow, I literally have no recollection of doing that.' I laugh a tinkling laugh. 'I must be more preoccupied with my results than I thought.'

I give him my very best smile. (For the record, I have a great smile. 'Dangerous', according to my ex-boyfriend Ram. Like Julia Roberts in *Pretty Woman*, according to Maxine, my boss at the salon.) The police officer just glares back, somehow immune to its usual powers.

'Can I go now?' I ask. 'It's just that I'm kind of running late.'

He sighs. 'Go on, then.'

I smile – maybe he's not so bad after all – and thank him, before continuing up the street.

'Er, what do you think you're doing?' he calls after me.

I turn back to face him. 'You said I could go.'

'Yes. Back the way you've come. This street is a crime scene.'

'A crime scene?' I ask, screwing up my face.

'Yes.'

I peer up Larwood Avenue. Apart from the cordon tape, a few police cars and some official-looking people milling about, nothing appears to be out of the ordinary. No blood splatters or chalk outlines or forensics tents.

'What sort of crime scene?' I ask.

'None of your business.'

'But if I don't cut down here, I have to go all the way around.'

'Not my problem,' the police officer says, walking me back towards the cordon.

Chapter 2

By the time I get to school, most people have been and gone and the foyer is empty apart from Mr Devi, the head of Year Eleven, and Mrs Schulman, the deputy head.

They're sitting at a table in front of the entrance to the main hall. They look weird in their off-duty summer clothes. I can see Mrs Schulman's lacy bra straps peeking from beneath the straps of her sundress, while Mr Devi is wearing a pair of truly hideous salmon-coloured shorts and some Velcro sandals so ugly I can barely bring myself to look at them.

'Frankie,' he says as I approach. 'Great to see you. Having a good summer?'

'Yes, thanks, sir,' I reply automatically.

The truth is, although I'm not having a bad summer exactly, it's far from the life-defining fun-fest I imagined it would be. It hasn't helped that for three weeks of it, Jojo has been ill with a horribly contagious virus. I hadn't realized just how many of my summer plans revolved around her until she suddenly wasn't available.

There are two boxes on the table. One marked A–M, a second marked N–Z. While Mrs Schulman delves into the second box, I attempt to peer into the first. Only three envelopes remain, but the box is too deep for me to make out whether one of them is addressed to Jojo or not.

'Here we are,' Mrs Schulman says, handing me my envelope. 'Ricci, Francesca.'

I thank her and take it outside, sitting down on the steps. The concrete is hot against the back of my thighs.

As I turn the envelope over in my hands, I can't help but think back to the last time I opened something so official-looking.

It was back in April and I'd just got home from school. The letter was propped up against the fruit bowl on the kitchen table, the Arts Academy's distinctive logo printed next to the postmark. My heart racing, I rang Jojo straightaway to check if she'd got her letter too, then we put our phones on speaker and opened them together on the count of three.

I can still remember the growing heat in my cheeks as I read the contents, my disappointment red-hot. And the cooling numbness that quickly replaced it when Jojo said the three little words that I'd been so sure were destined to be part of *my* script.

I got in.

I shove the memory away and slide my finger under the flap of the brown envelope, pulling out the computer printout tucked inside.

My eyes scan the list of grades.

A three in maths.

Fours, fives and sixes in everything else.

Except drama.

For drama, I got a nine.

The very top grade. Literally, the best you can get.

'Typical,' a familiar voice says. 'The second I finally nip off for a loo break, you turn up.'

I look up. My drama teacher, Ms Abraham, is standing over me, wearing a denim pinafore dress over a white vest top and a pair of canary yellow flip-flops.

I like Ms Abraham a lot. She's older than she looks (I know for a fact she's at least forty), but she still manages to be cool and fun at the same time as being a really good teacher. Before she did her teacher training, she was a professional actor in London, although she claims she never quite hit the big time. She reckons the closest she got was understudying Naomie Harris at the National Theatre.

'But that's massive,' I said when she told us one lesson. 'Why didn't you just keep going?'

She just shrugged. 'Dreams change, Frankie.'

I looked around the draughty drama studio and pulled a face. 'No offence, miss, but this is not my idea of a dream.'

That earned me a poke in the ribs from Jojo. Not that Ms Abraham seemed to mind what I'd said. She just smiled an enigmatic smile and told me I'd get it one day.

'What are you doing here, miss?' I ask as she sits down beside me, tucking her dress between her legs.

'Just helping out,' she says. 'It was absolute bedlam earlier.' She nods at the piece of paper on my lap. 'Congratulations on that nine, by the way.'

'Oh, thanks,' I say, shoving it back in the envelope, suddenly self-conscious.

'You should be really proud,' she adds. 'You worked bloody hard for that.'

I don't say anything.

'I mean it, Frankie,' she insists. 'Do you know what percentage of students manage a nine in drama?'

'No.'

'I'll tell you. It's five. Five per cent.'

'Is Jojo also one of them?' The question leaves my lips before I can stop it.

Ms Abraham tilts her head to one side. 'Does it make a difference if she is or isn't?' she asks.

I shrug. 'No.'

Yes.

There's a pause. Ms Abraham has painted her toenails coral. She must have done it at home herself because it's a bit messy, specks of polish clinging to her cuticles.

'Frankie,' she says. 'I know you may not want to hear this, but I'm really looking forward to having you in my A level class this coming term. Seriously, the Arts Academy's loss is my gain.'

'Thanks, miss,' I say. 'But you really don't have to do this.'

She raises an eyebrow as if to say, 'Don't I?'

'Honestly, miss, I'm not bothered. It was ages ago now. And yeah, I wanted to get in at the time, but I've had the summer to think about things, and the truth is, I'm not sure it's the right place for me anyway.'

'Really?' she says, continuing to look doubtful.

The Arts Academy is a free specialist arts college, the only one of its kind in the whole of the Midlands. Entrance for the acting strand is ultra-competitive and by audition only. Ms Abraham was the one who told Jojo and me about it in the first place; the one who encouraged us to apply for a place in Year Twelve; the one who wrote our references, and helped us pick out audition pieces.

'Really,' I say. 'I mean, I'm sure Jojo will get on just fine there, but, I dunno, it just struck me as a bit regimented, you know? A bit stuck up its own arse.'

'Oh,' Ms Abraham says, blinking. 'Right. Well, I have to say, I'm a bit relieved.'

I frown. 'Relieved? Why relieved?'

'Well, to be honest, I've been a bit worried about you, Frankie.'

'Me?' I say, screwing up my face.

'Yes. You.'

'Why?'

'I know how badly you wanted to get in. I hated the idea of you getting despondent based on this one disappointment. Especially when you've got so much talent.'

Have I, though? Surely if I was that talented we wouldn't even be having this conversation right now. I'd be too busy preparing for my first term at the Arts Academy.

'Yeah, well that was then and this is now, and I'm totally over it,' I say.

Ms Abraham continues to look unsure.

I laugh. 'Seriously, miss, there's no need to look so worried. It's ancient history, I swear.'

Finally her face melts into a smile. 'Well, that's great to hear, Frankie,' she says, nudging my shoulder with hers. 'Really bloody fantastic.'

My phone buzzes in my bag.

''Scuse me, miss,' I say, getting it out.

It's a WhatsApp message from Mum.

> Well???

My eyes drift to the time in the top right-hand corner of the screen. I'm supposed to be at the salon in less than ten minutes. Maxine's usually pretty good if I'm ever a bit late, but I don't want to take the piss when she's already given me the morning off as paid leave.

'I'd better get going,' I say, clambering to my feet. 'Work.'

Ms Abraham stands up to join me. 'Is Jojo on her way, do you know?' she asks.

'Why? Has she not come in yet?'

'No. Her envelope's still here. I assumed you'd come together.'

'Yeah, well, that was the plan . . .'

Ms Abraham's expression turns serious once more. 'Everything's OK between the two of you now, isn't it?'

'Course,' I say. 'Fine. Something must have come up, that's all. I'll give her a ring on my way to work and see what's up.' I pull my backpack onto my shoulders. The canvas straps are damp with sweat from where they've been wedged under my armpits.

'I'm really glad we got the chance to chat, Frankie,' Ms Abraham says. 'I'm so pleased you haven't taken the Arts Academy thing to heart.'

'Course I haven't,' I say. 'I mean, at the end of the day, it's just a school, right?'

14

She nods and smiles, and I know I've said the right thing.

We say our goodbyes and I walk briskly towards the gates, my lie reverberating in my ears.

Because it's not just a school.

It's *the* school.

And Jojo is going and I'm not.

Chapter 3

My colleagues at the hair salon have clubbed together and bought me a box of Ferrero Rocher and an oversized card with 'Congratulations' splashed across the front. It's really sweet of them, but I can't help but feel a bit embarrassed considering my pretty ordinary results. I keep the details vague to save face but can't help letting slip about my nine in drama, my voice glittering with automatic pride.

'Now, what's a nine again?' Alison, the receptionist, asks. 'It was just A, B, C, D, E or F back in my day.'

'A nine is like an A-plus I guess, only better,' I say.

They all make impressed noises.

'Just make sure you remember us when you're rich and famous,' Maxine says with a grin.

'Will do,' I promise.

Maxine's salon isn't remotely cool. The black and white photos of hair models hanging in the window are at least thirty years old and it caters almost exclusively for old ladies, but as part-time jobs go, it could be a lot worse. The work (making cups of tea, washing hair, sweeping the floor) is easy enough, and I like the other staff a lot.

I offer around the chocolates before stowing them away in the staff-room fridge. When I return, I'm straight on tea duty, making a cup of Earl Grey (not too strong, splash of milk, two sugars) for Ida, one of our regulars.

'Absolutely dreadful,' she says as I place it down in front of her.

'You haven't tasted it yet, Ida,' I joke.

She tuts. 'I'm talking about the baby.'

'What baby?' I ask, balancing a Rich Tea biscuit on the edge of her saucer.

'The missing baby,' Maggie – one of the senior stylists – says, pulling a comb through Ida's pure white hair. 'You know.'

'No. What missing baby?'

'The baby that's gone missing from Larwood Avenue.'

'Larwood Avenue? I tried to walk down it about an hour ago. It's all cordoned off.'

'Well, you know the petrol station?'

I nod. It's about halfway up the road, near the alleyway that comes out onto Heaton Way. They have a Krispy Kreme fridge. Jojo and I used to go there after school on a Friday and split an original glazed (Jojo's choice) or a chocolate-iced custard-filled (mine). I don't know exactly when or why we stopped doing it, only that it's been months since we did.

'Well,' Maggie says. 'Someone nicked a baby right out of the back of a car parked just outside.'

'When?' I ask.

'This morning,' Ida says. 'In broad daylight too!'

'Didn't the baby's parents or whoever try and stop them?'

'That's the thing,' Maggie says. 'The baby's mum was inside at the time, getting a coffee. She says she swears she locked the car door.'

'Only she clearly couldn't have,' Ida chimes in. 'Because by the time she got back' – she clicks her fingers – 'the baby was gone.'

'Isn't it all on CCTV?'

'No,' Maggie says. 'There are cameras on the pumps, but she was parked in the little car park bit, you know, round the side.'

'Are you talking about Olivia Sinclair?' a woman sitting at the next chair, her hair in pink rollers, pipes up.

'Who's Olivia Sinclair?' I ask.

'Keep up, Frankie,' Maggie says. 'Olivia Sinclair is the name of the missing baby.'

'Oh.'

I try to decide what would possess anyone to nick a baby. Going by my baby cousins, as far as I can work out all they do is dribble, cry, sleep and poo themselves. *Not* my idea of a good time.

'Awful, isn't it?' the woman in curlers says.

'Horrible,' Ida agrees.

'Just thinking about it makes me shudder. I mean, what kind of monster takes off with someone else's baby?'

'God knows. There's only so long they can hide, though. The whole country is going to be looking for them. And when they find them' – Ida pauses for dramatic effect – 'there'll be hell to pay.'

'Frankie,' Maxine calls from across the salon. 'Can you gown up Mrs Penrose for me?'

I leave the women to gossip and grab a gown from the pegs on the wall.

By the time Maxine tells me to take my break almost two and a half hours later, I've had it up to here with Olivia Sinclair. It's all any of the punters want to talk about. Not that I don't think it's a big deal that a baby's been kidnapped practically on our doorstep – I just don't see the point of going on and on about it, especially when there are so few facts to actually discuss.

I step outside and let out a sigh of relief. With its non-existent air con, the salon is pretty toasty at the best of times, but it's been almost unbearable the past couple of weeks.

I go to the newsagents next door and buy a white chocolate Magnum with the £1.50 tip Mrs Penrose left for me, and then head up the street in search of some shade from the throbbing sun. I find it in the form of the awning outside the greasy spoon on the corner. I sit down at one of the plastic tables set out on the pavement and take out my phone.

I have five new WhatsApp messages – another one from Mum badgering me about my results, two from my friend Ella about what I'm wearing to Theo's party tonight, one from my other friend Bex asking what booze I'm taking, and one from a boy in our year called Rory asking what time I'm planning on getting there. Quickly I tap out replies to everyone but Rory. He's a nice-enough boy, but I'm not really interested in him like that and I'm worried a swift response will only give him the wrong idea. Tonight is about having fun with my mates, Jojo especially. The last thing I want is a boy getting in the way of precious re-bonding time, especially one I'm not even really that into.

I scroll down to my most recent set of messages to Jojo. It's not just that they haven't been read: they haven't even been delivered, a sad grey tick next to each of them. Which means she's either run out of battery or switched her phone off, both of which strike me as highly unusual. Unlike me, Jojo never leaves the house without a fully charged phone and she always keeps a portable charger on her. I should know; I borrow it enough. As for turning her phone off, I just can't think why she would, unless it was by accident, and if that was the case, surely she'd have realized by now and turned it back on.

I think back to the last time I saw her face to face. It was less than twenty-four hours ago. She came over to mine yesterday afternoon and we lolled in the garden for a couple of hours, taking it in turns to choose what music to pump through my mini speakers. She looked even paler than usual, but I put that down to her still being ill. She claimed she was feeling much better but refused every offer of crisps or biscuits; she even turned down an ice lolly. She was quiet too. But then Jojo has always been prone to disappearing into her own little world every now and again so I didn't take it to heart.

'Are you OK?' I asked as she sat beside me, her freckled arms slick and shiny from where she'd applied sunscreen, her loose cotton T-shirt dress pulled down over her knees.

'I'm fine,' she said.

'You sure?'

She forced her lips into a smile. 'Course.'

She paused, plucking a daisy from the grass and slicing a hole through its stem with her thumbnail.

'Why'd you ask?' she added.

'Oh, no real reason. You just seem a bit preoccupied, that's all.'

'I'm probably just a bit anxious about results.'

I couldn't help but frown. What did Jojo have to be anxious about? She already has her place at the Arts Academy. Her grades make no difference. Even if she bombed. Which she wouldn't. Jojo has always been naturally academic, quietly sailing through her mocks with apparent ease.

I didn't say any of this, though. I knew I'd only look petty if I did.

If it was the other way round, you'd want Jojo to be happy for you, Mum keeps reminding me.

And she's right. Of course she is. But it's still hard.

'You'll be fine,' I said instead, scrolling through my phone for my next song choice.

'I know,' Jojo said. 'I'm just being stupid.' She wriggled her toes in the sun. 'You know what I'm like,' she added with a little laugh.

I did. Jojo is a worrier. She always has been, although she hides it well, burying her worries so deep the untrained eye would never ever guess anything was wrong. She can't fool me, though. I've known her for too long. If she were in front of me right now, I'd get to the root of what was going on in minutes, I'm certain.

I try to remember what else we talked about. Our song choices, Luca being a pain, Theo's party, how sick of the weather we were. Nothing important or particularly deep, just general chit-chat. I tried to get her to stay so we could watch *The Great British Bake Off* together, but she said she had to get back home for dinner.

'Next week, then?' I said.

'OK,' she replied.

Before she left, we made clear plans for today, plans we then confirmed later via WhatsApp. I scroll back to our most recent exchange. It was shortly before midnight, her last words:

> Night night. See you tomorrow xxx

Which only leaves one question: where the hell is she?

Chapter 4

On paper, Jojo and I probably make a pretty unlikely pair of best friends. We're opposites in practically every single way.

I'm tall; Jojo is petite.

I'm brunette and go brown the second I step in the sun; Jojo is a proper English rose who wears factor 50 practically all year round, even in deepest darkest winter.

I never stop talking; Jojo always thinks before she speaks.

I'm hopelessly messy; Jojo is forensically neat.

I'm impulsive; Jojo is calm and watchful.

I'm a night owl; Jojo is an early bird.

We once sat down and did one of those online personality tests. Our scores were polar opposites in every single category. Not that we were surprised. We've been best friends long enough to realize it's our differences that make us such a good team.

The bottom line is: I'm the one who forgets to charge her phone, not Jojo. Overnight, everything's gone topsy-turvy and I don't like it one bit.

As I walk up Jojo's driveway, the late afternoon sun beating down on my back, I realize that thanks to her mystery illness I haven't been to her house in well over a month now, at least not inside.

If there's ever a choice between which of our houses to hang out at, we almost always pick Jojo's, mainly because she's an only child so there are no obnoxious older brothers to contend with. Also, her mum and stepmum are really relaxed and cool and kind of just leave us to it, unlike my mum and dad who are distinctly uncool and can't resist showing off, even in front of Jojo who has known them since she was four and isn't the least bit impressed by their antics (although she's far too polite to admit it).

When Jojo first messaged me to let me know she was ill, I dropped off some sweets (Maoam Stripes, her favourite) and a stack of magazines from the salon, but Helen, her mum, wouldn't let me any further than the front door.

'Is it really that contagious?' I asked, peering up the stairs.

'Afraid so,' Helen replied, her hand resting on the door-frame. 'Maybe next week, eh?'

Standing in the exact same spot, I realize it never dawned on me to ask exactly what was wrong with Jojo.

I ring the doorbell.

No answer.

I try again, pressing for longer this time, just in case.

Still no answer.

I kneel down and poke my fingers through the letter box, wedging it open.

'Hello?' I call.

Nothing.

The house is silent in that thick heavy way that only empty houses ever are.

I straighten up and let the letter box fall shut, then cut across the grass to the side gate. I open it and follow the paved path round to the back of the house, where Jojo's bedroom is. I walk into the centre of the lawn and look up. Jojo's curtains are open and I can see the silhouette of her moneybox, a big fat ceramic pink pig she's had as long as I can remember, on the window sill. For a second I consider finding a pebble and lobbing it at against the glass, before quickly rejecting the idea.

I'm being stupid.

She's clearly not in.

No one is.

I sigh and walk back round to the front of the house.

I ring the bell one more time for luck before admitting defeat and trudging home.

'Frankie! Is that you?' Mum calls from the living room as I slam the front door shut behind me.

'Yes!' I yell back, kicking off my flip-flops at the bottom of the stairs.

'Can you come in here, please?'

I grin. I expect she's bought a cake or something to celebrate my exam results and this is the grand unveiling. My parents may not be very cool but they can be extremely cute when they want to be.

'Hang on, I'm just getting a drink,' I say.

That'll give her time to light the candles or sparklers or whatever.

I get myself a glass of water from the kitchen before heading into the living room.

But there are no sparklers. No cake. Just Mum, hovering by the mantelpiece, still wearing her uniform from the care home she works in – a generic polyester tabard – over her chinos and T-shirt, with Helen and her wife, Stacey, perched on the sofa, two untouched cups of tea sitting on the coffee table in front of them.

'Hi, Frankie,' Helen says with a tight smile.

'Hi. Is, er, everything OK?' I ask.

Helen and Stacey exchange a look too quick for me to interpret.

'We're sure it's fine . . .' Helen begins.

'It's just that we can't get hold of Jojo,' Stacey says, taking over. 'I don't suppose you've seen or heard from her today, Frankie?'

'No, sorry,' I say, my heart beating that little bit faster. 'I've sent her a ton of messages but she hasn't replied to any of them. Why? You don't think anything's wrong, do you?'

'No, no, nothing like that,' Helen says quickly. 'It's just not like her not to be in touch. And, well, we were just passing by so we thought we may as well pop in and check if she'd been in contact with you today.'

I shake my head.

'When did you last see her?' I ask.

'This morning.'

'What time? She was supposed to be calling for me at ten.'

'Before that,' Stacey says. 'I had to nip over to my mum's just after breakfast, about eight thirty, and by the time I got back, perhaps an hour later, she was gone.'

'I was already at work,' Helen adds.

'Maybe she left early to get her results,' Mum suggests.

'She didn't,' I say. 'Her envelope was still there when I got mine and that was about half eleven.'

'Yes, we called to check,' Helen says. 'No one at the school has seen her.'

'Did she take anything with her?' Mum asks.

Another indecipherable look passes between Helen and Stacey.

'Her purse and phone are gone,' Helen says. 'And a few other bits.'

'Well, there you go then,' Mum says encouragingly. 'I'm sure it's nothing to worry about. After all, this is Jojo we're talking about. Sensible is her middle name.'

Mum's right. If Jojo were part of the Mr Men and Little Miss universe, she'd be Little Miss Sensible for sure. She's the girl who never drinks, who always remembers her homework, who texts to let you know she's home safely; the girl who makes sure to get her five portions of fruit and veg and two litres of water, and eight hours of sleep; the girl who always knows the exact amount in her bank account and doesn't squander her pocket money on nail polish and *Heat* magazine and tops she'll only ever wear once from Pretty Little Thing. She is steady, practical, reliable. She is everything I'm not.

'She probably just forgot to charge her phone,' Mum adds, filling the uneasy silence.

'Maybe,' Helen says.

She doesn't sound convinced, though, and I don't blame her.

As if on cue, a phone on the coffee table buzzes with an incoming message, making all four of us flinch. Helen lunges for it.

'Is it her?' Stacey asks, looking over Helen's shoulder.

There's a beat where we all seem to hold our breath.

'No,' Helen replies, her voice flat, her shoulders slumping with disappointment. 'It's my bank. One of those stupid automated messages.'

'She'll turn up soon,' Mum says. 'She's got a party to get ready for, and if she's anything like Frankie she wouldn't miss a party for the world.'

She's talking about the gathering at Theo's later. A bunch of us (including Jojo) are supposed to be meeting at Ella's house at seven for pre-party drinks and snacks.

'Yeah, you're probably right,' Helen says.

Again, she doesn't sound convinced.

There's a pause.

Helen glances over at Stacey. 'We should get going.'

Stacey nods and they stand up, sliding their phones back into the pockets of their denim shorts.

'Sorry we didn't touch the tea,' Helen says.

'Oh, don't be daft,' Mum replies. 'It's too hot for tea anyway. Don't know what I was thinking.'

'You will let us know, won't you, Frankie?' Stacey says. 'If you hear anything.'

'Course,' I reply.

Mum and I walk them to the door together, waving them off as they head back down the path, their hands entwined.

'Well,' Mum says, the moment the front door falls shut behind them. 'You can tell Jojo doesn't do this sort of thing very often. If I went round to theirs every time I couldn't track you down straightaway . . .' She chuckles.

I stick my tongue out at her.

Mum has made an interesting point, though. I've always assumed Helen and Stacey are just really relaxed, but perhaps it's more the case that Jojo's simply never done anything to give them any cause for concern before now.

'Over the top or not,' I say. 'It is weird. For Jojo not to be in touch like this, I mean.'

'Maybe,' Mum says. 'But like I said before, Jojo is a smart girl. She wouldn't do anything daft.'

'Yeah, I suppose so,' I murmur.

Mum glances down at her watch. 'Aren't you supposed to be leaving soon?'

'In about an hour.'

'OK, well why don't you hop in the shower and I'll make you a quick bit of dinner.'

'There's going to be food at Ella's.'

Mum rolls her eyes. 'A few crisps does not constitute a meal, Francesca.'

'OK, fine. Just don't make me anything stinky, OK?'

'Oh, 'ello. Who are you planning on kissing tonight, then?'

God, she's embarrassing.

'No one,' I say. 'I just prefer not to turn up at social occasions absolutely honking of garlic, thank you very much.'

'I'll see what I can do. Now, go.'

Before getting in the shower, I grab my phone and compose a message to Jojo.

> What's going on?? Your mum and Stacey have been round. They're really worried. RING ME!!!! Love you xxx

I press 'send' and reach for my towel, hoping there'll be a reply by the time I return.

Chapter 5

The cake I'd anticipated materializes after dinner, complete with much fanfare and Mum's trademark sparklers.

'My clever girl,' Dad says, kissing me on top of my head as the sparklers fizzle out, his Italian accent just as thick now as it was when he moved here from Rimini twenty-three years ago.

Luca snorts.

'Luca,' Mum says sharply. 'You had your time last week – it's Frankie's now.'

'No offence, I'm just not sure a three in maths is anything to celebrate,' Luca says.

Ugh. Trust him to focus on my lowest grade.

'She can retake if she needs to,' Dad says. 'Can't you, Frankie?'

I screw up my face. The very last thing I want to think about right now are retakes. Luckily, I'm saved from answering his question by Mum.

'Look,' she says. 'They're talking about the missing baby on the news. Quick, turn it up.'

Luca is closest to the remote control. He picks it up and points it at the TV. I twist around in my seat so I can see the screen. People may have been banging on about this all day but I'm yet to see or read anything official about it.

'*Nearly nine hours after she disappeared, there have still been no confirmed sightings of missing infant, Olivia Sinclair,*' the reporter says in a grave voice.

A photo of a sleeping baby with chubby pink cheeks and wispy white-blonde hair flashes up on the screen. Mum lets out a gooey sigh.

'*Baby Olivia was snatched from the back seat of her mother's car shortly after nine a.m. this morning. Her parents Caroline and James Sinclair have made an emotional appeal for her safe return.*'

A clip is played from what looks like a hastily arranged press conference. A blonde woman holding a wad of tissues and a man with a beard sit behind a table with a jug of water and two microphones on it, cameras popping and flashing in their faces.

'Please don't hurt my baby,' the woman says directly down the lens. 'Please.'

'Bet they did it,' Luca declares.

'Oh, don't be so silly,' Mum says, tutting. 'Just look at them – they're beside themselves.'

'Either that or they're very good actors.'

'Oh, come on, Luca,' I say. 'Why would anyone kidnap their own baby? That literally makes no sense.'

'Does anything?' he replies airily. 'All I'm saying is, I wouldn't rule it out.'

I roll my eyes. Luca is always trying to say shocking things. I doubt he means them half the time.

'Who on earth would steal a baby?' Mum ponders, ignoring Luca. 'I mean, I just can't imagine what would make a person do such a thing.'

'If you two as bambinos are anything to go by,' Dad says with a wink, nodding at Luca and me in turn, 'they'd have to be off their rockers.'

'Shush!' Mum says, holding up her hand. 'The police are about to say something.'

We return our attention to the TV where a police officer is preparing to read an official statement.

'Time is of the essence and we are urging anyone with information, however insignificant it may seem, to come forward as a matter of urgency,' she says.

A series of telephone numbers scroll along the bottom of the screen as the camera zooms in on poor Caroline Sinclair's tear-stained face.

'Tenner they did it,' Luca says, sticking out his hand for me to shake.

'You're such a dick,' I reply, slapping it away.

Having polished off a slice of cake, I return upstairs. I left my phone up there on purpose in the hope I'd return to a message from Jojo. Alas, the only messages are from Ella and Bex sorting out logistics for tonight.

I remove the towel from my head and start the agonizing process of drying my hair. I'm already running late but my barnet will be a mass of frizz if I leave it to dry naturally. I'm forced to blast it in ten-second bursts, hanging with my head upside down in the gaps so it doesn't start sticking to my neck. It's during one of these gaps that I notice my phone glowing on the bed, Jojo's caller ID (a photo of her on her sixteenth birthday clutching the unicorn balloon I'd bought for her) flashing up on the screen.

Blood rushes from my head as I whip it back and make a dive for the phone.

'Finally!' I say. 'Where the hell have you been all day? I must have messaged you like twenty times!'

There's a beat before Jojo replies, almost like there's a delay on the line.

'Sorry,' she says. 'I only just managed to charge my phone.'

'What about your portable charger?' I ask.

'Oh. I, er, I've lost it.'

'Your mum and Stacey have been around and everything.'

'What did they say?'

'Nothing much. Just that you'd gone AWOL on them. Why? Haven't you spoken to them yet?'

'I'm going to ring them in a bit, straight after I've talked to you.'

Even though I'm irritated with Jojo for acting so blasé right now, I can't help but feel pleased she chose to ring me first.

'I had to go to school all by myself, Jojo,' I say. 'I looked like a right Billy No-Mates.'

'Sorry,' Jojo murmurs. 'Um, something came up.'

'Something more important than going to collect our GCSE results together?'

She doesn't answer.

I sigh, but don't push the issue. I'll get to the bottom of this later. Right at this moment, I have more pressing things on my mind. Like finishing my hair and getting to Ella's before all of her mum's home-made guacamole runs out. I eye the outfit I've picked out to wear tonight – a little red slip dress hanging on the back of my bedroom door – and for the first time since this morning, start to get excited about the night ahead. I hadn't realized quite how stressed I was about Jojo's non-communication until she finally got in touch.

'Listen,' I say. 'My mum's offered to drive us to Ella's. I'm running a bit late but I reckon I could be at yours for about twenty past if my hair decides to dry any time soon. That work for you?'

There's a pause.

'I'm really sorry,' Jojo says, her voice oddly faint. 'But I don't think I'm going to make it tonight.'

'What do you mean? This has been in the diary for ever.'

It really has. Theo's party marks the pinnacle of the summer, the end of an era. In less than two weeks I'll be back at school and Jojo will be at the Arts Academy and things will never be the same again.

'Are you poorly again or something?' I ask. 'Is that it?'

She didn't look great when I saw her yesterday. But if she's still unwell, surely she would have been at home all day.

'No, no, I'm fine,' Jojo says.

'What's going on then?'

'I'm at my dad's.'

'Your dad's?'

Jojo's parents split up when she was ten, and Helen got a place with Stacey soon after, taking Jojo with her. Jojo's dad lives in a flat on the other side of town.

'Yeah. I've been here all day.'

'How come?'

Jojo usually spends every other weekend with her dad.

It's rare she spends time with him midweek, even during the holidays.

'Um, he's in a bit of a bad place at the moment.'

I don't know Jojo's dad all that well, certainly not as well as she knows mine. He's a sales rep for a greetings card company and spends a lot of time on the road. Jojo's mentioned he struggles with depression every now and again, but I didn't think it was anything especially serious.

'Is he OK?' I ask. 'He's not done anything, you know, stupid, has he?'

'Oh no. No. Nothing like that.'

'He's going to be OK, then?'

'Yes, I think so.'

'Then you can come to the party!'

'I can't just leave him, Frankie!'

'But you literally just said you think he's going to be OK.'

'Exactly. *Going* to be.'

'But it's results day.'

'I know. And I'm sorry, but I . . .' She hesitates for a moment. 'I just don't feel right leaving him.'

I can hear crying in the background. 'What's that noise? Is that a baby?' I ask.

'It's the TV,' Jojo says. 'Listen, I have to go. I'll call you tomorrow or something.'

She hangs up before I have the chance to say anything else.

I stare at my phone.

I'll call you tomorrow or something.

Or something?

Is she taking the piss?

Immediately, I call her back. It goes straight through to

voicemail. She must be calling her mum. I continue drying my hair and try again a few minutes later. Once more, I get her voicemail. I try her another three times before leaving a message:

'Jojo, it's me. Listen, I hadn't finished talking to you. Can you call me back, please?'

As I hang up, I'm trembling with annoyance. I know it's her dad and everything, but if it's nothing urgent, couldn't her visit wait until tomorrow? Why today of all days? Worse still, she wasn't even especially apologetic about it. Yes, she said the word 'sorry', but it didn't exactly seem to be coming from the heart. If anything, she was trying to get me off the phone as quickly as possible. Or maybe this is the way things are going to be from now on. Maybe she's already preparing to cast me off to make space for all the fancy new friends she's going to make at the Arts Academy and this is just step one: *distance myself from Frankie.*

Well, if that's what she's got planned, I've got a few things to say about it. And she's going to listen to them whether she likes it or not.

Chapter 6

'Are you sure you don't want me to wait?' Mum asks.

We're parked outside the anonymous block of flats where Jojo's dad lives.

'Yes, thanks,' I say. 'We're probably just going to skip Ella's now and go straight to Theo's.' I paste a convincing smile on my face. 'Jojo's dad can drop us off,' I add for good measure.

I haven't shared my fears about Jojo with Mum. Mum adores her, she always has, and I know the second I suggest Jojo might be preparing to cast me off, she'll only try to convince me I'm wrong and attempt to talk me out of confronting her about it. I'm not wrong, though. I'm certain. It's literally the only explanation.

'Did she explain why she didn't let her mum and Stacey know where she'd got to?' Mum asks. 'I know her phone wasn't charged, but surely her dad could have let her use his. She must have known they'd worry.'

'No,' I admit. 'She didn't say.'

It's a good point. And yet another niggling aspect of our telephone conversation. The more I think about it, the more it doesn't add up . . .

I open the car door and get out, peeling my dress from where it's stuck to the back of my legs.

'If you're going to want a lift later on, make sure you give us a decent bit of notice,' Mum says. 'No SOS calls at three in the morning, please.'

'Will do,' I murmur, already distracted by the myriad things I want to say to Jojo before I lose my bottle. That's the thing about Jojo. She's got a vulnerability about her, a natural delicacy that can make it hard to get mad with her, even when she's in the wrong.

I head into the foyer of the building and press the call button on the lift. It's way too hot to even contemplate the two flights of stairs.

As I make my way down the bland corridor to Jojo's dad's flat, I try to decide what my opening gambit should be. After all, I'm just turning up here uninvited. Not that I had much choice – Jojo's phone is still going straight to voicemail, so I couldn't have warned her I was coming over even if I wanted to. Still, I can't help but worry this might not be the best idea. What if her dad really is in a bad way? The last thing he's going to want is his daughter's mouthy best friend turning up on his doorstep. But at the same time, I can't shift the feeling that Jojo wasn't being entirely truthful when we spoke on the phone earlier. Jojo is an excellent actor, but she's a shit liar, always has been.

I reach Jojo's dad's flat. I can hear the theme music to *The One Show* playing on the other side of the flimsy mock-pine door.

I take a deep breath and ring the buzzer.

Less than ten seconds later, Jojo's dad opens the door. He's wearing a gaudy Hawaiian shirt and eating a strawberry yoghurt. Now, this is probably going to sound really terrible and I know you don't have to *look* depressed to *be* depressed, but Jojo's dad seems completely fine to me, slightly confused perhaps, but otherwise perfectly chipper and very much enjoying his yoghurt.

'Frankie,' he says, blinking in surprise. 'Er, what can I do for you?'

I peer over his shoulder. The front door leads straight into the open plan kitchen/living room. I haven't been here in ages but it hasn't changed one bit. It's still typical clueless single-bloke territory – bare magnolia walls, ugly black leather sofa, standard issue IKEA coffee table, a recycling bin overflowing with empty pizza boxes and beer bottles.

But no Jojo.

She must be in her room.

'Hiya. Er, I wanted to speak to Jojo if that's all right. Is she through there?' I nod down the corridor towards the bedrooms.

'Frankie,' Jojo's dad says gently. 'Jojo's not here.'

'What do you mean, she's not here?'

'She's not due here until next weekend.' He frowns, concern suddenly flooding his face. 'Why? Did she say she was going to be here? It's just that Helen's been looking for her too.'

I hesitate. The last thing I want to do is freak him out. 'I must have got confused,' I say, styling it out as best I can. 'Mixed up my dates. Sorry to have bothered you.' I back out of the front door, into the communal corridor.

'Wait,' he says. 'Is everything OK? With Jojo, I mean.'

'Of course. Er, why do you ask?'

'No reason. I just haven't seen much of her lately. What with her being poorly the past few weeks . . .' His voice trails off.

'Honestly, I'm sure it's fine,' I say. 'This is my cock-up. It's the weather, I swear. It's turned my brain to mush.' I treat him to one of my winning smiles and it seems to do the trick, his shoulders visibly relaxing. 'Sorry to have bothered you,' I add. 'Er, enjoy your yoghurt. Bye.'

I stumble downstairs and out onto the pavement, my head spinning.

Everything Jojo told me on the phone was a pack of lies.

But Jojo isn't a liar.

She hates lies. Even silly little fibs. I remember once persuading her to ring Luca and pretend he'd won some competition to win a fancy mountain bike, and she fell apart after less than a minute, going bright red in the face and confessing. Despite my annoyance with her at the time, Jojo's complete and utter inability to be dishonest is one of the things I like best about her.

I sit on the edge of the kerb and try to decide what to do.

My phone is going berserk with messages from people wanting to know where Jojo and I are. I reply to them all with the same message: *Something came up. We'll see you at Theo's.*

I squeeze my eyes shut and try to come up with a plan. It's no good, though. My brain feels like it's been stuffed with cotton wool.

Think, Frankie, think. What stuff do you already know?

I know that Jojo disappeared from her house sometime between 8.30 and 9.30 this morning.

I know her phone has been off pretty much all day, despite the fact I've never once known her to run out of battery.

I know she called me not long after tea and told me she was at her dad's.

I now know this is a big fat lie.

I call her again.

It goes straight through to voicemail (surprise, surprise). I hesitate before leaving yet another message:

'Jojo, it's me again. I know you're not at your dad's. You really need to ring me.'

I hang up.

Now what?

Just wait for her to maybe call me back? But that might never happen. After all, I've been calling her and leaving her messages literally all day, and apart from that one weird conversation I haven't heard a peep out of her in response.

Perhaps I should just go to the party, forget about Jojo for twelve hours or so and deal with this in the morning.

I know I can't, though.

Jojo is my best friend.

If she lied, she lied for a good reason. I just have absolutely no idea what this reason might be. This is what's killing me the most right now. Because Jojo and I ordinarily tell each other everything.

And I mean everything.

From secrets to sleeping bags, there's nothing we haven't shared.

I know that until the age of eight, Jojo regularly wet the bed.

Jojo knows that when I was seven, I ate three of Luca's Easter eggs and successfully blamed it on our dog, Lola (R.I.P.).

I know that Jojo once sent an anonymous home-made Valentine's Day card to our physics teacher, Mr Ronson.

Jojo knows that I cried myself to sleep for five nights on the trot when Zayn left One Direction.

I know Jojo thinks she's the reason her mum and Stacey can't have a baby.

Jojo knows that my ex-boyfriend Ram's penis bends slightly to the right.

You get the picture.

Nothing is off the agenda.

If I'm entirely honest, the whole Arts Academy episode made things a bit scratchy between us for a while, but that's behind us now. I thought we were back on track. Or at least somewhere in the right direction. The realization that I might have been wrong burns.

Water fills my eyes. I blink it away. This is no time for tears. I need to stop being so bloody sentimental and focus.

Right. OK. So we've established that Jojo isn't at her mum's or her dad's.

So where else might she be?

I dismiss our mutual friends. If Jojo were with them, I'd know about it. Plus, it's rare that Jojo and I socialize without the other present. We come as a pair and always have done.

A thought hits me. Could she have a secret boyfriend? I had my suspicions she had a crush on someone earlier in the year when she started acting all cagey any time I mentioned the opposite sex, but she refused to admit to anything and eventually I stopped pushing her for details. Plus, even though Jojo can be a bit prudish about boys and sex and stuff, I just can't imagine her not telling me if she met someone she liked, unless maybe it was someone totally inappropriate.

Like someone really old and disgusting.

An image of Mr Ronson and his unkempt beard jumps into my head.

I thought Jojo's crush on him died the day he played the cat in *Dick Whittington* in the sixth form and staff pantomime two Christmases ago, dressed in nothing but a black body stocking. I remember the expression on her face as he crawled about the stage, his arse in the air – the mixture of horror and disappointment and sheer embarrassment etched all over her features.

But that was a while ago now. What if her crush had been reignited? And what if he was into it too?

No.

NO.

I'm being ridiculous.

Jojo has not run off with Mr Ronson. Plus, didn't he get married recently? I seem to remember Bex or Ella or someone tracking down his wife on Facebook and trawling through the honeymoon album she'd uploaded, chortling over pictures of a loved-up and rather sunburned Mr Ronson wearing Speedos on the beach, sipping a piña colada.

I reject the possibility of a secret boyfriend and take out my phone, double-checking Jojo's various social media profiles for clues. My search gleans very little. Jojo's never really been much of an online sharer and there's been nothing new for over three weeks now. The last thing she posted was on 27 July via Instagram – a photo of her grandma's dog, Pickle, fresh from the dog groomers.

I'm about to close the app when my eyes snag on something. The location above the photo of Pickle.

Newfield. Our home town.

Quickly, I scroll through my apps until I find the one I'm looking for.

Find Your Friends.

Jojo and I downloaded it years ago, when we both got our first ever smartphones for Christmas. It's this app that lets you see where your friends are. We used it all the time at first. Even though I generally knew where Jojo was and what she was up to at any given time, there was something comforting about being able to see it in the form of a pulsating blue dot on the screen confirming her exact location. I'm not sure when I stopped using it. Perhaps when I got together with Ram and felt guilty about not being as available as I once was. Not that Jojo ever made a fuss or indicated she felt neglected in any way. But then, that's Jojo for you.

I open the app and pray that Jojo hasn't deleted it. I select the 'Friend Finder' function and wait.

Jojo444 is offline.

Shit. Of course. The app only works if the person you're looking for has their phone switched on.

A second alert flashes up on the screen.

Would you like to see Jojo444's last known location?

I press 'yes' and hold my breath. It's all coming back to me now. If you're offline, the app saves your most recent location.

The map is taking ages to load.

Hurry, hurry.

Finally it appears, Jojo's location as of 18:49, indicated by a non-pulsating version of that familiar blue dot.

She's on Princes Way.

Princes Way?

Is that in Newfield? If it is, I've never heard of it.

I zoom out a little, my eyes searching for familiar road names or landmarks.

Nothing springs out at me.

That's when I see a train station symbol. I zoom back in.

Swindon station.

I frown.

I'm pretty sure I've heard of Swindon, but I have no idea where it is. I keep zooming out until I can make sense of where it is in relation to Newfield.

It's miles away.

My mind racing, I switch to the internet and type Princes Way, Swindon into Google Street View. It's a pretty bleak sight – mostly grey office buildings. I can't for the life of me think why Jojo might be there.

Then I see it.

A popular chain hotel, its sign aglow.

I go back to the app.

Boom! The locations match exactly.

I've found her.

I just have absolutely no idea why she might be there. Zero.

I think back to our telephone conversation. Was it really just an hour ago? Already the exact content is fading from my memory.

I squeeze my eyes shut and try to remember what she said, what I said, how she sounded.

That's when it comes back to me.

A baby. I heard a baby crying.

Jojo said it was the TV.

It didn't sound like the TV, though. It sounded like it was right there in the room with her, right next to the phone even. I was about to say that, I remember now, but I didn't get the chance because that's when she hung up, and in my annoyance and belief that she was where she said she was, I totally forgot about it.

Hurriedly, I put everything together.

Jojo left the house sometime between 8.30 and 9.30 a.m.

Olivia Sinclair was taken around 9.15 a.m.

Jojo hasn't been seen since. Neither has Olivia.

Jojo has lied about where she is, not only to me, but to her mum too.

Jojo has a baby with her.

My heart is galloping like crazy now.

Because, taking everything into consideration, there's only one possible explanation here.

Jojo, my best friend in the entire world, has stolen a baby.

Chapter 7

Oh God.

Oh God.

OH GOD.

I'm officially freaking out.

No.

NO.

I do not have time for this. I need to stop panicking and make a plan but my brain and body are refusing to cooperate. I know I have to get it together, though. I'm absolutely no good to Jojo flapping about like this. I need to focus. Unfortunately, focusing has never been one of my strengths.

I force myself to sit back down on the kerb and with trembling fingers type 'Olivia Sinclair' into Google.

And there it is. The same cherubic picture I saw on the news earlier.

I scan the article:

No confirmed sightings . . . police following several leads . . . public urged to come forward, etc. etc.

No mention of Swindon, but surely it's only a matter of time. Jojo looks young for her age, certainly too young to be a mother. People would notice her. She'll be on CCTV. She may have escaped it at the petrol station but there's no way she could have avoided it on the trip to Swindon – it's bloody miles away. And what is the statistic? That there's one camera for every ten people? Or is the other way round? Either way, it's a lot of cameras and Jojo and Olivia can't possibly have escaped them all.

I wonder what the punishment is for kidnapping a baby.

I Google it.

Up to fourteen years in prison.

How old will Jojo be in fourteen years? Thirty.

Ancient.

I think of all the things she'll miss. All the birthdays and milestones and rites of passage.

My eyes sting with panicky tears.

I have to get to her before the police do.

I look up train times to Swindon. The next train is at 20:22, changing in London.

I take a look at the prices. 'How much?' I gasp out loud. I don't need to check my bank balance to know I have nowhere near that amount at my disposal.

Maybe I can get a coach. I look up timetables but there's nothing until tomorrow morning and it calls at so many places in-between I wouldn't arrive in Swindon until mid-afternoon, by which time Jojo might have left the hotel and gone God knows where. I can't possibly leave it until then. I need to get there tonight, no matter what.

I need someone with a car.

Someone discreet I can trust.

Someone who won't insist we go to the police or get adults involved.

But who?

None of my mates are old enough to drive.

Then a photo pops into my head.

I saw it on Instagram just after Easter. I remember feeling a bit miffed by the caption – 'meet the new love of my life' – so much so I took a screenshot and sent it to Jojo, asking her if I had a right to be kind of gutted that I'd been so easily replaced by a heap of metal.

The photo was of my ex-boyfriend, Ram, a proud smile on his face, standing in front of a shiny black car.

I grab my bag and break into a run.

I'm nervous walking up Ram's front path. I don't know why. It's not like I haven't seen him since we broke up. Newfield isn't massive and we've crossed paths a couple of times and it's always been fine – a little awkward perhaps, but basically fine. This is different, though. This is his territory. And even though it was always a running joke that I got on better with Ram's mum and sisters than I did with him half the time, I'm still uneasy about knocking on their door unannounced. Unlike Ram, I haven't seen any of them since before we broke up and I have no idea how they feel about me all these months later. Certainly, I'm now regretting my decision to ceremoniously delete his number earlier this year. Calling him would have been so much simpler (not to mention quicker).

All the windows are open so there's definitely someone in.

I take a deep breath and ring the bell.

Ram's mum, Cheryl, answers; spotting me, she lets out a gasp of delight. My chest floods with relief.

'Frankie!' she says. 'What a gorgeous surprise. Come in, come in.'

Ram and I may have been doomed, but Cheryl and I liked one another from the start.

I let her usher me inside. Everything is exactly how I remember it, from the baby pictures of Ram and his two sisters on the sideboard, to the wonky shoe rack at the bottom of the stairs.

I've always loved Ram's house. It's not especially fancy or anything, just a narrow little terrace on an entirely ordinary street, but inside it's as cosy and welcoming as anything. Unlike my house, which is all very beige and cream and brown ('tasteful', according to my mum), Ram's house is a riot of colour. The living room, for example, is a symphony of reds and oranges, pinks and purples, from the cushions and throws on the sofa, to the framed posters on the wall and the shaggy circular rug in the centre of the floor.

'It reminds me of a sunset,' I remember telling Cheryl the first time I saw it.

'That's exactly what I was going for, Frankie,' she replied happily, before turning to Ram and saying, 'I like this one,' her eyes shining with approval.

'Now, let me get you a nice cold drink,' Cheryl says. 'I've got some of that posh elderflower cordial stuff in. I wasn't sure I'd like it, but I tell you what, it goes lovely with fizzy water, especially on a day like today.'

'Sounds great,' I say. 'Thank you.'

Cheryl totters towards the kitchen, her slippers clacking against the laminate flooring. Cheryl is the only person I know who wears slippers with a heel – satin pink mules trimmed with marabou feathers, a bit like the sort of the thing a film star from the 1950s might wear. Then again, she's glamorous full stop. Even today, probably the hottest of the year so far, she's in full make-up. I suspect most of my make-up slid off my face within moments of my leaving the house, but Cheryl's is immaculate. Even her double set of false eyelashes is refusing to wilt.

I follow her, lingering for a moment outside the living room. The door is ajar. On the mantelpiece, the shrine to Ram's dad sits as proudly as ever. Mr Jandu died in a car accident when Ram was fourteen, Laleh was nine and Roxy just four. In all the pictures, he's model handsome. The photos of him as a young teenager in Iran look uncannily like Ram. They have the same shock of black hair and intense gaze, the same loose-limbed ease, the same quietly devastating smile.

'Ice?' Cheryl calls from the kitchen. 'Or is that a silly question.'

'Yes please,' I say, scurrying after her.

'Now, what can I do for you?' Cheryl asks, setting my drink (complete with novelty ice cubes, a cocktail umbrella and a slice of orange) down in front of me on the breakfast bar. 'Not that there has to be a reason for your visit,' she adds quickly. 'You're welcome to drop in whenever you like.'

I take a quick sip. 'Um, I was just wondering if Ram was about actually?' I ask. 'I, er, don't seem to have his number in my phone for some reason.'

'Oh sorry, sweetheart, no. He's at work. He won't be back for another couple of hours yet.'

'Work?'

'Yes. At the rink.'

51

Ram has a part-time job working as a skate marshal at Nottingham ice arena.

'I didn't think he usually worked on Thursdays,' I say.

Thursday used to be one of our designated date nights. We'd watch Netflix, or, if we could be bothered and had the cash, go to the cinema, or out for a Nando's.

'He's been doing some extra shifts over the holidays,' Cheryl says.

'Oh. OK.'

'Why? Is it anything urgent?'

'Er, not exactly,' I say. 'I just kind of need to talk to him about something.'

'Oh yes?' Cheryl says, her eyes sparkling with interest.

'Nothing to do with us,' I say quickly. 'It's about a, er, mutual friend.'

'Oh, I see,' Cheryl says, her disappointment clear.

'Frankie!'

I turn towards the doorway. Roxy, dressed in her pyjamas, hurtles towards me, flinging her wiry little body into my arms. In addition to being a hit with Cheryl, I got on like a house on fire with both his sisters, especially little Roxy. When we broke up, she even made me a card. She covered it with sticky lipstick marks and scrawled the words 'I'll miss you!' across the front in red felt-tip pen, insisting on posting it through my letter box by hand.

While Roxy smothers me with kisses, Laleh emerges from the garden, her long dark hair tucked under a faded baseball cap. When she sees me, she breaks into a wide smile, the metal from her newly acquired braces glinting in the dipping evening sunlight.

'Oh my God, Laleh,' I say. 'When did you get so tall? You look like a supermodel or something!'

Laleh giggles and looks at her feet, proud and bashful in equal measures.

Wow, I've missed them. All of them. I hadn't realized how much. That's the sucky thing about breaking up with someone. It's not just them who you break up with.

'Do you love my brother again?' Roxy asks.

I hesitate, my face reddening. The last thing I want to do is give any of them false hope.

Cheryl saves me. 'Let Frankie finish her drink, Rox,' she says.

I throw Cheryl a grateful smile and ask them to fill me in on their news. They happily oblige. I quickly learn that Laleh has been chosen to represent the county in cross country running, Roxy broke her wrist and had to wear a sling for two whole weeks, and Cheryl has started going to Spanish classes at the local college. She tries some out on me but I'm not much of a linguist and we don't get very far, collapsing into giggles over Cheryl's hilariously bad attempts to ask for 500 grams of minced beef.

'Your turn, Frankie,' Cheryl says. 'How has life been treating you?'

'Yeah, fine. Same old, really.'

'Still acting?'

'Yep.'

I tell them a little about the production of *A Midsummer Night's Dream* our school put on in the spring (I'd played Helena opposite Jojo's Hermia) and my nine in drama.

'I always said you had star quality,' Cheryl says with a grin.

I glance at the clock. As much as I'm loving being back in the Jandus' cosy house, it's already gone eight and I'm still no closer to Swindon and Jojo.

I finish my drink and make my excuses.

'Do you want me to tell Ram you were here?' Cheryl asks, standing up.

'That's OK,' I say. 'I might just go down to the rink and see if I can catch him there.'

'Will you come back again soon?' Roxy asks, her eyes big and full of hope.

I glance at Cheryl. She nods encouragingly.

'Sure,' I say.

'Yay!' Roxy cries.

Cheryl walks me to the door. 'It really was good to see you, Frankie,' she says.

'Same.'

'I hope everything works out. For your friend.'

'My friend?'

'The mutual friend. Of yours and Ram's?'

'Oh! Oh. Yes. Me too. Thank you.'

She envelops me in a tight, floral-scented hug. 'Don't be a stranger now,' she says.

'I won't,' I promise.

Chapter 8

I take the bus to the rink. When I arrive, there's a girl I don't recognize behind the reception desk. I take a deep breath and plaster on an approachable girl-friendly version of my very best smile.

'Hiya,' I say. 'Are you OK to just let me through the gate? I'm not skating.'

'Sorry, skaters only,' she says in a bored voice.

'Seriously? I can't just pop up?'

'You can only spectate if you're accompanying someone who's skating.'

'Please,' I say. 'I'll literally be five minutes.'

She fixes me with a suspicious look. 'You want to spectate for five minutes?'

'Yes. Well, no. I need to talk to someone who's up there.'

'Sorry,' she says. 'No solo spectators allowed.'

'But I really need to talk to them!'

'If you're that desperate, then you can pay to skate.' She points at the screen advertising the admission prices.

'Seriously? You're going to make me pay seven quid just to go through the gate?'

She shrugs. 'I don't make the rules.'

Time for a change of approach.

'Listen,' I say, 'If you really must know, I'm here to see Ram Jandu.'

She snorts. 'You and half the female population of Nottingham.'

'But I am,' I say indignantly, resisting the temptation to slip in the fact he was, for a full seven and a half months, my bona fide boyfriend.

'He expecting you, is he?' she asks.

I hate the way she's looking at me – like I'm a massive chancer – her lips twitching with amusement.

'Not exactly,' I begin.

'Not that it matters either way,' the girl says, talking over me. 'You could be Ram's mum for all I care. If you wanna go through the gate, you've got to pay.'

I get my purse out of my bag and slam a ten-pound note down on the desk.

The girl is entirely unmoved, handing me my change and a receipt before letting me through the gate.

I haven't been to the ice rink in ages. Not since Ram and I broke up. I haven't missed it especially. I never was a natural, despite all the hours I clocked up here. I'm all legs and my centre of gravity's too high – 'like a giraffe on ice', Ram used to say.

I push open the double doors, my nostrils immediately assaulted by the stench of feet. I'd forgotten how bad this place reeks, especially the moment you first walk in. I take a deep breath, holding it until I'm safely past the skate hire desk, the main source of the smell.

The rink is packed. It doesn't take a genius to work out why. This is probably the coldest I've been in weeks, goosebumps breaking out on my arms and legs.

On Thursday, Friday and Saturday nights, eight till nine is 'disco' hour. Justin Bieber is blaring, and darting multi-coloured lights illuminate the ice. I make my way around the edge of the rink, peering through the Perspex barrier for Ram.

It doesn't take me long to spot him. I just have to follow the besotted gazes of the various groups of girls dotted about the ice. I swear, Ram should go to the manager of this place and demand a percentage of the takings for all the business he brings in.

To put it lightly, the boy is beautiful – a tall, dark handsome cliché of a teenage dream – fifty per cent boy band member, fifty per cent brooding male model. One hundred per cent drop-dead gorgeous.

And for over half a year, he was all mine.

Ram and I initially met as little kids, under the care of the same childminder – an unfailingly jolly woman called Diana. Ram was a school year ahead of me, but there was actually less than six months between us and we often played together. Unlike Luca, who's always been almost aggressively masculine in his interests, Ram was quite happy to play 'schools' and 'mums and dads' and help me build dens out of old bed sheets, and prepare pretend picnics. For a while we were as tight as anything, then, when I was about six, my school started offering an after-school club and we stopped going to Diana and I more or less forgot about Ramin Jandu.

I didn't see him again until spring last year when his school's football team played ours at home. I didn't usually make a point of watching matches but I'd recently started fancying the boy in goal so I persuaded Jojo to come with me. I didn't recognize Ram right away but I most definitely noticed him. All the girls did, and some of the boys too, their nudges and whispers racing down the side-lines like a Mexican wave. I was as shocked as anyone when, at the end of the game, he jogged straight over to me and said, 'Hello, stranger.'

'Er, hello,' I replied, slightly confused.

'I thought it was you,' he said, a grin on his face. 'Then I heard you laughing and I knew for sure.'

That was when the penny dropped. The gorgeous creature standing in front of me was the dark-haired little kid who played 'Dad' to my 'Mum' all those years ago.

We swapped numbers and met in town the following weekend. It was only supposed to be for coffee, but we ended up hanging out for the entire day.

I made him laugh. A lot. More than anyone had in ages, he said. And I loved that, played up to it, always ready with a quip or impression or funny observation.

We slipped into a relationship easily, with little discussion or negotiation. Somehow, our friendship as kids created a foundation that allowed us to skip a lot of the weird awkward stuff that comes with the territory when you first start going out with someone. We were comfortable with each other from the start. Perhaps too comfortable. It's only now I realize this was probably our downfall.

Ram is flying effortlessly around the rink, his dark eyes on alert for possible injuries or reckless skating. Unlike several of his colleagues who are clearly in the job primarily to show off and pick up girls, Ram has always taken his position as a marshal very seriously.

'Ram!' I call as he whizzes past.

But it's too noisy, my voice swallowed up by the thumping music and squeals and shouts of the punters on the ice.

Eventually, Ram glides to a stop at the opposite end of the rink, his hands on his hips, a whistle dangling from his lips as he keeps a close eye on a group of boys mucking about in the centre of the ice.

I will him to stay where he is and start to make my way around the perimeter of the rink. I reach the exit closest to where he's standing.

'Ram!' I yell. 'Ram!'

I swear he's about to turn in my direction when one of the boys shoves his mate. The boy goes flying into a group of girls, sending them scattering.

Ram blows his whistle and skates over, helping up the girls and scolding the boys. They're probably only a couple of years younger than him but they take their telling off, their heads bowed, before skating off, looking sheepish. Ram stays where he is, in the centre of the ice. There's no way he's going to hear me from there. I wave my arms but the rink is way too busy for me to stand out enough to attract his attention.

I could go and hire some skates, but I don't have any socks with me, and the idea of putting my bare feet into a pair of those gross smelly boots makes me want to vom.

There's only one thing for it.

Gingerly, I place a flip-flop-clad foot on the ice. Then another. It's unsurprisingly slippery. I put out both my arms for balance and shuffle my way towards Ram, feeling more than a little vulnerable with so many blades whizzing past my bare toes.

I'm maybe two metres away when he finally notices me, his face clouding with confusion. His gaze falls to my feet.

'You're missing something,' he says.

'Ha ha,' I reply. 'I'm not here to skate.'

'I can see that.'

'I need to talk to you.'

'I'm working, Frankie.'

'But it's urgent.'

He raises an eyebrow. 'Genuinely urgent or Frankie urgent?' he asks.

'Genuinely urgent!' I cry, pouting.

And just like that, I'm reminded of one of the (many) reasons why Ram and I split up – his complete and utter lack of patience for my tendency to exaggerate a teensy bit every now and then.

'I'm serious, Frankie,' he says. 'I'm working right now. I can't be distracted.' His eyes dart over my shoulder.

'You used to let me distract you,' I point out in a teasing voice.

'Yeah, well, I used to do a lot of things, Frankie.'

'Ouch,' I murmur.

'Look, I don't know why you're here, but you can't be on the ice in a pair of flip-flops. It's dangerous.'

'But I need to talk to you.'

'There's nothing left to talk about, Frankie.'

Oh, wait a second. He thinks I'm here to talk about 'us'.

True, in the immediate aftermath of our break-up last

October, despite being the one who initiated it, there were a couple of slightly undignified episodes where I attempted to lure Ram back. But that was absolutely ages ago now. Does he seriously think I'm still harbouring feelings for him, all these months later?

'It's nothing like that,' I say.

He doesn't look convinced.

'It's about Jojo,' I add.

'Jojo?' he says, his face softening slightly.

'Yes,' I say.

'Well, what is it?' he asks, his protective big brotherly instinct kicking in, just as I knew it would the second I mentioned her name. 'Is she OK?'

'I don't know. I hope so.'

'What do you mean?'

I lower my voice. 'I can't tell you here.'

'Why not?'

'Too many people.'

His frown deepens. 'You better not be messing with me, Frankie.'

'I'm not. I swear.' For good measure, I swipe my finger across my heart.

He glances up at the massive digital clock mounted above the rink and sighs. 'Go wait over there,' he says, pointing up at the plastic seating surrounding the rink. 'I'll be with you in ten.'

Chapter 9

'OK, let me get this straight,' Ram says. 'You think Jojo has kidnapped a baby.'

'Not any old baby. *The* baby. Olivia Sinclair.'

'OK, so you think Jojo has kidnapped Olivia Sinclair and taken her to Swindon, of all places. And now you want me to drive you nearly two hundred miles so you can bring them both back.'

'In a nutshell, yes.'

There's a beat before Ram bursts out laughing.

'What?' I say. 'Why are you laughing?'

'Why am I laughing? Are you seriously asking me that?'

'Yes!'

'Oh my God,' he splutters. 'You've come out with some crazy shit in your time, Frankie, but this? This really takes the biscuit.'

'But I'm serious. I honestly think Jojo's gone off with this baby.'

He laughs even harder. There are actual tears in his eyes.

'Stop it!' I cry. 'It's not funny.'

'Oh, yes it is.'

'On what planet? She could get in real trouble over this!'

'No she won't, because there is no way on earth she'd do something as batshit crazy as this. Now, if it was the other way round and Jojo was sitting in front of me telling me she thought you'd legged it with someone else's baby, it might be a different story . . .'

'Oh, I should have known you'd act like this,' I snap.

'Like what?'

'Like a patronizing arsehole.'

Ram's face falls. 'Oh, come on, Frankie, I was only messing.'

'Yeah, well, it wasn't funny.' I fold my arms and look out over the rink, empty now apart from the ice resurfacer chugging around in circles.

Ram sighs. 'Look, I'm sorry,' he says. 'That was a low blow. It's just kind of hard to take seriously, that's all.'

'Is it, though?' I ask. 'You only have to look at the evidence!'

'What evidence?'

For the second time I go through the timings, the multiple lies, the weird phone call, the baby crying in the background.

'But she said it was the TV, didn't she?'

'Only it wasn't,' I say. 'If the TV was on, I'd have heard it before then. And the crying was really loud and clear as anything, like it was right there in the room. I swear to you, Ram, it was a real-life baby.'

'OK, fine. But we don't know the baby was Olivia. Maybe she just happened to be walking past a baby when she was talking to you.'

'No,' I say. 'She was indoors, I could tell.'

'OK, then maybe she's gone to stay with someone who has a baby.'

'She doesn't know anyone with a baby. Plus, if she was visiting people, why would she be in a hotel? Surely she'd just stay with them.' I shake my head hard. 'I'm telling you, Ram, Jojo has Olivia.'

He sighs again.

'C'mon, you have to believe me,' I say.

'Well, I can't. Yes, Jojo is clearly acting a bit weird at the moment, but your "evidence" as you put it is flimsy to say the least.'

'It's more than that,' I say. 'It's a feeling.'

'A feeling,' he repeats.

'Yes. In here.' I pat my belly.

'Maybe she just wants a bit of a break from stuff,' Ram says, shrugging. 'And made up the lie about being at her dad's to buy herself a bit of time.'

'She's spent most of August ill at home. How much more time out does she need?'

'She's been ill?' Ram asks.

'Yeah. Since the beginning of the month.'

'Anything serious?'

'Just a virus. It properly knocked her out, though. I didn't see her for like three weeks.'

He frowns. 'That doesn't sound like Jojo.'

He's right. It doesn't. Despite her delicate appearance, Jojo hardly ever gets ill. Tacked on the inside of her wardrobe door is her impressive collection of 100% attendance certificates, one for every school year since reception. She even managed to avoid the mass chickenpox outbreak in Year Two, baffling everyone with her superhuman immune system.

'Is she better now?' Ram asks.

'Yeah. I think so. I mean, I only saw her yesterday and she said she was . . .'

I pause.

'What?' Ram says. 'What are you thinking?'

'Being ill. You don't think it messed with her head, do you?'

'How do you mean?'

'This virus. Could it have done something weird to her brain?'

Ram screws up his face. 'I doubt it, Frankie.'

'But how do you know that? It's got to be worth thinking about. Jojo, who is never ill, suddenly gets really ill for like weeks on end, and the moment she's apparently better she does the most un-Jojo thing possible and steals a baby.'

'Only she hasn't,' Ram says.

'I can't believe you won't accept there's even the tiniest possibility she's done this.'

'I'm sorry, Frankie, but I can't. I think you've put two and two together and got, I dunno, eleven billion, five hundred and twenty-six thousand, three hundred and sixty-six point nine recurring.'

'But what if she has?' I say.

'She hasn't,' he replies, not missing a beat.

God, he's irritating.

Time for a new angle.

'OK, fine, let's reverse things then. Let's say Jojo hasn't taken Olivia. Then why is she in some random hotel room in Swindon? And why has she lied about it? You can't deny there's something strange going on, baby or no baby.'

Ram hesitates, genuine worry finally flickering across his face. 'Are you absolutely certain she doesn't know anyone in Swindon?' he asks. 'No distant relatives or anything?'

'Positive.'

'What about online friends? There might be people you don't know about.'

'No,' I say firmly. 'She would have told me.'

'Do you know that for sure?'

I blink in surprise. I'm offended he's even asking this. He knows how close Jojo and I are, he's witnessed it first-hand.

'Of course,' I say. 'Jojo and I tell one another everything.'

'Everything?'

'Yes.'

'You don't think she might keep things from you? I'm not talking sinister stuff. I'm just wondering if there might be things she prefers to keep to herself.'

'No,' I say, my face hot with indignation. 'Why would she? We're best friends.'

'Hey, don't get mad at me,' he says, holding his hands up. 'I don't know the answers here. I was just asking.'

I hesitate, suddenly unsure of myself. Could it be possible that Jojo's been keeping secrets from me? The idea makes me feel sick.

'Was there anyone else in the room when you spoke to her?' Ram asks. 'Did you hear anyone in the background or anything?'

'Just Olivia.'

He gives me a sharp look. I return it with one of my own.

There's a long pause.

'So, are you going to help me or not?' I ask.

Ram sighs and rubs the back of his neck. 'Why me, Frankie? We haven't seen each other in months and all of a sudden you're wanting me to drive you halfway across the country. It doesn't exactly make sense.'

'Do you want the honest answer?'

'Well, preferably, yeah.'

'You're the only person I know with a car.'

'Aha.'

'It's not just that, though!' I add quickly. 'Jojo likes you. She trusts you. I can't turn up with just anyone. I have no idea what I'm walking into here.'

Another pause.

Ram lets out a heavy sigh.

I hold my breath.

'I'll need to be get back before morning,' he says. 'I've got a shift at ten.'

Is that a yes? I think it might be a yes.

'No problem,' I say, trying to keep the excitement out of my voice. 'If we get going soon, we'll be back in loads of time.'

'Hang on, I haven't agreed yet.'

'Well, hurry up and do it then. Jojo needs us and we're wasting time.'

Ram rakes his hands through his hair. 'You're certain this hotel is where she is?'

'She was there as of just before seven o'clock. I'm guessing she's paid to stay for at least one night so I can't see why she'd go anywhere else until tomorrow morning at the earliest.'

He swears under his breath. 'You'll have to navigate,' he says then.

'Oh my God, thank you!' I cry. I want to hug him but it feels like too much of an overstep so I just do a little dance on the spot instead.

'But just to be clear,' Ram says, as I follow him down the steps. 'I don't for one second think Jojo's taken this baby, OK?'

'OK,' I reply.

'That's not why I'm doing this. I'm doing it because Jojo's all alone in a random town and might need our help. Right?'

'Understood.'

'OK. Good. Now, why don't you go wait in the foyer while I collect my stuff.'

Ram has parked down a side road a few minutes' walk away from the ice rink. Despite the dimming light, it's still boiling. After the cool of the rink, it's like stepping into an oven.

He's changed out of his black 'Skate Marshal' polo shirt and into a white T-shirt. He looks good in white. I always used to tell him so.

'Don't touch the car until I've unlocked it,' he says, rummaging in his bag for his keys.

'How come?' I ask.

'The previous owner went to town on some fancy alarm system. It's ridiculously sensitive. You only have to brush the car and it goes off.'

'What, like this?' I ask, pretending to nudge the bonnet.

'Frankie!' Ram scolds. 'I mean it.'

'Oh, calm down, I was only joking.'

'Well, it wasn't funny. The alarm is really bloody loud. We'd wake half the street.'

I roll my eyes as he unlocks the car. I'd forgotten what a stickler for the rules he can be.

'Did you pass first time?' I ask as I climb into the passenger seat.

'My driving test?'

'Yeah.'

'Uh-huh.'

'Thought so. How many lessons did you have? No, let me guess.' I think for a moment. 'Fifteen? No, twelve.'

'Close. Eleven.'

I'm not remotely surprised. Ram is one of life's golden boys – naturally good at everything. It used to impress me and drive me mad in equal measures, the way he could turn his hand to almost anything with little to no effort (at least that's what it looked like from the outside). Of course he passed his driving test first time after only eleven lessons. Of course he did.

'How many minors?' I ask.

'Three.'

'Hmmm.'

Despite the fancy alarm system, Ram's car is not especially posh (a second-hand Citroën) but it is immaculate. Empty, apart from one of those magic tree air fresheners dangling from the rear-view mirror, both the exterior and interior are pristine. Not that I expected anything less. His bedroom was the neatest of anyone I've ever met. The first time I went inside, I felt like I was stepping into one of those show bedrooms at IKEA.

'Nice wheels,' I say, putting on my seat belt.

'Thanks,' he murmurs. 'You're OK to navigate, right?'

'Yeah. I'm not sure how long my battery will last, though.'

'I've got a charger in my bag.'

'OK, cool.' I type the postcode into Google Maps. It's further than I thought.

'What's our estimated arrival time?' Ram asks.

'Um, elevenish,' I say, rounding down by almost an hour and angling the phone away so he can't see the screen. The last thing I need is for him to get put off by the distance and change his mind.

'Shit,' he says. 'I'm going to be driving all night pretty much. You best not fall asleep.'

'What do you mean?' I ask, feigning innocence.

'Frankie. The entire time we were going out I don't think you once made it to the end of a film without conking out. And we watched a lot of films.'

He's right. We did. Especially towards the end when it was becoming increasingly obvious we had hardly anything in common.

'I promise I won't fall asleep on you,' I say. 'Scout's honour.'

'Since when were you a scout?'

'Oh, don't be so picky. You have my word I won't fall asleep, OK?'

Ram looks sceptical but starts the car.

As the engine roars into life, a shiver dances up my spine.

'Ready?' Ram asks.

'Ready,' I reply.

Chapter 10

Ram and I have been on the road for less than fifteen minutes and already we appear to have run out of conversation.

Excellent.

'Mind if I put the radio on?' I ask. I'm not very good with silences. Just a few minutes of quiet makes me feel antsy. I'd be such a bad monk.

'Sure,' Ram says.

I lean forward and fiddle with the buttons until I find KISS. I turn up the volume and lean back in my seat.

My phone buzzes in my lap with yet another text message asking why Jojo and I aren't at the party. I've been replying to them all with the same cut and pasted response.

> Something came up. Have fun! Mwah, mwah. F&J xxx

'You're popular tonight,' Ram says as I press 'send'.

'I'm supposed to be at a party right now,' I reply. 'GCSE results day and all that.'

'Oh shit, of course. How'd you do?'

'Not bad,' I say. 'No horrible surprises. One really nice one.'

'Oh yeah?'

'Yeah. A nine in drama.'

'That's wicked,' he says. 'Well done.'

His happiness for me seems genuine. I'd forgotten how supportive he always was, especially of my acting ambitions.

'How'd Jojo do, do you know?' he adds.

'No. She never picked up her envelope, did she. Oh, it's a left here, by the way.'

He flicks on his indicator. 'So, what you going to do?' he asks. 'Stay on for sixth form? Go to college? Hey, what happened with that acting place you and Jojo used to talk about all the time?'

He means the Arts Academy.

I hesitate. The day I found out I didn't get into the academy was one of the worst of my life. I'm not exactly in the mood to relive it.

'I didn't end up auditioning,' I say.

'Really? But you wanted to get in so badly.'

'Yeah, I know. But the more I looked into it, the more I realized it maybe wasn't for me.'

'How come?'

'Well, the commute to start with. It's a train and a bus. And you know what I'm like in the mornings. Totally useless.'

I laugh. I think it's pretty convincing but Ram doesn't join in.

'Do you still want to act?' he asks.

'Of course I do,' I say indignantly. 'More than anything. I can act anywhere, though. I don't need to go to the Arts Academy.'

There's a pause.

'What about Jojo?' he asks. 'Did she audition?'

'Uh-huh,' I reply lightly, my fingers tracing the window frame.

'And? How'd she do?'

Once more, I hesitate. I can't exactly lie again, though. Not when we're going to be seeing Jojo in a matter of hours.

'She got a place,' I say.

'Really?'

'Yeah.'

'Wow. How many people apply again? Isn't it loads?'

'Thousands,' I admit.

'Wow,' he repeats. 'What an achievement. Good for her.'

'Yeah,' I murmur.

'You happy for her?' he asks.

'What's that supposed to mean?' I snap. 'Of course I'm happy for her, she's my best friend.'

'Calm down, I was just asking.'

'Yeah, well, it was a stupid question. As if I wouldn't be happy for her. What do you take me for?'

'I was going to say: it would be OK if you weren't. You're only human, after all.'

'Well, I am, OK? Happy for her, I mean.'

'OK, OK. I'm sorry I asked.'

We don't speak for another three songs.

Although it was Ms Abraham who first told Jojo and me about the Arts Academy, I was the one who sent off for the prospectus and booked Jojo and I on the open day and initiated practically all our conversations about it. Not that Jojo wasn't interested. In her own quiet way, I believe she wanted to get in just as much as me. I know for a fact she practised her audition speech way more than I did mine. Which begs the question, why would she jeopardize her place by doing something as crazy and downright criminal as this? She's due to start at the academy in less than two weeks. She can't exactly do that if she's on the run with Olivia Sinclair.

My brain hurts.

Nothing makes sense.

And yet I know my instincts are right.

Jojo has Olivia.

I just have no idea why.

'What are you doing?' Ram asks.

We've been travelling for over an hour, although it feels like much longer. It's fully dark now, but no less stiflingly hot.

'Googling why people steal babies,' I reply.

Ram rolls his eyes.

I ignore him and scan the results page. 'There are entire articles about it,' I report, clicking on the first result.

'And?' Ram asks.

'What happened to you thinking I've made this whole thing up?'

Ram sighs. 'I don't think you've made anything up. I just think you've made some pretty massive assumptions based on very little. It doesn't mean I'm not interested. I mean, someone's taken Olivia, haven't they?'

I don't answer him, skim-reading an article on a psychology website. The content is not what I was expecting.

'OK, this is going to sound really weird,' I say. 'But most people who steal babies are women who are trying to keep their relationship together.'

'Huh?'

'I know.'

'But how does that even work? The woman just turns up with a baby one day and expects her boyfriend or whoever not to ask any questions?'

'Not exactly. According to this, she'll have probably faked an entire pregnancy.'

'But that's insane.'

'I know. Plus, Jojo doesn't even have a boyfriend.'

'You know that for definite?'

'Yes. Why?'

'No reason.'

Apart from a three-week relationship with Christopher Wan in Year Nine, during which they exchanged maybe eleven words at the most, Jojo has always been single despite my best efforts to matchmake.

I go back to the main results page and scroll down. I click on some more links, most of which repeat the same theory, until I find something a bit different.

'OK, here we go,' I say. 'This article refers to a case from 2013 where a woman abducted a newborn from a hospital, and when they delved into her history it turned out she'd had loads of miscarriages.' I sigh. 'But that doesn't make any sense either. Jojo's never even had sex.'

Ram glances over at me. 'She hasn't?'

I pause, suddenly aware I've said too much.

'You won't let on I told you that, will you?' I ask.

'Of course I won't. It's none of my business.'

'Thanks. It's just that Jojo's kind of private about that sort of thing.'

'I won't say a word.'

I close down the tabs and rest my phone on my lap. 'So, how about you?' I ask. 'You seeing anyone at the moment?'

There's no evidence of a girlfriend on Instagram, but then Ram was never especially into flaunting our relationship online. I managed to persuade him to pose for a few photos but he always did so grudgingly, the look in his eyes screaming that he had a million better things he'd rather be doing than cuddling up to his girlfriend in front of a camera lens. It was one of the many things we used to argue about.

'It wouldn't kill you to look like you're having a good time,' I'd say.

'That's just it,' he'd reply. 'I *was* having a great time until the precise moment you pointed a camera in my face. Can't we just enjoy hanging out without having to document it?'

'It doesn't mean he loves you any less,' I remember Jojo saying when I complained to her about it. 'He just isn't keen on having his private life splashed all over the internet.'

'It's not like I'm posting pictures of him naked or on the loo,' I muttered.

'I know,' Jojo said gently, ever the diplomat. 'But I'm worried you're confusing him not wanting to pose for selfies with you with him not being proud to have you as his girlfriend.'

They were both being totally reasonable, of course. I knew that deep down, which was probably why I was acting like such a brat about it. The fact was, despite Ram's explanation and Jojo's reassurances, I still couldn't help but worry that his reluctance to appear in photos was a reflection of his feelings towards me, and that with another girl – a prettier, cleverer, more interesting, all-round better girl – he'd behave totally differently.

I realize Ram hasn't answered my question.

'Well?' I prompt.

'No,' Ram says. 'I'm not seeing anyone.'

'Have you seen anyone since we broke up?'

'No.'

I'm surprised. And also a little pleased.

'How come?' I ask, unable to resist the temptation to fish.

He shrugs.

'It's not like you've not got the opportunity,' I point out. I think of all the girls I saw giving him heart eyes tonight. He could have a different girlfriend for every day of the week if he wanted to.

'I haven't really had the time,' he says.

'If you meet someone you like, you make time.' *You did for me*, I add silently.

'Well, clearly I haven't met anyone I like then.'

I wait for him to return the line of questioning, but he doesn't, and I get the feeling he's not overly keen on the topic in general. I've seen a few boys since breaking up with Ram, but it's always fizzled out after a couple of weeks. I don't know why. I just haven't met anyone who's held my interest.

'I haven't met anyone either, by the way,' I say. 'You know, in case you were wondering.'

'OK,' he says, shrugging.

'That's not a hint by the way,' I add quickly. 'I'm not suggesting we get back together or anything like that.'

'Noted.'

'OK, good.'

We sit in silence for a few moments.

'Do you regret it?' I ask.

'Regret what?'

'Asking me out in the first place.'

'No. Why?'

'Just curious.'

'Do you regret saying yes?' he asks.

'No.'

'Why did you ask me out?'

'Do you really want to get into this, Frankie?'

I shrug.

Ram sighs. 'If you must know, I asked you out because of your laugh.'

'My laugh?'

'Yeah. You're the only person I've ever met who laughs with their entire body.'

'I do?'

'You do.'

'And you liked that?'

'I liked that.'

It's true we laughed a lot in the first few weeks of our relationship. One time I made Ram laugh so much he thought he was going to throw up. It's kind of hard to imagine now. It feels like a lifetime ago.

'What went wrong?' I ask. It comes out in an unintentional whisper.

Ram looks pained. 'I thought we'd gone over all this.'

'That was ages ago, though.'

Ram and I broke up last October. We were in the hallway at my house (Mum, Dad and Luca were all out) and we were arguing. I have no idea how we ended up in the hallway or even how the argument started, only that it quickly evolved into the sort where you say the kind of things that you can't take back, and before I knew it we were breaking up.

Although I was the one who voiced it first, it was a mutual decision; a joint acknowledgement that we'd be happier apart, which makes it sound like it was easy and pleasant. It was neither of these things. We both shouted, even Ram who rarely raises his voice. I cried. I like to think Ram cried on his way home, but I guess I'll never know.

'We were just a wrong fit,' Ram says now, his voice gentle. 'It was no one's fault.'

'Yeah,' I murmur. 'I know.'

Because we went to different schools, I at least didn't have to endure the torture of seeing him in the corridors every day, but Ram still invaded my thoughts almost constantly. Although I knew we were better off apart, his sudden absence in my life left a massive hole. I missed him. I missed his arms around me, and his smell, and his grey Uniqlo hoodie, and the way he looked at me when I was being funny or cute or charming. I missed his mum and sisters, and their cosy little house, and even his annoying best friend, Maxwell. I missed him making me cups of tea and rubbing my feet and helping me with my maths homework.

But there were things I didn't miss too. The arguing, freezing my arse off standing on the sidelines at his football matches, his choice of Netflix films, wobbling about on the ice while groups of girls gave me daggers, the sneaking suspicion that I was massively intellectually inferior to him and he was just too polite to say so.

Gradually, though, the hole after our break-up filled, largely thanks to Jojo who was downright heroic in those early days, always on hand with sage advice and a giant bar of Dairy Milk, and by the New Year, I was back on form – single and very much ready to mingle once more. I'd got my first big relationship out of the way and I'd emerged more or less unscathed. It was a necessary rite of passage, and I'd made it out the other side. I felt wise, worldly, womanly.

At least, I did then. Right now, I feel none of these things. I don't get it. It's not like I want him back or anything like that. Ram is right. We're the wrong fit, we always were. There's just something about being in such close proximity with him that's stirring up all those old feelings, making me doubt myself and wonder if I could have done something differently, if I could have tried harder, or just been better . . .

'You OK?' Ram asks.

'Fine,' I say. 'Mind if I change the station? I fancy a change of mood.'

'Go for it.'

I lean forward and begin scrolling through the stations. I want something comforting and familiar.

'Magic OK?' I ask.

My parents listen to Magic. I like to take the mick out of them about it, but secretly I love the cheesy music selections.

'Magic's fine,' Ram replies.

'I'm Still Standing' by Elton John is playing. I murmur along with the lyrics and start to feel a bit better. I was being silly before, letting nostalgia and doubt get the better of me.

The next song is 'Superman' by Black Lace. 'Oh my God, blast from the past!' I say, laughing.

'Can you turn this off?' Ram says abruptly.

'Oh, come on, my singing isn't that bad.'

'It's not that. I've just changed my mind about Magic. Can you stick Classic FM on instead?'

'Classic FM? Are you serious?'

'Or anything else. Just not this.'

'Fine,' I say, tutting and changing the station.

I can't bring myself to put Classic FM on so I compromise with Radio 2.

'This better, Your Highness?' I ask.

'Yes,' Ram says, his gaze straight ahead. 'Thank you.'

Chapter 11

'I need to fill up,' Ram announces.

They're the first words he's spoken since he got all pissy about my choice in music about half an hour ago.

I glance at the dashboard. The red light is illuminated. It feels like we've been in the car for ever, but according to Google maps we're not even two thirds of the way there yet.

'OK,' I say. 'I wouldn't mind a wee actually.'

We agree to stop at the next services. When we arrive, the service station is eerily quiet. The few concessions that are still open are manned by kids barely older than us, with pallid complexions and zombie-like gazes.

Large TV screens mounted on either side of the food court are showing the news. The photo of Olivia flashes up. I grab Ram's arm and point up at the closest screen. There's no sound, but the scrolling banners suggest the police have no new leads, at least none they're willing to share with the general public. It appears we're one step ahead of them. For the time being anyway.

I glance across at Ram. He gives me one of his 'I'm still not buying this for one second' looks and gently removes my hand from his arm.

'I'm going to the loo,' he says. 'I'll meet you back at the car.'

The lighting in the toilets is bright and harsh. I attempt to touch up my make-up, but it's a lost cause. In the end I just make do with blotting my sweaty face with a tissue and re-doing my bun. It's not like I've got anyone to impress, right?

Before returning to the car, I go to WHSmith and stock up on bottles of Coke, a jumbo packet of Haribo, a grab bag of pickled onion Monster Munch and a couple of chunky Kit Kats in the hope it'll distract Ram from the fact I'm probably not going to be able to make much of a contribution to the petrol costs.

I pay for my items and head for the exit.

Ram is just outside the double doors with his back to me. He's on the phone.

'Stop right there, Mum,' he's saying. 'I mean it. There is no way Frankie and I are getting back together, no way at all.'

At the sound of my name, I freeze.

'I'm just helping her out with something,' Ram adds. He sighs and rubs the back of his neck. 'I know you do. But you need to understand that it's not going to happen. We tried it and it didn't work. It more than didn't work. It was a disaster.'

I blink. I know we had our ups and downs but 'disaster' seems a bit strong. What happened to us just being a 'wrong fit'?

'No,' he continues. 'It's nothing to do with what happened at New Year. I told you, that was a non-starter. Look, I've got to go . . . Of course I'll drive safely . . . Love you too. Bye.'

As he hangs up I dash back through the automatic doors. I watch through the glass as he slides his phone into the back pocket of his shorts and walks towards the car.

I count to twenty before following him.

'Provisions,' I say, shoving the bag of drinks and snacks into his lap.

He takes a brief look inside before handing it back. 'Why didn't you tell me you'd been over to my house?' he says.

Ah.

'It didn't come up. And I had no choice but to go over there. I didn't have your number.'

'Why not?'

'I just didn't. Look, is it really such a big deal?'

'Yes.'

'Why?'

'Because. You've got them all riled up.'

'Riled up?'

'Yeah. It'll be Frankie this and Frankie that for weeks now.'

'It's not my fault we got on so well. Or would you rather I'd just been a complete cow to them?'

He sighs. 'Of course not. I just . . .' His voice trails off. 'They just get attached,' he says after a pause.

'Well, I was attached too,' I shoot back.

'I know.'

There's another pause.

I dive into the bag and rip open the packet of Haribo. I'm a bit too rough with it and half of them end up on the floor. Ram winces.

'Sorry,' I mutter, bending down to pick them up.

'Don't put those ones back in the bag,' he says.

'As if I would,' I mutter.

I sit back in my seat, the sweets I picked up off the floor already going soft and squishy in my warm fist.

'Are the Cokes cold?' Ram asks.

I nod.

'Can I have one, please?'

I wrap the dirty sweets in a tissue then pass Ram one of the bottles. He thanks me and takes a long swig.

'We should get going,' he says, screwing the lid back on and sticking the bottle in the cup holder.

'OK,' I reply.

Ram doesn't speak again until we're back on the motorway. 'So, what's the plan?' he asks.

'Plan?'

'Yeah.'

'How do you mean?'

'For when we arrive.'

'Oh God, I don't know. I was just going to improvise.'

He shakes his head. 'Of course you were.'

'Well, excuse me, but I don't think I have a whole lot of choice. I mean, Jojo's clearly lost her mind. Who knows how she's going to react.'

'You honestly think she's got Olivia, don't you?'

'How many times have I got to tell you this? Yes!'

'Even though it's totally out of character.'

'Yes.'

Ram pauses. 'OK,' he says. 'Let's just say you're right and Jojo has got her, what's your goal here?'

'My goal?'

'Yeah. What are you going to do when we arrive?'

'I told you, I'm going to improvise depending on what we discover.'

'Yeah, but you must have some sort of outcome in mind.'

'Well,' I say slowly. 'I suppose I'm going to start by talking to Jojo and persuading her she's made a massive mistake. Then we'll all go back to Newfield and return Olivia to her parents.'

'And how are we going to do that without getting the police involved?'

'We'll do it anonymously.'

'How?'

'I don't know,' I say, prickling with irritation. 'I haven't ironed out the details in my head yet.'

'No shit.'

'Fine,' I snap. 'You come up with a plan then.'

'Why should I? I'm not the one who thinks Jojo has kidnapped a baby. I'm just the chauffeur.'

There's a pause.

'Why are you even here?' I say.

Ram blinks. 'What do you mean?'

'If you're so convinced I'm just some silly drama queen who's imagined this all from nothing, why did you even agree to come?'

'I told you earlier.'

'So tell me again.'

'Because you asked me to. No, you *begged* me to.'

'And since when did what I want make the slightest bit of difference?'

Ram sighs. 'Please don't do this, Frankie.'

'Do what?'

'Turn this into another argument.'

'I'm not!'

'Yes you are. You literally can't help yourself.'

'So, what, you're calling me a liar now?'

'What? No. That's not what I said.'

'Well, that's what it sounded like.'

'Well, that wasn't my intention.'

'Well, that's how it came across, so maybe you should think before you start spouting off in future.'

No one says anything for about thirty seconds. Ram is the one who breaks the silence.

'Look, I don't think you're a liar, Frankie,' he says softly.

I don't say anything.

'I'm just tired. I'm not used to driving long distances.'

'OK.'

'I don't want to fight,' he adds.

'Me neither,' I say.

There's another long pause.

'I'm sorry I had a go at you,' I say.

'And I'm sorry I had a go back. Truce?'

I hesitate before answering. Despite Ram's apology, I still feel a bit upset. Not that I'm going to let on. It'll only prove his point if I do.

'Truce.'

Chapter 12

The hotel car park is for residents only so we're forced to park on a side road.

We walk to the hotel in silence. Now that we're finally here, just moments away from Jojo and the baby, the nerves are kicking in.

The hotel foyer is stuffy and painfully bright. The receptionist, a skinny man with massive sweat patches under his arms and a badge informing us his name is 'Reece' pinned to his sky-blue shirt, eyes us wearily as we approach the desk.

'Can I help you?' he asks, not even bothering to disguise the yawn that breaks his question in half.

'Hopefully,' I say. 'A friend of ours checked in earlier. I wonder if you could just tell us what room she's in?'

'What's the name?' he asks.

'Jojo Bright.'

He taps away at his keyboard. 'No, sorry.'

'Joanna Bright, then?'

'No, sorry.'

'Are you sure?'

'Positive.'

I look to Ram. He shakes his head.

Then it comes to me. 'OK, how about Amelia Wylde?' I say.

When we were about thirteen, Jojo and I spent an entire afternoon coming up with stage names in case ours were already taken by the time we joined Equity, the acting union. After much deliberation, I went with Kristin Winters, while Jojo plumped for Amelia Wylde.

'Winters and Wylde,' we used to chorus as we practised our signatures in preparation for all the autographs we'd one day sign.

This time Reece doesn't bother to look at his screen. 'Oh yeah, her,' he says. 'The girl with the baby. Checked in about three.'

'I'm sorry, what did you just say?' Ram asks.

'That she checked in around three.'

'No before that. Something about a baby?'

'Oh yeah. She had a littl'un with her.'

'Told you!' I exclaim.

'Are you absolutely sure about that?' Ram asks Reece, his voice trembling.

Reece frowns. 'Yeah. I had to sort her out with a cot for it.'

'Can you tell us what room she's in, please?' I ask, gripping the edge of the reception desk.

'Ah, sorry, no can do.'

'What? Why not?'

'It's against the rules, innit?'

'What rules?'

'Hotel rules. We can't go round giving out our guests' room numbers willy-nilly.'

I glance at Ram, who has sunk onto the fake leather sofa next to the vending machine, his eyes wide with shock at the realization that I was right all along. I turn back to Reece.

'But she's my best friend,' I say.

'Makes no difference, I'm afraid.'

'But I can prove it. Look!'

I get my phone out.

'See!' I yelp. 'She's my wallpaper.'

I hold it up so he can see. It's a picture of Jojo and me in our *A Midsummer Night's Dream* costumes, our arms around each other's shoulders.

'Sorry, I can't,' Reece says. 'I'd get it in the neck if she complained.'

'But she won't!'

'Can't risk it.'

I look over at Ram for help but he's staring at the floor, his head in his hands.

I'm on my own.

Time to channel my not-so-inner drama queen.

'What if it's an emergency?' I say.

Reece narrows his eyes. 'What kind of emergency?'

'It's the baby,' I say. 'The baby needs regular medication. And the thing is, Jojo, I mean, Amelia left home without it and we need to get it to her as a matter of urgency. We've driven all the way from Nottingham.'

'What kind of medication?' Reece asks, narrowing his bloodshot eyes. 'What's wrong with it?'

'It's a genetic condition. Very rare.'

'And what happens to the kid if they don't take it?'

'They'll get really sick. They'll probably have to go to hospital.'

Reece hesitates.

'Please, Reece. It's important.'

He sighs and starts tapping at his keyboard. 'Room four-two-six,' he says with a sigh. 'Fourth floor. Lift's over there.'

'Thank you, Reece. You're a star.'

I pull Ram to his feet and drag him towards the lifts.

'I'm not sure I should be here,' Ram says.

These are the first words he's spoken since Reece confirmed Jojo and Olivia's presence at the hotel.

'What are you talking about?' I ask. We're in the lift. It's moving excruciatingly slowly.

'Yeah, I think I should wait downstairs,' Ram says.

'But why?'

'Jojo isn't expecting either of us. We don't know how she's going to react to seeing you, and you're her best mate. Do we really want to add me into the mix?'

Maybe Ram's got a point. He and Jojo always got on, but it's not like they kept in touch after the break-up. The last thing I want is to freak her out or have her totally clam up on us. Yes, we're relying on Ram to drive us home, but I can introduce that detail later, once I've got the situation under control.

'Yeah, perhaps,' I say.

'I just think it's for the best, you know.'

The doors open onto the fourth floor. I step out into the corridor.

'I'll be just downstairs if you need me,' Ram says.

'OK.'

'Good luck,' he adds.

The lift doors judder shut. And I'm on my own.

I set off down the corridor. It's way past midnight, and apart from the buzz of the vending machine outside the lifts, it's silent.

Under my breath, I count the room numbers.

401, 402, 403, 404, 405 . . .

Room 426 is right at the end of the corridor.

I stop outside. There's a 'do not disturb' sign hanging from the handle. My heart hammering in my chest, I listen at the door.

Silence.

I take a deep breath and knock.

No answer.

I knock again, harder this time, using the side of my fist instead of my knuckles.

Still no answer.

'Jojo,' I call. 'It's me, Frankie. Are you in there?'

Nothing.

Maybe she's popped out? But where? And why? It's gone midnight. She could be asleep, I suppose, but unlike me, Jojo has always been a light sleeper, forever marvelling at my ability to sleep through thunderstorms and Luca's obnoxious heavy metal and Mum's early morning vacuuming sessions. There's no way my banging wouldn't wake her, I'm almost certain.

I knock again.

Still nothing.

Doubt ripples through my body.

Maybe Reece got it wrong. Maybe he confused Jojo (or

Amelia) with someone else. But that makes no sense either. She's here, I'm certain. So why is she ignoring me?

'Jojo, can you hear me?' I call. 'Seriously, open up!'

But all I'm greeted with is heavy silence.

I back away from the door.

Now what? I can't just keep knocking. I'll wake up the entire corridor. In which case, do I just wait? After all, she's got to come out sometime. But that might not be until morning, hours and hours from now. I can hardly sit in the corridor all night.

The ripple of doubt morphs into a wave of panic. What if something's happened to her in there? Something bad. And that's the reason she's not answering the door?

My hand trembling, I get my phone out of my pocket to call Ram for a second opinion.

That's when I hear it.

I terminate the call and press my ear against the door.

And there it is.

The unmistakeable cry of a real-life baby.

And not just any old baby.

Olivia Sinclair.

And then the gentle creak of the mattress as someone – no, not someone, Jojo – gets out of bed.

I keep knocking.

And this time, I'm not going to stop until I get a response.

PART TWO

JOJO

Chapter 13

When I was seven, we went on a family holiday to St Ives in Cornwall. It was a long drive so to break up the journey home we stopped off for lunch in Swindon, a town in Wiltshire. After the picture-postcard snowy white beaches and dinky little lanes of St Ives, Swindon, with its boxy concrete buildings and pedestrianized high street, felt like the most boring place on the planet. So boring, in fact, I'd flat out forgotten all about its existence until this morning – when I found myself with a baby in my arms and the pressing need to go somewhere no one would ever think of looking for me.

I bring up the A–Z station finder on the ticket machine screen and type in 'Swindon'.

At over £100, the ticket is way more expensive than I was expecting. For the first time since I left the house, I hesitate. I didn't anticipate spending so much all in one go.

On the way to the station, I stopped at the cashpoint and withdrew as much money as I could from my savings account. Along with my wages from the odd bit of babysitting and several chunks of unspent Christmas and birthday money, I've built up quite the nest egg. Still, am I really prepared to spend that much on a single train ticket?

As my right index finger hovers over the 'buy' button, my phone buzzes against my hip bone. My heart racing, I reach into the pocket of my baggy shorts and take it out.

Stacey.

She must have just got home. I picture her walking through the empty house, calling my name, confusion at my absence quickly melting into panic. I need to get a move on. I've got a head start but not a huge one. If she suspects I've headed for the train station, it would only take twenty minutes for her to get here, fifteen if there's not much traffic.

My phone stops buzzing. Before Stacey has the chance to call again, I turn it off and press 'buy', my hand visibly trembling as I feed notes into the slot.

As the tickets are printing, I kiss my baby on his head.

'It looks like we're going to Swindon, Albie,' I whisper.

The first leg of my journey requires me to travel to London. The train is already at the platform when I arrive. I walk its length, peering through the windows to work out which is the quietest carriage. I settle on coach C because it has the fewest reservation cards.

As I inch my way down the aisle, I catch sight of my reflection in the window. It takes me a second or two to make the connection and acknowledge that the girl with shadows under her eyes and a sleeping baby strapped to her chest is actually me. I avert my gaze and keep moving, coming to a stop when I reach an unoccupied table with no reservations. I slide into the forward-facing window seat, placing my backpack beside me.

If I crane my neck, the departure board is just about visible. We're leaving in four minutes. Even though I'm pretty sure Stacey couldn't possibly get here in time now, my stomach still churns as the seconds crawl by, my heart lurching every time I glimpse someone with blond hair making their way down the platform.

In the final couple of minutes before departure, the carriage begins to fill up. I dig into the backpack and spread baby paraphernalia across the table – bottles and nappies and wipes, hoping the debris will put off my fellow passengers. It works. Although plenty of people pass by, no one sits opposite me.

Finally, the doors beep and close and the guard blows his whistle. A few seconds later, we're moving. It's only then I realize I've been holding my breath. God knows for how long. When I let it out, my exhalation is shaky.

As the train chugs through the outskirts of Nottingham, I count trampolines, satellite dishes, roof skylights, solar panels – anything to distract me from the enormity of what I have done. What I *am* doing.

I place my hand on Albie's head, searching for that soft spot where the skull is yet to fuse. I always thought it was a myth, but there it is, ever so slightly squidgy under the gentle pressure of my thumb pad. Instantly, I feel a lot calmer.

My breathing back to normal, I reach for the book I grabbed from Stacey's bedside table – *Keep Calm: The New Mum's Manual* – and turn to the first page.

'Anyone sitting here?'

I look up. A middle-aged woman dressed in a tropical print kaftan is standing in the aisle. She's panting slightly and her hair, the colour of a ripe tangerine, is sticking to her forehead in sweaty kiss curls.

'I'm sorry?' I say.

'I was just wondering if anyone was sitting here?' she says, gesturing at the two empty seats opposite me.

I glance around. The carriage is busy, spare seats at a premium. The woman continues to look at me, her expression patient but expectant.

'Oh, no, I don't think anyone is,' I say, setting aside my book and scooping up the bottles and wipes and things and returning them to my bag.

'Oh, don't you worry about that,' she says, plonking herself down. 'I've got plenty of space.' She places a huge rattan bag on the table. 'I thought I'd missed it,' she continues. 'They've closed Larwood Avenue for some reason so my bus got diverted.' She buries her nose inside her bag, producing a packet of tissues and a compact mirror in the shape of a seashell. She opens the compact, placing it in the palm of one hand while she blots her forehead. 'I don't suppose you could spare me one of your wipes?' she says, snapping the compact shut. 'Don't worry if you can't.'

'No, of course,' I say. I pluck a wipe from the packet and pass it to her.

'Thank you, sweetheart,' she says, swiping it under each armpit in turn. She leans across the aisle and tosses it in the bin along with three soggy tissues. 'This weather, eh?' she adds, pulling at the loose material of her kaftan and wafting it about. 'I know we shouldn't moan, but my God, it's getting to be a pain. I never thought I'd say this, but I'd kill for a bit of rain.' She reaches back into her bag, taking out a plastic carton of grapes and placing them in the centre of the table. 'Would you like some?' she asks, snapping off a small bunch for herself.

'Oh. No, thank you.'

I'm not hungry. I haven't felt hungry in weeks now. In fact, it's been so long since I had an appetite, I can't quite remember what the sensation feels like, the days of polishing off extra-large Domino's pizzas with Frankie some weird, distant memory.

'Well, they're here if you change your mind,' the woman says, leaving the grapes in the centre of the table.

'Thank you,' I say.

'How's your little one coping?' the woman asks.

Your little one. She accepts he's mine, no questions asked. I want to kiss her.

'In the heat, I mean?' she adds when I don't respond right away.

'Oh, OK, I think,' I say.

'That's good,' she says, popping a couple of grapes in her mouth and chewing loudly. 'Especially with all that hair. Takes after his dad, does he?'

My body tenses.

'He's got quite the headful,' she adds.

The implication being that he couldn't have possibly got it from me. My hair has always been thin and as straight as a poker, hanging in uninspiring wisps around my face. I had it cut into a bob last autumn in an effort to make it appear thicker, but I'm not sure it made much difference, if any.

'Did he come out like that?' she asks.

'Er, yes.'

'Bet that was a shock,' she says, chuckling.

'Yes,' I murmur. 'You could say that.'

Chapter 14

Three weeks ago

The first day of August is chilly and grey.

'Where's this heatwave the forecasters keep banging on about?' Stacey demands at breakfast. 'That's what I want to know.'

'Patience, babe,' Mum says, setting identical plates of scrambled eggs on toast down on the table in front of Stacey and me.

'But it's August and I'm wearing leg warmers!' Stacey extends one of her long slender legs. As promised, she's wearing a pair of bright purple leg warmers over the top of her skinny jeans.

Mum just shakes her head and sits down with her own plate of food.

'It's not right,' Stacey continues, shovelling scrambled eggs onto her fork. 'The summer holidays are supposed to be all about lazing in the garden getting a tan! How am I supposed to get a tan in this?' She motions at the window. Even the pair of sparrows perched on washing line look a bit chilly. 'It's not right,' she repeats, shaking her head.

Mum and I exchange grins. Stacey has been complaining about the weather ever since she finished work for the summer holidays (she's a university lecturer).

'Are you not hungry, sweetheart?' Mum asks, nodding at my plate. She's taken the week off work, hence our leisurely breakfast.

I glance down. I haven't even picked up my fork. 'Sorry, no, not really. I woke up with a stomach ache.'

'Time of the month?' Stacey asks with a sympathetic tilt of the head.

'Oh. I don't know. Maybe.' I've been getting periods for almost two years now but, annoyingly, they're yet to settle into a regular pattern and I often go for months at a time without having one at all.

'I think there are painkillers in the junk drawer,' Mum says.

'Thanks.'

I cross over to the junk drawer and prise it open. Amongst the batteries and Sellotape and tape measures and ballpoint pens, I find a packet of paracetamol. I pop two into my hand.

'Best to take them with food,' Mum says as I return to the table. 'Maybe try a bit of toast.'

I nod and carefully scrape the eggs off the toast, nibbling the corner of one slice before swallowing the pills down with a swig of orange juice.

'So, what's on the agenda for today, Jojo?' Mum asks as I wipe my mouth on a piece of kitchen roll.

'I don't know,' I say. 'Maybe nothing. Frankie's at her gran's all day so I doubt I'll see her. How about you guys?'

'The paint hunt continues,' Stacey says.

'Seriously?'

'Unfortunately, yes,' Mum says, sighing.

Mum and Stacey have been searching for the perfect shade of paint for their bedroom for what feels like weeks now. Dozens of paint swatches with daft names like 'Phantom Mist' and 'Whispering Swallow' are stuck to their wall with Blu Tack.

'Want to come?' Stacey asks, wiggling her eyebrows.

'Thanks, but no thanks.' I love hanging out with Mum and Stacey, but when it comes to DIY, they're complete nightmares, fretting over every single tiny detail, and I have no desire to be dragged into the ongoing paint debate.

'We might go for a cheeky Wagamamas afterwards,' Stacey adds in a singsong voice.

Ordinarily, the promise of a vegetarian katsu curry might just about win me over, but the dull ache in my stomach has killed off all my usual cravings.

'I think I'm just going to stay here,' I say. 'Take it easy until my stomach feels a bit better.'

Mum and Stacey leave about an hour later, by which time I've migrated to the living room, clutching the hot water bottle Stacey insisted on preparing for me.

'We won't be long,' Mum says, popping her head behind the door to say goodbye.

'Yeah, right,' I say, rolling my eyes. 'You'll be gone for hours and you know it.'

She laughs. 'Ring if you need anything, yeah?'

'Will do.'

'Bye, Jojo!' Stacey calls from the hallway. 'Hope you feel better soon!'

'Thanks!' I call back. 'And good luck!'

'Cheeky!' she replies.

I wait for the front door to slam shut before returning to the episode of *The Good Place* I'd paused.

The credits are rolling and I'm waiting for the next episode to kick in when I get a message from Frankie.

> I've only been here for about 12 minutes and my gran is already driving me CRAZY!!!

Frankie's gran (her mum's mum) is notoriously demanding and Frankie is stuck with her all day. I smile as I tap out a sympathetic reply. After a tricky few months, following the whole Arts Academy thing in the spring, I finally feel like my friendship with Frankie might be back on track. Although the guilt hasn't gone away exactly, it's definitely not as intense as it was and, with only weeks to go until the term begins, I'm stupidly relieved that things seem more or less back to normal.

My phone buzzes with another message.

F: What you up to?
J: On the sofa. Worst period pains ever!!

As if on cue, pain shoots through my abdomen. I squeeze my eyes shut and wait for it to pass.

J: How long does paracetamol take to kick in?
F: I dunno. Half an hour maybe?
J: Jesus, I hope so.
F: Is it really only 11 a.m.? I swear time slows the second I enter my gran's house.

F: Ugh. I've got to go. She wants to go to Lidl.
#Funtimes
J: Enjoy!
F: Ha! Hope the pills kick in soon xxx
J: Thanks. Me too xxx

I continue to watch the TV but the shooting pains keep coming in waves, making it harder and harder to concentrate.

I press pause and roll off the sofa. Taking my hot water bottle with me, I hobble upstairs to the bathroom where I manage to force out a poo. Instead of bringing relief though, the pain only intensifies. I go over what I've eaten the past few days, but nothing stands out as potentially dodgy. No, it must be my period: it's the only explanation. I wipe myself and reach to pull up my knickers. They're halfway up my legs when I notice the crotch is stained with a weird gluey discharge.

Gross.

Grimacing, I scoop up the jelly-like substance with a wad of toilet paper and flush it down the loo, before removing my knickers altogether, tossing them in the laundry basket.

I shudder. I will never get used to having periods. Ever.

I go to my room and put on a fresh pair of knickers, pressing a sanitary towel into the crotch, then grab my duvet and drag it downstairs. Back in the living room, I pull it on top of me and continue to watch TV. I manage another one and half episodes of *The Good Place* before the pain in my stomach gets so bad I'm forced to return to the bathroom.

There's more weird discharge in my pants. Some of it has soaked into the sanitary towel but some of it is too thick and remains sitting there on the pad. I wonder if Frankie has had it before. I reach for my phone.

> Gross question alert but do you ever get clear discharge in your pants before your period??

More shooting pains. They hurt so much I have to grit my teeth together and grip onto the sink with both hands, to stop myself from crying out.

Finally, the pain subsides a little. Blinking, my eyes fall on the bathtub. Maybe a hot soak would help?

I turn on the taps, and while the bath is filling up, limp back downstairs for some more paracetamol. I take two more – isn't that about the maximum dose in twenty-four hours? – and lie down on the sofa while I wait for them to take effect. If anything though, the pain just gets more intense. I know I don't have much actual experience, but I cannot kick the feeling this is something more serious than normal period pain. That's usually more of a dull ache. This feels like my entire torso is being squeezed and tightened; my insides yanked and twisted in every possible direction. The pains aren't confined to my abdomen any more either. They're in my back and thighs and bottom too.

Worried my bath might be about to overflow, I try to stand up but my body refuses to cooperate and I'm forced to make my way back up to the bathroom on my hands and knees.

I need Frankie's gran's stair lift, I think, as I heave my body up the stairs. Really, this is ridiculous. I'm sixteen for God's sake, not sixty. I'd probably laugh if it didn't hurt so much.

The bathroom is cloudy with steam. Pulling myself to my feet, I switch on the extractor fan and turn off the taps before removing my pyjamas and knickers. I stick my hand into the water and let out a yelp. It's way too hot but far too full (almost to the brim) to risk adding any cold. I'll have to wait for it to cool down a little before getting in.

Unable to face any more physical exertion, I curl up on the rainbow-striped bathmat, naked and exhausted.

What a pathetic sight I must be right now. Frankie will think it's hilarious when I tell her about it later.

Actually, where is my phone?

I look up. It's on the edge of the sink, where I left it. I stretch to reach for it and open up Instagram in an effort to distract myself from the pain with photos of sunsets and cupcakes and cute dogs. I have a fleeting idea of posting a selfie – #periodpain #itsucksbeingagirl #paracetamoldoesnotwork!!!

A fresh stab of pain, perhaps the worst one yet. I let out a gasp, fresh tears brimming in my eyes.

What the hell is happening to me?

I go to ring Frankie. Then I remember – she's in Lidl getting bossed around by her grandmother.

With shaking fingers, I call Mum instead.

It rings out before going through the voicemail. I don't leave a message. I don't want to worry her. Instead, I send her a text.

> Paracetamol not really working. Can you pick me up something stronger on your way home? Thanks! Xx

There's a sudden surge of moisture between my legs. Gingerly, I reach down. I pull my hand away to discover my fingers are coated with the same sticky discharge I found in my knickers earlier, only this time it's lumpy and flecked with blood. I wash my hands, then retrieve my phone and decide to give Frankie a ring after all.

I'm scrolling to her name when another pain shoots through me; so strong and sharp it takes my breath away and the phone slips from my hand, bouncing off the edge of the bath before plunging beneath the surface.

I go to stick my hand into the water in an effort to retrieve it but the pain between my legs stops me, forcing me to grab onto the edge of the bath to stop myself from crumpling to the floor. I grit my teeth and squeeze my eyes shut.

I get this overwhelming urge to push.

But push what?

I look down.

There's something there.

Between my legs.

What the fuck?

I blink.

Look again.

It looks like the top of a head.

No.

It can't be.

It's not possible.

Another urge to push.

I don't fight it. I can't fight it.

I squeeze my eyes shut once more and push again. And again. And again.

In the gaps I scream and howl and pant, the pain like nothing I've ever experienced before.

Until finally, it is out of me.

A baby.

My baby.

Chapter 15

'How old is he?' the woman asks.

I pause before answering. 'Three weeks today.'

On the one hand, it feels like yesterday; on the other, I can't imagine my life now without Albie in it.

She lets out a whistle. 'You're brave,' she says. 'Out and about already. I think my oldest was nearly three months before I dared even give the local bus a try.' She laughs again. 'Is he your first?'

She makes it sound like such a normal question.

'Er, yes,' I say, my cheeks flushing. I look out the window. We're on the very fringes of the city now, the countryside beckoning.

'I had mine young too,' the woman says.

That gets my attention.

'Bit of a scandal at the time actually,' she continues. 'We proved them wrong, though. Me and my Eric. Forty years and three grown-up kids later and he's still the love of my life.'

She smiles proudly and I feel a strange ache in my chest.

'Here, I'll show you,' she says, producing a fat red leather purse, bulging with cards and receipts and loose change from her bag. She opens it up and pulls out a photograph, sliding it across the table towards me.

I pick it up and peer closely. A much younger version of the woman opposite me is sitting in front of a tinsel-laden Christmas tree with a chubby-cheeked baby on her lap. Next to her, a broad-shouldered man with an impressive moustache is holding a slightly startled-looking toddler on his lap. A third child, a boy of around four, is sitting cross-legged at their feet, a toy car in his hands.

'Christmas 1985,' the woman says, her voice rich with love and pride.

She leans over and points out the children in turn.

'Steven, Michael and David,' she says. 'Plus my Eric, of course.'

She looks up, her cheeks proud and pink. 'And I'm Annie,' she adds. 'As in Little Orphan.'

I realize this is my cue to introduce myself in return. 'I'm Amelia,' I say.

'And the little one?'

'Oh, this is . . . this is Luca.'

I don't know why I pick Luca. Only that it's the first male name that pops into my head.

'Luca!' Annie exclaims. 'How very exotic! Have you got Italian blood then? Or does he get it from his dad?'

'No,' I say quickly. 'It's from my side. My dad is Italian.'

She glances down at my pale white arms.

'I take after my mum,' I stammer.

'I was going to say! You look like quite the English rose to me.'

I manage a polite smile before returning to my book. I've lost my place and have to start again.

'Helpful?' Annie asks.

'Sorry?'

'Your book.'

'Oh, I'm not sure yet. I've only just started.'

'Well, if I can offer you any bit of advice, it's this: follow your instincts.'

'OK,' I say slowly.

'Because you're going to have loads of people trying to tell you how to do this and how to do that, but at the end of the day, you have to do what feels right for *you*.'

'But how do you know what that is?' I ask.

Annie smiles. 'You'll know. And from what I can make out, you're doing pretty well so far.'

I smile tightly.

'So, what will you be doing in London?' she asks. 'Visiting family?'

'Er, yes,' I say.

'Lovely. I'm going to stay with my sister for a few days. She's just had an op on her knee so she's feeling a bit sorry for herself. I'm going to try to cheer her up a bit. She's in Crystal Palace. Whereabouts are your lot?'

'Ealing,' I say.

Frankie has an aunt and uncle who own a pub there. We stayed with them last summer, after a visit to the Globe Theatre.

'Very nice,' Annie says. 'I bet they're all excited to see little Luca.'

'Yes,' I say, the lies tripping off my tongue. 'They can't wait.'

'I expect some of them haven't met him yet.'

'No.'

'They're going to be gaga for him, I'm telling you. I'm nutty about my grandkids. Absolutely besotted. I was quite strict with my boys when they were growing up, but when it comes to their kids I'm a right soft touch. And boy, do they know it. Wrapped around their little fingers, I am.' She chuckles. 'Dad not with you then?' she asks.

'*My* dad?' I ask.

I wonder if Stacey and Mum will look for me at his place. I hope not. I hate the idea of him worrying about me. I already feel guilty enough about ignoring so many of his calls and texts lately.

'Luca's dad,' Annie clarifies.

'Oh,' I say, swallowing hard. 'No. It's, er, it's just me.' I look down at my fingernails. I've started biting them again, the skin around the cuticles pink and angry.

'Is he not on the scene?' Annie asks, her voice gentle.

I look up. 'Um, no. I mean, not exactly. It's complicated.'

Her face crumples with sympathy. 'Oh, sweetheart,' she says.

'It's fine,' I reply quickly. 'It's best this way, really.'

Although my delivery sounds convincing enough, I can't help but feel like I'm delivering lines from a badly written play.

'Well, it's his loss,' Annie says, leaning over and placing her hand on top of mine. Her hands are warm and soft and she wears rings on almost every finger, the metal hot against my skin. 'Do you want to talk about it?' she asks. 'I know I can rabbit on, but I promise you, I'm an excellent listener too.'

'No,' I say. 'Honestly, it's fine. Thank you, though. That's really kind of you.' I plaster on my very best smile.

Annie doesn't look convinced. She wears her concern on her sleeve, head tilted to one side, eyes soft and sad.

Carefully, I slide my hand from beneath Annie's. 'Really,' I say, sitting up a little straighter and wrapping my arms around Albie's warm little body. 'We're fine. More than fine.'

Albie chooses that exact moment to let out a yowl.

Time for his bottle. 'Excuse me,' I say, turning away and reaching into my bag.

As I'm preparing Albie's bottle, we pull into the next station. According to the departure board it's twelve minutes past ten. I was due at Frankie's over ten minutes ago. She'll be wondering where I am. She might even have started to worry already. After all, I'm hardly ever late, especially when it's something important.

I close my eyes.

I'm sorry, Frankie.

For everything.

Chapter 16

Three weeks ago

The clatter of a trolley rouses me.

I blink my eyes open just in time to see a cheerful-looking woman with curly jet-black hair bustle in and plonk a tray on the over-bed table.

'Tea time,' she says as she wheels it into place.

I push myself up into a seated position and lift the plastic cover to reveal a mug of soup of unidentifiable flavour accompanied by a rock-hard bread roll, a portion of what I think might be cottage pie and a cup of pale pink jelly. Just the smell makes me want to puke. Hurriedly, I replace the cover and attempt to push the table away, only the wheels must be locked because it doesn't budge an inch.

A nurse, the one with startlingly pale skin and pillar-box-red hair who looked after us when we arrived, pokes her head round the side of the door. 'Ah, Jojo, you're awake,' she says.

I nod numbly.

As she makes her way towards me, my eyes drift to the plastic badge pinned to her light blue uniform. 'Staff Nurse Hayley', it says.

'How're you feeling?' she asks.

'Er, OK, thank you,' I mumble.

It's a lie. But I don't know what else to say.

'In case you were wondering where your mum and stepmum have disappeared to, they asked me to let you know they've just popped out to get you some bits.'

'Bits?'

'Pyjamas, toiletries, that sort of thing, I think.'

'Right.'

At the moment I'm dressed in a hospital-issue nightie – baggy and shapeless with tiny yellow flowers printed all over it. Instead of knickers, I'm wearing an adult-sized nappy that rustles every time I make the slightest movement.

'They shouldn't be long,' Hayley adds.

'OK. Thank you.'

'In the meantime, can I get you anything?'

'Would you mind taking this away?' I ask, pointing to the tray in front of me.

Hayley peers under the cover. 'You really should try and eat something, lovey,' she says. 'You need to keep your energy up.'

'I'm sorry but I really don't think I can.'

She stands back, her arms folded. 'Hmmm, how about I check with catering services and see if they can whip you up a bit of toast instead?'

Even the thought of toast makes my stomach turn over but I don't want to come across as rude so I nod and thank her.

'In the meantime,' she says. 'Maybe try to get some of the jelly down you. The sugar will do you good.' She hands me the cup of jelly and a teaspoon before wheeling the table into the corner of the room. 'He's doing well by the way,' she says over her shoulder.

I frown.

He?

Then it clicks.

He is the baby.

My baby.

'Another twelve or so hours on SCBU and he should be right as rain.'

SCBU.

The Special Care Baby Unit.

I have a baby.

He's in the Special Care Baby Unit being treated for low blood sugar.

'Right,' I murmur.

'We can go up and see him later on if you like.'

I don't reply, focusing instead on the flower print on my nightie, my eyes tracing a path between the petals. Until now, motherhood has always been an abstract thing, something I'll maybe do one day, decades from now, with a person I'm probably still years away from meeting. Hayley doesn't need to know that I don't want to see him. After all, what kind of person doesn't want to see their newborn baby?

I know I can't, though. Because seeing the baby makes all of this real. Tucked away in my little room, on a totally separate floor from him, in a totally separate department, I can trick myself into believing he doesn't exist, that I'm in hospital for an entirely different reason – an appendix removal or a broken bone.

Hayley leans across and gives my shoulder a sympathetic

squeeze. She must think I'm such an idiot. I wouldn't blame her. How on earth did I miss the fact I was growing an actual human being inside me? How? I'm supposed to be clever. For my GCSEs I'm predicted a string of eights and nines. Just how did I manage to mess this up quite so spectacularly? I've spent my entire life priding myself on my observation skills, my attention to detail. More than that, I thought I knew myself.

'Well, if you change your mind . . .' Hayley says.

I smile weakly. 'Thank you.'

'In the meantime, I'd better go see about that toast. If you need anything else, remember, you just press the button, OK?' She points out the nurse call button next to my bed.

'Thank you,' I repeat.

I wait until she's left the room before setting aside the jelly and spoon.

I look for my phone before remembering its watery demise. With no other method of telling the time, I make a guess. Judging by the quality of light peeping through the narrow slits between the blinds and the evening meal festering on the tray in the corner, I plump for some time between five and seven.

My mouth is dry. I reach for the jug of water on the cabinet next to my bed. It's made of plastic and is only half full, but to my shock I can barely lift it, and most of the water ends up spilling on the bedclothes, soaking through the sheets to my bare legs beneath.

It's not just my upper body that feels weak. An experimental attempt to get out of bed is abruptly abandoned when I realize I don't trust my legs to keep me vertical. The dominant pain, though, is between my legs. Sore doesn't even cover it. It feels like I've been kicked there repeatedly.

I haven't, though.

I've had a baby.

No matter how many times I tell myself this single fact, it fails to sink in, to even penetrate.

I've had a baby.

It was Stacey who found me.

Us.

I was on the bathroom floor when she walked in, naked, a slippery pink alien thing covered in sticky white residue in my arms, the bathmat beneath us soaked with blood.

She staggered back a few steps in shock as if she'd stumbled across a dead body.

There was a beat before she flew into practical mode, yelling for Mum, calling an ambulance, grabbing clean towels.

After that it was all a bit of a blur.

The entire time, I could only manage a single sentence. Over and over again.

'I didn't know.'

Mum and Stacey say they believe me. Not that it matters. At the end of the day, it doesn't change anything. The end result is still the same.

I still have a baby.

A baby I didn't in any way plan for.

I'm prodding at my plate of dry toast when Mum returns, armed with bulging carrier bags.

'Where's Stacey?' I ask as she dumps them in the corner of the room and pulls up a chair.

'Just getting a cup of tea,' Mum replies, pushing her hair out of her eyes. 'She'll be here in a bit.'

I eye the mound of bags. M&S, Mothercare, Next, John Lewis. 'How much did all that cost?' I ask. They must have spent a fortune.

'Oh, don't you worry about that,' she says, sitting down. 'I'm sorry we were gone so long. We had some things to discuss.'

'What kind of things?'

'Your . . .' She pauses, clearly searching for the right word. 'Your situation.'

'And?'

'And. I think we might have come up with a plan of sorts.'

'A plan? What kind of plan?' I ask, my stomach fluttering with nerves.

'One that should hopefully work for everyone.'

'OK,' I say slowly.

Mum scoots her chair a little closer to the bed, the legs scraping against the lino. 'OK, this might sound a bit much at first, but just hear me out.'

I have no choice but to nod.

Mum takes a deep breath. 'The baby,' she says. 'Stacey and I will raise him.'

My mouth falls open into a silent 'What?'

'Just think about it,' Mum says, her eyes shining. 'It's the perfect solution. You get to continue your life as normal, while Stacey and I bring up the baby as our own.'

'What do you mean by "as our own"?'

'Exactly what it sounds like. Stacey and I will be the baby's parents.'

'And what about me? What will I be?'

'Well, his big sister, of course.'

'But that's crazy,' I stammer.

'That's what I thought when Stacey first suggested it, but the more we talked it through, the more sense it started to make.'

'This is Stacey's idea?'

'No. I mean, initially perhaps, but as I say, we've discussed it in detail now and we're both in full agreement that it's the best option going forward.' She leans in closer, taking my hands in hers. 'The thing is, we've always wanted more children,' she says. 'You know that. Things just haven't gone our way before now. This way Stacey and I get to be parents together after all. Just like we've always dreamed.'

Cue a pang of guilt deep in my belly.

'But neither of you have been pregnant,' I say. 'Won't people be suspicious if you suddenly have a baby?'

'Don't worry, we've thought about all that. We'll tell people we used a surrogate and the reason we didn't tell them about it sooner was because we were worried about being let down at the last minute; that we didn't want to jinx things by telling people before things were official. They'll understand.'

'And what about Dad?' I ask.

He has no idea where I am right now; no idea he's just become a grandfather. I picture him alone in his boxy little flat, pottering about the kitchen, a ready meal whirring in the microwave, oblivious to all of this.

'We'll tell him the same thing,' Mum says.

She sounds so calm, like she's proposing the most normal thing in the world. Maybe she is and I'm the crazy one here? Either way, the whole concept makes my head hurt.

'You just need some time to let it sink in,' Mum says, massaging my palms with her thumbs.

She's talking like this is some years-in-the-planning scheme.

'What, like you have?' I say, removing my hand.

Mum sighs. 'Listen to me, Jojo. I'm fully aware that this is all very new and strange, but trust me when I say we've thought it through. We've sat down and gone through every possible scenario and this is without doubt the route that makes the most sense. This way nothing has to change. You can still go to the Arts Academy, just as planned.'

The Arts Academy. I'm supposed to be starting there in September, just over a month from now. I've been counting down the days, crossing them off an invisible calendar inside my head.

I look down at my hands. There's blood under my fingernails. I ball them into fists so I can't see it.

'It's a win-win, Jojo,' Mum says. 'You'll get to see him as much as you like but not at the cost of your education, your future.'

'What about the baby's dad?' I ask.

Mum flinches slightly. 'What do you mean?'

'Don't we need to at least run this by him?'

She pauses before answering. 'Stacey and I have discussed it and we've concluded that it'll be a lot simpler and easier if we just keep this between the three of us.'

'You mean, we just don't say anything?'

'Jojo, you said so yourself earlier – you're not ready for a baby. And if you're not ready, I doubt the father, whoever he may be, is ready either.'

I bite my lip. I can see her point, but doesn't he at least have the right to know? The opportunity to decide if he wants in or not?

'The more people we have involved, the more complicated things will get,' Mum says. 'What if his family started interfering? It could get messy. This way, we avoid any unnecessary drama.'

'But the baby, what will we tell him when he gets older? He's bound to want to know.'

'We can think about that further down the line.'

'It doesn't feel right, Mum.'

None of it does. And yet Mum continues to smile serenely like it's a done deal. She reaches to tuck a loose strand of hair behind my ear. Her fingers are cold. I want to recoil from her touch but I don't, tensing up instead.

'Of course it doesn't now,' she says. 'But it will. I know what you're like, sweetheart, and I know you're going to want to do the "right" thing here, but you need to think very carefully about what the actual right thing for you and the baby is. It might not be entirely clear right away.

'Bringing up a child is gruelling,' she continues. 'Even when it's planned. It's all-consuming, nothing like the romantic adventure Hollywood films might have you believe. It's exhausting and brutal and unforgiving.'

'There must be some good bits?' I say.

'Of course there are. There'd have to be or no one would actively plan to have a baby ever again.' She pauses to smile. 'I just need you to know that parenthood is no walk in the park. Even with the best will in the world, it's going to derail your life, whether you like it or not. And I'm not going to stand by and let that happen to you, Jojo. Not when you've got so much talent and potential, not when there's a perfect solution right here in front of us.'

I don't say anything.

'We have to be realistic here. You can't go to the Arts Academy *and* bring up a baby. It's just not going to be feasible.'

She's right. The commute to the academy is already over an hour and a half each way. And the hours are long, much longer than if I stayed on at school for sixth form. And there are evening and weekend rehearsals. They told us all about them at the audition; kept reiterating we'd have to be prepared to work harder than we'd ever worked before. I'm not an idiot. There's no way I can juggle motherhood with the demands of the course. Not unless I have some serious help in place.

I close my eyes and try to imagine a world where the baby that slithered into my arms less than twelve hours ago is not my baby at all. Could I do it? Could I pretend he was my little brother? Could I be comfortable with that? Could I deceive that many people?

I just don't know.

'We'd be lying to everyone,' I say. 'The baby, the father, Dad, all our family and friends . . .'

Frankie.

I'd be lying to Frankie. And it wouldn't just be one lie. If I go through with this, I'd have to lie to her for the rest of my life.

Mum shakes her head. 'You've got to stop looking at things this way, sweetheart. You need to start thinking with your head instead of your heart and focus on what's best here. For you *and* the baby.'

'But how am I supposed to know what that is?' I ask.

Mum reaches for my hand once more, her grip tighter this time. 'By trusting Stacey and me. We wouldn't be putting this proposal forward if we didn't think it would work. This way, your life goes on as if nothing has happened. You get to continue your studies and the baby is safe and happy and well looked after. By us.'

She makes it sound so easy.

Too easy.

'Plus, you always said you wanted a little brother or sister,' she adds playfully.

'But he isn't my brother,' I say flatly.

He's my son.

'I know that,' Mum says. 'But a few months down the line, once we've settled back into our usual routines, I'm sure things will slide into place.'

'But . . .'

'Like I said before, you just need to let it sink in,' she says, talking over me. 'And remember that Stacey and I have your best interests at heart here.' She pauses and looks me straight in the eye, her gaze intense. 'You do know that, don't you?'

The fact is, Mum and Stacey have always had my back, from the very beginning. They are and always have been a great team. And together they'll be great parents too, of this I have no doubt.

'Well, don't you?' Mum prompts.

'Of course I do,' I say. 'It's just a lot to take in . . .'

'I know, sweetheart, I know. But remember, you're not doing this on your own. We're all in this together – you, me and Stacey.'

Chapter 17

The first time I met Stacey I didn't have the slightest clue that in a little over a month's time I'd be living with her. I didn't even know that she was my mum's girlfriend. All I knew was that my mum had become friendly with a lady called Stacey who she met on an Open University residential weekend (Mum was a student, Stacey her lecturer) and that she wanted me to meet her.

The meeting took place at a city centre branch of Pizza Express in late June. I was ten and about to enter my final year of primary school.

Stacey was already there when we arrived. She looked nothing like what I was expecting.

Because of her job, I'd pictured someone older and stern-looking, possibly dressed in tweed, but Stacey was none of these things. She was tall and young and pretty with cropped bleached-blonde hair and bright pink lipstick and immaculate black eyeliner flicks. She wore black skinny jeans and sequinned Converse and a black T-shirt with 'This Old Thing' emblazoned across it in hot pink lettering that matched the colour of her lips almost exactly.

When she and Mum greeted each other, they hugged for a very long time with their eyes closed, their chins resting on each other's shoulders.

'And you must be Jojo,' Stacey said when they finally separated. She smiled at me and held out her hand for me to shake. 'It's so nice to meet you finally,' she said. 'Your mum talks about you all the time.'

I glanced at Mum for confirmation, but she was too busy looking at Stacey, her eyes aglow in a way I wasn't sure I'd ever seen before.

Over lunch, Stacey asked me lots of questions about school and my hobbies. When I admitted I liked drama, she asked me if I'd ever seen a play in the West End and when I said 'no', she promised to take me to see one, which I thought was nice but also a little bit strange considering I'd only just met her and I was pretty sure West End tickets were kind of expensive.

At the end of the meal, Mum suggested I use the toilet before we left.

'I'm OK, thanks,' I said.

'I'd prefer it if you went,' she replied. 'We're going to run some errands after this so you might not get another chance until you get home.'

She seemed insistent so I relented and traipsed across the restaurant to the loos.

Returning to the table a few minutes later, I noticed that Mum and Stacey were sitting very closely together, their foreheads almost touching. The second they spotted me they straightened up and scooted apart, forcing their lips into matching closed-mouthed smiles.

Stacey insisted on paying the bill, despite Mum's protestations.

'No, I insist,' she said, pushing Mum's hand away and slapping her credit card down on the little silver tray. 'It's the least I can do.'

When it was time to say goodbye, Mum and Stacey hugged for a long time again.

'Did you like her?' Mum asked on the bus ride home.

'Who?' I asked. 'Stacey?'

'Yes.'

'Yes, she was nice,' I replied. 'She was funny.'

Mum beamed. 'Good,' she said, squeezing my knee. 'I'm glad.'

'It is a bit weird, though,' I said.

Mum's face twitched. 'What is?'

'Being friends with your teacher.'

I couldn't imagine going out for lunch with my teacher, Mrs Ambrose, in a million years.

'Oh,' Mum said, relaxing into a smile. 'Well, I think it's a bit different when you're our age – the student/teacher divide doesn't really exist when you're both grown-ups.'

'Oh. OK.'

We sat in silence for a moment as the bus edged through the afternoon traffic.

'Is Stacey your *best* friend?' I asked.

Although Mum was friendly with lots of people – other mums from school, the women in her book club, the old school friends she met for dinner every Christmas – she didn't have a designated best friend. She didn't have a Frankie in her life.

'You know, I think she just might be,' Mum replied, putting her arm round me and kissing me on the top of my head.

'That's nice,' I said.

I liked the idea of Mum having a best friend. The idea of life without one seemed unspeakably lonely to me.

'Oh, you're a good girl, Jojo,' she said.

I smiled and snuggled into her arm.

The following week, I was in the kitchen raiding the biscuit tin after school when Mum asked me to come through into the living room. I was surprised to find Dad already there (he didn't usually get home from work until much later, often missing dinner). He was perched on the edge of the sofa, a nervous expression on his face. The second our eyes met, he tried to hide it, rearranging his features into a smile, but it was too late. I was officially spooked.

My heart beating fast, I sat down in the big squishy armchair, my favourite spot, and began to nibble at my chocolate bourbon, not really tasting it. Mum hesitated before joining Dad on the sofa. They sat at opposite ends, their knees angled away from each other, their backs straight and hands placed neatly in their laps, instead of leaning back against the cushions the way they usually did. I remember thinking they looked like bookends.

Mum spoke first. 'Jojo, we've got something to tell you,' she said. She glanced at Dad before continuing. 'Your dad and I have decided to split up.'

Appetite lost, I placed my half-eaten biscuit down on the arm of the chair. 'Why?' I asked.

Mum glanced at Dad once more. He didn't meet her gaze, staring into his lap instead.

'I've fallen in love with someone else,' she said.

'Who?' I asked, instinctively looking at Dad, his head still lowered.

'You've already met them actually.'

'What do you mean?' I asked, racking my brains as to who it could possibly be.

'Pizza Express,' Mum said gently. 'Stacey.'

Suddenly, everything made sense.

The way Mum used to come home from her residential courses so pink-cheeked and cheerful; the minute-long hugs she shared with Stacey; Stacey's sincere promises to take me to see a West End show.

'Anyway,' Mum continued, 'I'm going to move in with her and I'd like you to come with me.'

'Where does she live?' I asked.

I couldn't move away from Newfield. There was no way. Frankie was here.

'She lives on the other side of Nottingham at the moment but we're going to get somewhere together, here in Newfield so you don't have to change schools.'

'What about Dad? Where will be live? Will he stay here?'

I didn't like the idea of Dad rocking around the house on his own. It wasn't a big house. It was a very ordinary semi with three bedrooms and a conservatory that was too hot in summer and too cold in winter. And yet, the idea of him living here alone made my chest ache.

'We're going to sell the house,' Mum said.

'And once it's gone through, I'm going to look for somewhere of my own close by, so I can still see you lots,' Dad added, the brightness in his delivery at odds with the sadness in his eyes.

My gaze drifted to a magazine on the coffee table. The Duchess of Cambridge was on the cover, smiling and waving. She was wearing a navy-blue dress and pearl earrings and had her hair up in what I was pretty sure was known as a chignon.

Mum and Dad both seemed very calm. There was no scream-ing or shouting like when people split up in soap operas. They spoke in soft, low voices, which somehow gave the illusion of making everything they said sound perfectly reasonable. I didn't scream or shout either. I just listened and nodded and pretended my head wasn't about to explode.

'Does this mean you're gay now?' I asked as Mum tucked me in that night.

'I don't think there's any need to put a label on it,' she replied, sitting on the edge of the bed. 'I just happen to be in love with a woman now.'

'What about Dad? Are you not in love with him any more?'

She hesitated before speaking. 'If I'm honest, I'm not sure I've been in love with your dad for quite some time now.' She sighed. 'Grown-up relationships are complicated, sweetheart. Things change. People change.'

'OK,' I said doubtfully.

'You'll understand one day,' she added, smoothing down the duvet with the palm of her right hand. Then she reached across and stroked my hair. Her hands were warm and smelled of washing-up liquid. 'You're a good girl, Jojo, do you know that?'

I forced a smile and nodded.

She kissed me on the forehead and turned off the light, plunging the room into darkness.

I lay awake for hours, trying to make sense of the news. I hadn't seen it coming one bit, and yet, the more I thought about it, the more it became clear that Mum was telling the truth – she hadn't been happy for a very long time now. In fact, the happiest I'd ever seen her was probably in Pizza Express, sitting opposite Stacey, her eyes full of stars.

*

Mum and Stacey got married on a blazing hot afternoon in mid-July, almost a year to the day since our lunch at Pizza Express.

Unlike Mum and Dad's wedding, which from the looks of the photos that once graced our mantelpiece had been very traditional – a chocolate-box church, a quartet of bridesmaids in pink satin dresses, Dad looking uncomfortable in a top hat, etc. – Mum and Stacey's was cool and casual. Instead of a frothy white gown and lacy veil, Mum wore an emerald-green silk dress and a vintage headband while Stacey sported a Paul Smith tuxedo suit, and instead of an ancient church organ honking out the Wedding March, Mum and Stacey walked up the aisle to 'At Last' by Etta James.

The service, in the function room of a boutique hotel, was simple and short on religion, filled instead with quirky readings and Mum and Stacey's favourite songs. I performed a Maya Angelou poem entitled 'Touched by an Angel' and Mum cried.

After the service, there was dinner and speeches (when Stacey opened her speech with 'My wife and I . . .', the guests roared with delight). Then the tables were pushed aside and everyone danced to a playlist Mum and Stacey had spent the last few weeks putting together. It was fun, but as Frankie and I whirled around the dance floor, giddy on the tiny sip of champagne we'd been allowed, I couldn't stop picturing Dad alone in his new flat – a poky place on the other side of Newfield he'd recently moved into following the sale of our old house.

Two weeks later, following a brief honeymoon in Copenhagen, Mum and Stacey sat me down and told me they had something important to speak to me about.

As they perched on the sofa, I had flashbacks to the afternoon when Mum and Dad told me they were splitting up. Only this time Mum and Stacey were holding hands and smiling, their thighs smushed up together.

'How would you feel,' Mum began, 'about maybe having a little brother or sister at some point?'

My eyes immediately flew to Mum and Stacey's stomachs.

Mum laughed. 'No one's pregnant,' she said.

'Yet,' Stacey added with a grin.

'We wanted to talk to you first,' Mum said. 'Before we got the ball officially rolling.'

'OK.'

'So, what do you think?' Mum asked. 'You always used to say you wanted a sibling.'

This was true. Most of my friends had brothers and sisters, and when I was younger, I'd often ask why I didn't. Not because I desperately wanted one; I was mostly just curious as to what made us different to all the other families we knew. As soon as I was old enough to understand, Mum explained the reason. When I was born, there were complications and Mum had almost died during labour. The doctors had made it very clear that any further attempts to conceive would be unwise. From that moment on, I stopped asking and pushed the idea from my head, figuring I'd sacrifice having a brother or sister if it meant I got to keep my mum.

'But I thought you couldn't have any more children,' I pointed out.

'I can't,' Mum said. 'But Stacey can.' She rubbed her shoulder up against Stacey's.

'The thing is, I've always wanted kids,' Stacey said. 'Ever since I was tiny. I've just never met the right person to have them with until now.' She looked at Mum and they smiled dreamily at one another.

'Who would be the dad?' I asked.

'We'll use a sperm donor,' Stacey explained.

'Who?'

'No one we'll ever meet. It'll be from an anonymous database.'

'Does that mean the baby won't know who its dad is?'

'Well, yes, technically.'

'So it could be anyone?'

'Well, not exactly.' Mum said. 'The donors are very carefully screened. And we get basic profile information – height, eye colour, profession, that sort of thing – to help us pick.'

'And you'd both be its mums?'

'Yes,' Mum said. 'Stacey would carry the baby but yes, we'd both be its mum.'

'Where would it sleep?' I asked.

'We'll convert my office into a nursery,' Stacey said.

'Don't worry, sweetheart,' Mum added with a laugh. 'We've given it a lot of thought.'

'OK,' I said, mainly because I didn't know what else to say, but also because I got the sense they'd already taken my blessing for granted.

'I knew you'd be on board,' Mum added, beaming. 'My good, good girl.'

Within days, the bathroom cabinet was filled with ovulation kits and pregnancy vitamins. Although Mum claimed they hadn't wanted to get the 'ball rolling' until they'd spoken to me, it was clear they'd done plenty of research before doing so, and just a few weeks later they announced they had chosen their donor (a blond, blue-eyed structural engineer from Denmark) and Stacey was ready to be inseminated.

Mum and Stacey came home from the clinic all giddy and excited. As we ate dinner, they pondered over whether Stacey could already be pregnant.

'How soon will you know?' I asked.

'It varies,' Stacey replied. 'Some tests claim they can tell right away but we're going to wait a couple days before I do one.'

That was a Tuesday. On that Friday, Mum and Stacey ceremoniously trooped to the bathroom to do the test. I stayed in the living room. Although I'd got used to the idea of a baby brother or sister, I still hadn't made up my mind how I really felt about it. Mum and Stacey had clearly taken care to include me in their conversations, but I still couldn't help but feel separate from the entire venture – a spectator, rather than a member of the team. Perhaps it would feel different when the baby was actually here, but until then it was hard to pinpoint my exact thoughts on the subject.

They returned a few minutes later.

'Well?' I asked.

'Not this time,' Stacey said, sighing.

'It's only been a few days,' Mum said. 'It might not show up yet. We'll check again on Monday.'

They did.

The result was still negative.

'Can you have another go?' I asked.

'Of course,' Mum said, giving Stacey's knee a firm squeeze.

The following month, they went through the insemination process again.

Once more the result was negative.

'I just don't understand,' Stacey said, chucking the negative test in the kitchen bin. 'I had all the tests. They said everything looked fine.'

'And it will be,' Mum said. 'We'll get pregnant next time, you'll see.'

But the next month was the same. No baby.

*

I relayed all of this to Frankie on our walks to and from school.

'Maybe they need to do IVF,' Frankie said.

'What's that?'

'I don't know what it stands for, but my auntie Lorna was having trouble having a baby and she had it and now she's got twins and is so knackered she put her toothbrush in the freezer the other day.'

I suggested this over dinner that evening.

Mum and Stacey exchanged looks.

'We're not eligible,' Mum said eventually.

'Why not?'

Mum hesitated. 'It's a postcode thing.'

'But that's not fair.'

'I know, sweetheart, but that's the way it is.'

At that point, Stacey stood up, the legs of her chair screeching against the tiled floor, and left the room.

'Did I say something wrong?' I asked.

'No, of course not,' Mum said, her eyes on the door. 'Stacey's just feeling a bit sad, that's all.'

About a month later later, I woke in the night feeling thirsty. I climbed out of bed and ventured towards the kitchen to fetch a glass of water.

I was almost at the kitchen door when I heard Stacey crying.

I peered through the crack. Mum and Stacey were sitting at the table, a half-empty bottle of red wine between them. Both their faces were flushed.

'Nothing's wrong with you,' Mum said, leaning across the table and taking Stacey's hands firmly in hers.

'So why can't I get pregnant?' Stacey asked, her eyes shining with sadness.

'I don't know,' Mum admitted. 'But it's not your fault.'

'Then whose fault is it if it's not mine? It's my body that's defective, no one else's.'

'We don't know that. We've just had a run of bad luck.'

'Bad luck?' Stacey spat. 'We've had three attempts now. Three! It was supposed to be a seventy per cent success rate.'

'I know,' Mum said. 'I've been there right beside you through all this, remember?'

Stacey shook her head.

'Maybe we could look into doing IVF privately,' Mum said gently.

'We can't afford it, Helen. We've already ploughed pretty much everything we had into these three cycles.'

'Perhaps we should try the NHS route then?'

'We can't. We're not eligible, remember?'

'We'll find a way around it.'

'How? Just deny Jojo exists?'

I flinched. What did *I* have to do with any of this?

'No, of course not. Maybe we can appeal?'

'There's no point, Helen. They were very clear. If either of us have a child from a previous relationship, no matter what the circumstances, it automatically counts us out. I love Jojo, you know I do, but she's not my child and she never will be. How on earth can they think it's the same thing?'

I froze.

It was because of me.

It wasn't a postcode thing at all. Mum and Stacey couldn't have a baby because of me.

My head reeling, I stumbled back to my room, my glass of water forgotten.

Chapter 18

Annie and I chat for the rest of the journey but the mood has shifted, the balance in our dynamic slightly off-kilter now that she's made up her mind that I'm a poor single mum, cruelly abandoned by the father of her newborn baby. I can't exactly blame her. After all, she doesn't know the full story. All she has are the scant details I've given her, some of them true, others not so, and she's filled in the gaps accordingly.

When we get off the train at St Pancras, she stays close, sticking to my side as we pass through the barriers.

'Have you got anyone meeting you?' she asks, her eyes scanning the people waiting on the other side.

'No,' I reply.

'Really?'

'It's a surprise,' I say quickly. 'My visit, I mean. My family don't know I'm coming.'

Annie breaks into a smile. 'Oh, Amelia, how lovely,' she says. 'My goodness, they're going to be absolutely thrilled when you turn up on their doorstep.'

I smile. 'Hopefully.'

'Do you know where you're going from here?' Annie asks. 'I can walk with you down to your platform if you like, make sure you're going the right way.'

'No, no,' I say. 'Thank you, but I'll be fine. I've done this journey loads of times. Honestly, I could do it with my eyes closed.' I glance up and spot a sign for the toilets. 'Actually, before I go anywhere, I should probably get him changed.' I pat Albie gently on the bottom.

'I could wait for you,' Annie offers. 'I'm not in any sort of hurry.'

'You really don't have to. In fact, I might, er, stay and get a bit of lunch before I get on the tube. You know, split up the journey a bit.'

'Well, as long as you're sure,' Annie says doubtfully.

We're at the bottom of the escalators now. A few metres away, a boy a few years older than me is sitting at one of those public pianos, his black hair flopping in front of his eyes as he plays the introduction to 'Bohemian Rhapsody'. He's good; a small circle of spectators is gathered around him with their phones out, filming his performance. The entire station is crammed with people and luggage and noise. I've been to London before, with Mum and Stacey, with Dad, with school, but I've never been here alone and certainly never in sole charge of such a tiny human being. Instinctively, I wrap both my arms around Albie. If I could swaddle him in bubble wrap right now, I would.

'Well,' Annie says. 'It was lovely to meet you, Amelia. And you too, Luca.' She reaches forward and strokes Albie gently on the cheek.

'It was really nice to meet you too,' I say.

She opens her arms and I let her envelop me in a hug. She smells of sweat and sugary perfume and Elnett hairspray. 'It'll be

OK,' she whispers, her breath warm on my skin. 'I can sense what a fighter you are and I'm telling you, it will all be OK.'

My tears take me by surprise. What's wrong with me? I'm not a crier. I'm a worrier, a brooder, a dweller, definitely. But I'm not a crier. That's always been Frankie's role. I used to envy her. She cries so easily and often, and almost always seems to feel better afterwards – revived and refreshed.

'It's – what's the word? – cathartic,' she often says, cheerfully wiping away her tears.

It helps that Frankie has one of those faces that bounces back almost immediately. Her skin never goes blotchy and her lashes are naturally long and dark enough for her to forego mascara, meaning she never has to deal with unsightly stains down her cheeks. Crucially, Frankie is free with her emotions in a way I've only ever been able to replicate on stage, when playing someone else. She laughs and cries and shouts and squeals and rages in a way I don't think I ever have.

Until now.

Because ever since Albie came into my life, I feel on the brink of tears almost constantly; my emotions, previously so neat and ordered, are suddenly wild and unpredictable and out of my control. It doesn't feel free though, the way Frankie makes it look – it makes me feel scared and vulnerable, and with Albie strapped to my chest, I want to feel the exact opposite of those things.

I want to feel strong and capable and in control.

I blink away my tears just in time for Annie to release me from her embrace.

'Right,' she says. 'Duty calls. Have a lovely time with your family, sweetheart.'

'Thank you,' I say. 'You too.'

She gives me one last sympathetic smile and we go our separate ways.

The second she disappears from view, I experience a wave of anxiety. Quickly, I push it away. Now is not the time to panic or fall apart. Now is the time to step up and prove what I've suspected all along – that I can do this by myself.

I take a deep breath and with my head held high follow the signs towards the loos.

There's a queue for the baby change. The other parents waiting are all much older than me. Their babies are older too. They writhe in their pushchairs and chew on soggy rice crackers and regard me with weary eyes. One of them is old enough to talk and whines, 'Mummy, Mummy, Mummy,' over and over. I do my best to ignore it all, keeping my focus on Albie.

Finally, a harassed-looking mother emerges pushing a double buggy and it's my turn.

I lock the door behind me and assess my surroundings before carefully lowering the changing bench. As I remove Albie from the carrier, I catch sight of my reflection in the mirror.

I look terrible.

My T-shirt is criss-crossed with sweat marks from where the carrier has been and there are greyish shadows under my eyes. It's not just that, though. It's almost like the fear and worry and confusion of the last few weeks has taken over every muscle in my face, dragging it down, making it appear tense and drawn. I look like the oldest sixteen-year-old in the world.

I tear my eyes away from my reflection and concentrate on the task in hand, laying Albie down on the bench. The second his body touches the plastic he wakes up and begins to howl, his tiny hands scrunching up into tight balls as he screams.

'Shush, darling,' I whisper, as I sift through my bag for a fresh nappy and wipes.

I haven't changed any nappies before. I've wanted to, but Stacey or Mum always get in there first, shooing me away, crouching over Albie, forming a human barrier between me and him. I always paid attention though, despite their efforts to discourage me from watching, peeking over the tops of their heads as they deftly changed him, making mental notes on their technique.

I undress Albie and remove his soiled nappy before carefully cleaning his bottom. He's a little red, so I apply a thick layer of nappy rash cream with my index finger, then put on a fresh nappy, taking extra care to make sure it's tight but not too tight, before redressing him. The entire time he cries, his tiny pink tonsils trembling. In response, I sing to him.

I sing 'Wind the Bobbin Up', and 'Jack and Jill', and 'Humpty-Dumpty'. I don't stop singing until Albie is back in his carrier.

I wash my hands, open the door and walk back out into the crowded, sweaty concourse. Sunlight streams through the glass ceiling, making me blink after the dim artificial light of the baby change.

I resume my singing, under my breath now. 'Rock-a-Bye-Baby' and 'Twinkle Twinkle Little Star' and 'Incy-Wincy Spider'.

Nothing seems to do the trick. Albie just continues to scream, his little face pressed up against my chest, turning redder and redder.

Perhaps he knows what I've done. And *this* is his protest. The thought that I might be causing him distress makes my stomach flip. I dismiss the thought and keep moving.

One foot in front of the other.

One step at a time.

You can do this, you can do this.
You. Can. Do. This.

The tube is hotter and dimmer and deeper and noisier and smellier and busier than I remember from my previous trips to the capital. As the train approaches, I place my hands over Albie's tiny ears, his cries competing to be heard over the rumble and screech of the engine.

The moment I step onto the train, a woman wearing a hijab offers me her seat.

'I'm fine, thank you,' I say.

'No, you sit down,' she says, standing up. 'I'm getting off at the next stop anyway.'

I hesitate before sinking gratefully into the seat, setting my backpack between my legs. I double-check my route on the underground map, counting the stops before I have to change lines. Reassured I have enough time, I get Albie's bottle out, then release him from his carrier so I can feed him. His head is clammy, his hair damp.

The second the teat of the bottle touches his lips, he stops crying.

My shoulders slump with relief.

He was just hungry.

As Albie sucks, I keep my face lowered, my grown-out fringe flopping in front of my eyes. I can tell people are looking at us, though. I can feel the heat of their gaze, their eyes boring into the top of my head.

I'm not used to being looked at this way. At least, not in real life. I'm short and slight and mousey-haired, my features small and even, yet entirely unremarkable in their symmetry. It's almost like

I've been designed specifically with invisibility in mind. People tell me I have nice eyes, but it's generally an observation they make after a long period of time in my company – a revelation they have to put in the time to earn. I'm a slow burn and I always have been. I don't mind. Not being noticed gives me something far more precious in return – the time and freedom to notice others, to observe. It's a luxury someone like Frankie doesn't have. Frankie is always being looked at. Within the last couple of years she's grown tall and leggy and acquired boobs and hips. Adding in her inky-black waist-length hair and a smile that stops traffic, it's a combination that demands attention, whether she likes it or not.

On stage it's different. On stage, I love being looked at, love the sensation of multiple eyes tracking my every move. Because they're not watching me, they're watching me play a character; and if I'm doing a good job, they should forget about me entirely. I think that's why I like acting so much. It's nothing to do with showing off. I like taking on other characters, delving into someone else's life so deeply I almost disappear altogether.

I'm under no illusions that the people currently looking over at us are actually interested in me, at least not independently from the tiny warm body currently nestled in my arms. Without Albie, I would sit here entirely unnoticed, like a ghost. With him, I am a curiosity, a mystery to be unravelled. I know what they're thinking. They're looking at me and trying to work out how old I am, if I'm his mother or not. They're making their mind up about what kind of person I am.

At the next stop, a group of girls around my age pile on, chatting animatedly while passing round a bottle of Coke.

One by one, they clock me and Albie, nudging each other until they're all looking in our direction. I can feel my face reddening. It's one thing to have older people stare and make silent judgements, quite another to be confronted with a group of girls my own age.

It only takes a few more seconds before one of them, a girl with a tangle of long dark hair, speaks up.

'He's well cute,' she says, pointing at Albie.

'Oh, thanks,' I say.

'You should think about getting him into modelling.'

I smile, unsure how to respond.

'Why not? He could make a packet.'

I just continue to smile, playing the part of the bashful yet proud mum.

'What's he called?' another girl asks.

'Albie,' I reply, immediately kicking myself for using his real name.

'Aw!' the girls chorus. 'Albie!'

They look so young and carefree, fresh-faced and bright and summery in their denim shorts and crop tops, long hair swishing around their shoulders, bulging Primark bags at their feet. They remind me of Frankie and me. And yet I can tell from the way they just addressed me, that it hasn't even crossed their minds that we might be peers, that just over a month ago I was just like them – a normal teenage girl who went shopping with her mates and cooed absent-mindedly over cute babies, confident mother-hood wouldn't be part of my reality for at least a decade, probably longer.

When they get off at the next stop, they all cry 'Bye, Albie!' in unison, tumbling off onto the platform in a noisy rabble, cueing a deep ache in my belly I can't quite interpret.

Chapter 19

Three weeks ago

I can't sleep.

Although my room is quiet enough, I can sense the hustle and bustle in the rest of the building on the other side of the door. That's not the problem, though. Even with the darkest, quietest, most comfortable room in the world, I would struggle to sleep right now. I keep replaying my earlier conversation with Mum in my head. A big part of me is swayed by her argument. This way, I still get to go to the Arts Academy and my friendship with Frankie is preserved. Plus, it's my chance to put things right, to give them the child they've always wanted – the child I've prevented them from having. And yet every time I think about surrendering to the plan, a mass of panic as big as a bowling ball takes residence in my belly. And with it, a picture of the baby – his skinny little body covered in blood and goo, his hair, thick and black as ink and totally unlike my mousey-brown wisps, sticky and matted against his tiny skull – embeds itself in my head, always accompanied by a single, confusing word.

Mine.

I roll onto my back, my horrible nappy rustling, the pain between my legs making me wince.

My jaw clenched, I reach for the remote and turn on the TV so I can find out the time.

2:11 a.m.

Before I can stop myself, I press the call button Hayley pointed out earlier.

It's a few minutes before a nurse I don't recognize appears. She's young, possibly only six or seven years older than me. With her long limbs and dark hair and olive skin, she reminds me of Frankie.

Frankie. She has no idea I'm here. The thought of her tucked up in her bed, fast asleep and oblivious, makes my heart twist.

'Hiya, Joanna,' the nurse says. 'I'm Lacey. Now, what can I do for you?'

'Is it too late for me to visit the Special Care Baby Unit?' I ask.

Her face softens. 'Of course not. You sit tight and I'll go grab a wheelchair.'

The SCBU is on the floor above.

As Lacey pushes me through the brightly lit corridors, she showers me with questions.

What's his name?

How much did he weigh?

How early was he?

Standard baby stuff.

Only I don't know the answers to any of them.

'Don't you worry,' she says when I apologize. 'Your brain does funny things when you've just given birth.'

When we arrive at the unit, a different nurse takes over from Lacey, pushing me over to a plastic cot in the corner of the dimly lit room.

'He's doing really well,' she says. 'In fact, if he keeps going like this, he should be able to join you on the ward as early as tomorrow afternoon.'

I wait until the nurse has moved away before using the wheelchair arm rests to push myself up into standing position. I shuffle a little closer and peer into the cot.

For some reason, I'd expected him to be naked apart from a massive nappy, and hooked up to lots of machines, like I've seen on the TV. Instead, he's wearing a lemon-yellow babygro and there are no machines in sight. As I remembered, his hair is black and thick, nothing like my pink bald head when I was born. He's fast asleep.

'Hello,' I whisper.

He has the tiniest nose. Like a button. And pouting pink lips that look like they're about to blow a kiss. And the longest, darkest eyelashes I think I've ever seen.

He's beautiful. Breathtakingly so.

Did I really make him? The thought makes my brain ache with wonder and confusion.

'Would you like to hold him?' the nurse asks, coming up behind me and making me jump.

'Is – is that allowed?' I stammer. 'I mean, will he be OK?'

'Of course. You sit down and I'll pass him over.'

I settle into a comfortable chair and watch as the nurse scoops up the baby with ease.

'Here we go,' she says, lowering him into my arms.

He barely weighs a thing.

'Is the way I'm holding him OK?' I ask.

'Perfect,' she says.

'He's so warm.'

She laughs. 'I know. Regular little hot water bottles, they are.'

I smile.

A real smile.

Perhaps my first since I arrived at the hospital.

'I'll leave you to it,' she says. 'If you need me for anything, just give me a wave.'

I look back down and just stare at my baby for ages, studying every centimetre of him, not daring to move a muscle in case I disturb him but at the same time willing him to wake up so I can look into his eyes and say 'hello' – a proper one this time.

The nurse comes over to check how I'm doing.

'Good, thanks,' I murmur, unable to tear my eyes away.

'Does he have a name yet?' she asks.

At the moment, according to the plastic bracelet around his wrist, he's just 'Baby Bright'.

'Albie,' I say slowly. 'I think I'm going to call him Albie.'

The nurse smiles. 'It suits him already,' she says.

I hold Albie until I can't feel my right arm any more and the sun is peeping through the crack beneath the lowered blinds.

A few hours later, I'm moved from the private room onto a ward where I'm the youngest patient by at least ten years.

The other women's bedside cabinets are cluttered with congratulations cards, pink or blue helium balloons proclaiming 'It's a boy!' or 'It's a girl!' bobbing gently above their heads. Steady streams of visitors troop in bearing oversized teddy bears and bundles of impossibly tiny clothes.

I'm the only one who doesn't have their baby with them.

'Soon,' Hayley tells me just after breakfast. 'In the meantime, would you like these?' She holds up a stack of gossip magazines. It's not the sort of thing I'm usually interested in, but right now mindless and glossy is exactly what I'm craving.

'Yes, please,' I say. 'Oh, and would you mind drawing the curtain around my bed?'

She glances around the ward and then back to me, her face soft with sympathy. 'Of course, lovey,' she says.

Shortly afterwards, the woman in the bed next to me is discharged. I watch through the gap in the curtain as she and her husband carefully transfer their baby from its cot to an obviously brand-new car seat, their faces full of worry and wonder. I can tell, just by looking at them, that this baby was very much planned. I picture them huddled over a pregnancy test, whooping with joy when the two pink lines or whatever appeared in the little window. I envy their joy, their togetherness, their cosy little family of three.

The woman catches my eye through the curtain. Quickly, I look back down at my magazine, reading the same paragraph over and over again, my cheeks on fire, until I'm certain they've left the ward.

I'm relieved when Mum and Stacey turn up. They looked tired yet happy, the dark circles under their eyes offset by the flush in their cheeks. Stacey in particular is buzzing, chatting merrily about all the things we're going to need for the baby, making a list on her phone.

'He'll be OK in a Moses basket in our room for now,' she says.

'But we're going to have to think about kitting out a proper nursery for when he's a bit bigger.'

'I wish I'd hung on to Jojo's baby things,' Mum says.

'You weren't to know,' Stacey replies, kissing her on the cheek. 'Plus, it'll be nice to get new stuff, don't you think?'

At no point do they ask for my opinion. It's like I'm not even in the room, their upbeat chatter clearly not requiring my input. I want to tell them to slow down, that I'm not ready to agree to something this big, but I don't know how. They seem so happy, so excited, and I don't want to be the one to break the spell.

Shortly after lunch, Albie, his blood sugar levels now normal, is delivered to the ward. As his cot is wheeled into place next to my bed, I sit up straight, eager to see him again, to check if anything has changed in the few short hours we've spent apart.

'Can I hold him?' I ask.

Mum and Stacey look at each other. I've failed to mention my 2 a.m. visit up to the SCBU.

'Perhaps it's best if you don't right now,' Stacey says, positioning herself in front of the cot, blocking my view.

'Sorry?' I say, convinced I must have heard her incorrectly.

'The thing is, your mum and I have been talking, and if this plan is going to work, we're going to need to put some boundaries in place.'

I throw Mum a desperate glance.

'It's for the best,' Mum says as Stacey turns away, scooping Albie into her arms. 'Don't worry,' she adds. 'You'll have lots of chances for cuddles later on. It's just that these early days are so crucial for bonding.'

So I sit in bed while Stacey holds my baby in her arms, her body subtly angled away from me. And when he wakes up, it's her eyes he connects with, not mine. The pain almost takes my breath away.

'It's for the best,' Mum repeats.

And even though all I want to do is rip Albie from Stacey's arms, a big part of me knows Mum must be right. And so I sit and watch, trying my hardest to ignore the desperate ache in my chest.

Chapter 20

I have over half an hour to kill before the next train to Swindon leaves. Albie, drunk on milk, is on the brink of sleep, his eyes drifting shut, his body slack in the carrier.

I browse around the Paddington Bear shop and on a whim buy him a cuddly Paddington Bear. Handing over the money to the cashier, I feel vaguely foolish. I only have limited funds. Should I really be spending my money on a cuddly toy? At the same time, I desperately want Albie to have something from me and only me.

'Can you remove the tag, please?' I ask the cashier.

'Of course.'

De-tagged, I place Paddington in my backpack, his head poking out the top.

As we leave the shop, my stomach lets out an angry rumble. Although I can recognize that my belly feels empty and hollow, I don't feel remotely hungry. Still, I know I need to eat something. I need to keep my strength up.

For Albie's sake, more than anything else.

I queue at Upper Crust and buy a tuna baguette, then head to WHSmith where I purchase a chocolate flapjack and a bottle of water.

The moment the platform is announced, I heave my backpack onto my shoulders and head for the barriers, my fingers gently circling Albie's skinny little ankles. On board, I select a non-table seat in the furthest standard carriage.

I eat my baguette robotically, barely tasting it. The flapjack is starting to melt. I polish it off quickly, in five mindless bites, the chocolate coating my teeth and tongue. The lot is gone before we even set off.

With Albie well and truly in the land of nod, I take my book out of my bag and try to read. I can't concentrate though, and end up reading the same passage over and over.

The conductor comes through the train to check tickets. He inspects mine, scribbling on it with a biro before handing it back.

'And the little one's ticket?' he says.

'I – I don't have one,' I stammer. 'I didn't think he needed one.' I didn't even think to check. It's not like he's taking up a seat. I'm not going to get fined, am I?

'Just messing with you,' the conductor says. 'Of course he doesn't need a ticket.'

'Oh, right,' I say, my face reddening. 'Ha ha . . .'

He winks and keeps moving down the train, my heart still thumping like mad.

About forty-five minutes into the journey, I realize I need the loo. It makes sense. I haven't been since I left the house this morning.

I assess my fellow passengers. Across the aisle, a girl in her early twenties is hunched over a laptop.

'Um, excuse me,' I say, waving to attract her attention.

She removes her earphones.

'Would you mind keeping an eye on my stuff while I nip to the loo?' I gesture at my backpack.

'Sure,' she says. Her eyes drift to Albie, lighting up at the sight of his snoozing form. 'I could watch him too, if you like,' she adds.

'No, no, that's OK,' I say quickly.

'Are you sure? I'm dead good with babies.'

'I'm sure,' I say. 'Thank you.'

Just the idea of letting Albie out of my sight make my stomach churn. For a moment I get an insight into how Mum and Stacey must be feeling right now. This is different though, I tell myself. I'm not some random stranger.

Albie belongs with me.

'Next stop Swindon, next stop Swindon.'

I blink my eyes open.

I was dreaming. Frankie was in it and she was shouting at me, but every time I tried to respond an aeroplane would swoop over our heads, drowning out my words.

I look down. Albie is still strapped to my chest, still fast asleep.

I glance to my left. My backpack is on the seat where I left it, Paddington's nose poking out the top, his sewn-on eyes looking directly at me. The girl across the aisle, though, has gone.

Groggy from my impromptu nap, I gather up my things, shoving my rubbish in the nearest bin and pulling my backpack onto my shoulders before stumbling towards the doors, clinging onto the rail with one hand, my other arm wrapped protectively around Albie as the train sways into the station.

I step out onto the unexpectedly pretty platform. A wave of accomplishment sweeps through my body.

We made it.

It's mid-afternoon and the sun is blazing down. I stop to retrieve Albie's hat from my bag and slip it on his head, before hurrying to follow the flow of people towards what I guess must be the town centre.

I walk down the vaguely familiar high street, past the usual shops and restaurants – New Look, Nando's, Argos, Poundland, McDonald's, Boots. I head straight into Boots and buy another pack of nappies, a big bottle of water and a reduced-price egg and cress sandwich to eat later.

Next step: find somewhere to stay.

Somewhere safe. Somewhere anonymous.

Somewhere Albie can sleep horizontally after an entire day strapped to my body.

Somewhere I can recalibrate and gather my thoughts behind closed doors.

I still don't dare to turn my phone on, so I'm going to have to rely on my instincts. It doesn't take long before I stumble upon the perfect candidate – a budget chain hotel on a nondescript road about ten minutes' walk away from the high street. Clean, basic, comfortable (enough), not too expensive.

The hotel foyer is empty. I press a buzzer on the reception desk and a few moments later, a man appears, holding one of those plastic portable fans a few centimetres away from his neck.

'Can I help you?' he says.

'I'd like a room, please.'

'Have you got a booking?'

I shake my head.

He taps at his keyboard. 'How long you staying?'

I hesitate. I have absolutely no idea. 'If I say one night for now and end up deciding to stay for longer, is that easy enough to sort out?' I ask.

'Sure. Just let us know before eleven a.m. tomorrow.'

'OK, thank you.'

'One night for now then?'

'Yes please.'

'Just the one guest?'

'Well, me and him.'

For the first time, the man behind the desk registers Albie. 'Need a cot then?' he asks.

'Oh. Yes, please.'

'I'll have to see if they have one available. First come first served, you see.' He taps away again. 'You're in luck. I'll get someone to send one up in a bit.'

'Thank you.'

He taps at his keyboard some more, then says. 'That'll be fifty-nine pounds. Cash or card?'

'Cash,' I say, fumbling for my purse.

I count out the requisite amount of notes and slide them across the counter.

'Just one more thing,' he says, handing me one pound in change. 'What's the name?'

'Sorry?'

'The name. For the booking.'

'Oh,' I say. 'It's Amelia. Amelia Wylde.'

Chapter 21

Yesterday

I take extra care getting ready, covering up the shadows under my eyes with concealer and swirling Mum's bronzer across my pale cheeks. I even get my straighteners out for the first time in three weeks and make a half-hearted attempt to coax my lank hair into soft waves.

Choosing an outfit is harder. It's a hot day but anything strappy or flimsy is out. In the end, I tug a long loose T-shirt dress I haven't worn in ages over a pair of calf-length leggings. I'm going to be way too warm in them but I daren't risk Frankie catching a glimpse of the bulky maternity pad currently pressed into my knickers. At least my boobs have finally stopped leaking. Mum and Stacey decided that a bottle would be best, right from day one, so the milk is drying up now. My boobs are still tender and swollen, though, and twice as big as they used to be. I only hope Frankie won't notice.

I stand in front of the mirror and stare at my reflection.

To the untrained eye, I probably look totally normal. A little tired perhaps, but other than that, a perfectly average teenage girl.

What a joke.

'You look nice.'

I turn around. Mum is standing in the doorway to my bedroom.

'Thanks,' I murmur.

'Looking forward to seeing Frankie?'

I shrug.

The truth is, I'm desperate to see her. This is the longest we've ever gone without seeing each other and I've missed her hugely. At the same time, the thought of seeing her face to face makes me so nervous I want to throw up.

'It's good you're getting out of the house,' Mum adds. 'Being cooped up all day can't be good for you.'

'Mmm.'

'What are you going to tell her?'

'I haven't decided yet. Maybe nothing for now.'

'You're going to have to tell her sometime.'

She's not talking about the truth, though; she's talking about the story she and Stacey have concocted.

'Would you like a lift?' she asks.

'No thank you,' I say. 'I'm going to walk.'

'OK, sweetheart. Well, if you need picking up later, you know where I am.'

I'm nervous as I approach Frankie's front door.

What if she can tell? What if she sees through my lies and figures it all out?

My palms prickle with sweat as I ring the bell. Seconds later, the front door flings open and Frankie launches herself at me.

It hurts. After three weeks I'm still feeling tender. I don't let on, though. I just hold on for dear life, frantically blinking away the tears in my eyes.

I get back home to find Mum and Stacey in the garden with Albie. He's lying on his back on a blanket, Mum and Stacey on their sides, framing him. I watch from the patio doors. They look so happy. A perfect little family of three. My heart twists.

Mum glances up.

'Oh, hello,' she says, propping herself up on her elbows. 'You're back early. I thought you might stay for *Bake Off*.'

The new series is starting tonight, and for the past few years Frankie and I have made our weekly viewings a ritual, making mug cakes in the microwave during the ad breaks. She'd asked me to stay but I'd made up an excuse.

'I was tired,' I reply.

'You should have called me for a lift.'

'I wanted to walk.'

'Did you have fun?'

I bite down hard on my lip. As afternoons go, it was probably one of the hardest of my life. I put everything I had into trying to appear as normal as possible and I'm exhausted. I knew lying to Frankie was going to feel horrible but the reality was even worse than I'd feared. And this is just the beginning.

'It was OK,' I say eventually.

'See,' Mum says, smiling triumphantly. 'I told you getting out the house would do you good.'

'Yeah,' I murmur.

The entire time, Stacey doesn't take her eyes off Albie.

*

'Aren't you hungry?' Mum asks, frowning at my full plate.

It's dinner time. A plate of aubergine parmigiana, one of my all-time favourite dishes, sits in front of me but I've barely touched it. I can't remember the last time I ate with gusto. If I think hard enough I can picture myself wolfing down pizza and making crisp sandwiches and scoffing entire packets of Jaffa Cakes in one sitting, but that feels like another version of me, one I can't quite imagine being ever again.

'I had loads of snacks round at Frankie's,' I say.

It's a lie. I refused everything Frankie offered, blaming my lack of appetite on my phantom illness.

'Sorry,' I add. 'I didn't think.'

'Well, get down what you can,' Mum says. 'I don't like the idea of you just filling up on crisps and biscuits. You need to keep your strength up.'

I force a forkful into my mouth. It tastes like glue.

'So,' Mum says, wiping the corners of her mouth with her napkin. 'I was thinking. Well, we were thinking' – she pauses to glance at Stacey – 'that we should probably look into getting Albie's birth registered next week.'

My heat begins to beat that bit faster.

'Why next week?' I say, putting down my fork. 'I thought we had ages.'

'It has to be done within forty-two days of the birth,' Stacey says. 'And we've already used up twenty-two of them.'

'I don't think I'm ready,' I stammer.

'I know it feels that way, sweetheart,' Mum says, reaching for my hand. 'But we're trying to be practical here. The new term is starting soon. Better we get this sorted now rather than have to fit it around school and things. Don't you think?'

She gives my hand a squeeze. I don't return it; just let my hand hang limply in hers before pulling it away.

'I know it feels like a big step,' Mum says. 'But all it is really is a bit of paperwork.'

'You'll feel relieved once it's done,' Stacey adds, her voice overly bright.

I don't say anything.

'And once we've done that,' she continues, 'we can think about making things official. We've spoken to a solicitor and the process is surprisingly simple.'

I look up sharply. 'When did you speak to a solicitor?'

Mum and Stacey exchange a guilty glance. 'Does it matter?' Mum asks. 'It was just a chat on the phone, very informal. And well, because of our circumstances, it's just a case of filling out the relevant paperwork. We could have the whole process done and dusted in under a month.'

'A month?' I say. But that's no time.

'Yes,' Stacey says, her eyes sparkling. 'Great, isn't it? I mean, there's no point in dragging things out, is there?'

I throw Mum a panicked look. It doesn't seem to register. She smiles and tucks a strand of my hair behind my ear – her signature move. I have to resist every urge in my body not to bat her away.

'The sooner we get things sorted, the sooner we get out of this limbo and move on properly. It's for your own benefit, I promise.'

That's what they keep telling me. Over and over and over again.

It's for the best.

We're only thinking of you.

Time heals everything.

But I'm still waiting for it to make sense and click into place. If it's all for my own benefit, then why does it feel so very wrong?

They take my silence as agreement.

'That settles it then,' Stacey says, topping up her and Mum's wine glasses in turn. 'I'll ring up the town hall tomorrow and make an appointment.'

After dinner has been cleared away, Mum and Stacey retire to the living room. I hover in the doorway as they get themselves comfortable, trying and failing to ignore the clutch of 'new baby' cards displayed on the mantelpiece and window sill, all of them addressed to 'Stacey and Helen'.

'We're going to try that new Netflix show,' Mum says, flopping down on the sofa as Stacey uncorks a fresh bottle of wine. 'The one Auntie Jen was talking about the other day. Fancy it?' She pats the sofa cushion next to her.

'No thanks,' I reply.

'Are you sure? The acting's supposed to be great.'

'I'm sure. I'm just going to go and read for a bit.'

'OK, sweetheart. I'll pop up and see you in a little while.'

'OK.'

I leave them to it and head upstairs to the bathroom. The soundtrack of summer evenings – lawnmowers and children playing and the distant chimes of an ice-cream van – leaks in through the open window. I have a wee. My urine is dark yellow. I make a mental note to drink more water. I used to be really on it, diligently draining my water bottle every few hours before filling it up again, but over the past few weeks all my usual habits and rituals have fallen by the wayside. My eyebrows are untidy, my toenails overgrown, my teeth unflossed. I haven't even looked at a razor.

I flush the loo and wash my hands. Reluctantly, I raise my eyes to meet my gaze in the mirror above the sink. Despite the heatwave, I'm as pale as anything. Apart from today, I haven't left the house since we got back from the hospital, two whole weeks ago. It feels like longer – life before Albie a fuzzy memory. The days and nights have all melded together. If it wasn't for the calendar in the kitchen, I wouldn't have a clue what month it is, never mind what day.

During this time we've had a small but steady trickle of visitors – just close friends and family for now. Not one of them has questioned the surrogacy explanation. To give them credit, Mum and Stacey are pretty convincing, fleshing out their story with so many specific details that I almost start to believe it. Luckily, they haven't insisted on telling Dad yet so at least I haven't had to lie to him. I will eventually, though, and I'm dreading it. I avoid most of the visitors, hiding in my bedroom with my earphones in, only making an appearance if summoned, dutifully playing 'big sister'. No one cares about me, though. Albie is the star of the show with Mum and Stacey in supporting roles. I'm a bit part at best. A glorified extra.

Unlike pretty much every other new mum on the planet, I've actually lost weight. My cheeks are sunken and my collarbones are protruding. Gingerly, I run my finger along them. They feel pointy and sharp. I stand back and lift up my dress. I can see my ribs, the very same ribs the midwife reckoned Albie was tucked behind the entire time I was carrying him, hence the complete lack of baby bump. I turn so I'm in profile and try to picture Albie inside me. I can't, though. No matter how many times I tell myself he was in there for eight whole months, I can't quite accept it as truth. It's just too outlandish for me to get my head around. I let my dress fall back into place and venture out onto the landing, lingering outside Mum and Stacey's bedroom.

The sound of the TV floats up the stairs. I can hear Mum and Stacey talking over it, the way they always do when they're watching anything. I picture them making a toast, clinking their glasses together and saying something like 'here's to us and our beautiful baby boy!'.

My phone buzzes in the pocket of my dress. It's a message from Frankie, asking if I'm watching *Bake Off*. I ignore it and move towards the door. It's ajar. I peer through the gap. The blackout blinds are lowered, the only light source a lamp in the shape of a crescent moon, a gift from one of Stacey's work friends, balanced on the chest of drawers next to Albie's Moses basket. I step inside, pulling the door to behind me, then pick my way over towards it. I peer in. Albie is fast asleep, his tiny chest rising and falling in a steady rhythm. I kneel down next to the basket so my face is level with his. I study his features, searching for bits of me, but only seeing his dad.

I straighten up and slide my hands under his warm little body, carefully lifting him to my chest. I sniff his head. He smells sweet and sour at the same time. I sit down on the edge of Mum and Stacey's bed and cradle him in the nook of my arm so I can look at him properly.

Even after almost three whole weeks, he still blows my mind. I can't imagine a time when he won't.

I don't know how long I sit there for, only that every time I think about returning Albie to his Moses basket, I can't quite bring myself to do it. One more minute, I tell myself. Over and over and over.

He begins to squirm in my arms. I stand up and jiggle him slightly, the way I've seen Stacey do. For a moment, I think it's worked and I go to sit back down, but then he lets out a cry – sharp and piercing. I keep pacing back and forth, singing softly under my breath in an effort to soothe him.

A few seconds later, the door bursts open. I whirl round. It's Stacey, clutching the baby monitor in her left hand.

'What are you doing?' she asks, striding towards me. 'Did you wake him up?'

I take a couple of steps backwards. 'No. I was holding him and he started crying.'

'Why were you holding him?'

'I just wanted to.'

She tuts. 'We're trying to get him into a routine, Jojo. Do you know how damaging it is for a baby to get used to being held when they're supposed to be falling asleep?'

'He didn't fall asleep in my arms, though. He was already asleep when I picked him up.'

'Well, you shouldn't be disturbing him like that.'

'I just wanted to hold him. You never let me.'

'That's not true.'

'Yes it is.'

She won't let me anywhere near him half the time. She does it all with a laugh and a smile, but the subtext is clear: he's mine, not yours, so get used to it and keep your hands off.

'We've discussed this, Jojo. It's for the best. We don't want you getting too attached.'

It's too late, I want to yell. *I'm already attached.*

'Just give him here,' she says, tossing the monitor on the bed and holding out her arms.

For a second I imagine pushing past her and running down the stairs with him and out the front door. It's a stupid idea, though. Where would I even go? Not to mention the fact Stacey wouldn't let me get as far as the landing.

'Jojo, I mean it,' Stacey says, her arms still outstretched.

Reluctantly, I hand him over.

As she takes him, she turns away from me. 'It's not just cuddles, you know,' she says over her shoulder. 'Motherhood.'

'I know that,' I say. 'I'm not an idiot.'

Slowly, she turns to face me. 'I never said you were, Jojo,' she says, her voice low and measured. 'But it's been three weeks now. I know this is a big adjustment, but it's an adjustment for us all. I think you forget that sometimes. That this isn't just about you.'

I feel like I've been slapped.

'All this interference isn't helping anyone,' she continues. 'You need to step back and let your mum and I get on with raising Albie, OK? For his sake if nothing else.'

She turns away, rocking Albie in her arms. As he begins to settle, my heart wants to break in two.

That's my job, I want to shout. *I should be the one who stops him crying, not you! I'm his mum!*

But I can't.

I agreed.

I owe them this.

A big fat tear slips down my cheek. I duck out of the room before Stacey sees it.

I fix up the arrangements with Frankie for tomorrow, for results day, then I'm reading when Mum knocks on my door.

'Come in,' I mutter.

'Hey, sweetheart,' she says, padding across the carpet towards me. 'All right if I sit down?'

I shrug and draw my knees under my chin to make room on the bed.

As Mum sits down, she picks up my book, a battered childhood copy of *The Enchanted Wood* by Enid Blyton, and smiles at the cover. 'I remember reading this to you,' she says. 'You always used to ask for the chapter where they go up to the Land of Birthdays.'

She's right. In the end, I knew it so well I could recite the entire chapter on demand and would be word perfect every time. I wish I could go to a magical land right now. Maybe not the Land of Birthdays, though. A land where it's calm and quiet; a land where I can actually think.

'You missed out,' she says, placing the book back down on my pillow.

'On what?'

'The Netflix thing. It was fab. Great acting. At least we thought so.'

'OK.'

There's a pause.

'Stacey told me what happened before,' she says.

I don't say anything.

She strokes my cheek. 'I know it seems harsh but she's right, darling. You need to leave the parenting to us.'

'I was just holding him, Mum.'

'I know. But maybe it's best if you don't for a bit.'

'What are you saying? That I can't ever hold him?'

She sighs. 'I'm saying, you need to take a step back, Jojo. Being a mother is all Stacey has ever wanted. You need to give her the time and space to do it.' She looks around. 'It's not like you haven't got other things to keep you occupied,' she adds, reaching over to my desk and picking up the Arts Academy equipment list I've been ignoring.

At the beginning of June I was sent a list of items I'd need for my first term – black sweatshirt and jogging bottoms, black

T-shirts, black character shoes, black practice skirt, notebooks, a yoga mat, etc . . . I remember the excitement rippling through my body as I read the list, setting aside a specific day to go out and buy them all. But that was before. Back when getting into the Arts Academy was the biggest thing that had ever happened to me.

'Hey,' Mum says. 'I've got an idea. How about we go shopping for this lot on Saturday? We could make a day of it. Go for lunch, maybe watch a film. What do you reckon? It's been ages since we had any proper mother/daughter time.'

'I don't know. Maybe.'

'I really think we should, darling. You've barely left the house these past few weeks. It'll be good for you. I'll have a look at the film listings, see if there's anything interesting on.'

I don't reply, just fiddle with the edge of the duvet.

Mum pushes herself to her feet. 'Don't stay up too late now,' she says. 'You need to start getting back into a routine. Especially with all those early starts you're going to have to get to the academy on time. Perhaps we should do a couple of dummy runs next week, get you used to the commute so it's not too much of a shock to the system.'

'Perhaps,' I echo.

She pauses in the doorway. 'It's going to get easier, sweetheart,' she says. 'I promise.'

I nod.

I don't believe her, though. Not for one second.

*

I'm still in bed when Stacey bangs on my door the following morning. I slept badly, waking up every half an hour or so. I drag myself out of bed and open the door.

She looks stressed. Her hair is free from product and her trade-mark statement lipstick is missing.

My first thought is Albie.

'What's going on?' I ask, panic rising in my belly. 'Is everything OK? Where's Albie?'

'Everything's fine. It's my mum,' she says. 'She's locked herself out and needs me to go over with the spare key. You're not going anywhere in the next little while, are you?'

'I'm supposed to be at Frankie's at ten so we can pick up our results,' I say.

'OK, that's fine. I should be back by then, no problems. Can you stay with Albie? I'd take him with me but the car seat is in your mum's car. We forgot to swap it over.'

'Of course,' I say.

'He's asleep in our room. He's just had a feed so he shouldn't wake up until after I'm back, so if you'd just leave him to sleep, I'd appreciate it.' She puts extra emphasis on this part, her gaze intensifying.

'Fine,' I say, looking away.

'Thank you, Jojo. I'll be as fast as I can.'

I sit down on my bed and listen as Stacey gallops down the stairs, pausing to grab her keys from the hook before slamming the door shut behind her. A few seconds later, I hear the familiar roar of the faithful engine of her ancient Fiesta as she pulls out of the cul-de-sac.

I count to ten before standing up and making my way straight to Mum and Stacey's bedroom.

Albie is in his Moses basket. I look down at him and I'm flooded with a love so strong it almost knocks me over. You can't just take a step back from something like this. Mum and Stacey keep making out that it's a decision, that I'm simply not trying hard enough, that if I put my mind to it, I'll simply forget that's he's my son and happily get on with my life and never think about it ever again. But the reality is, I can't step away. Just the idea of turning my back on him, of standing aside and letting someone else be his mother while I sit by and watch from the sidelines, makes me want to let out a never-ending silent scream.

In that moment I know what I've got to do.

Before I can talk myself out of it, I run to my room and start packing a bag.

Chapter 22

Room 426 is at the very end of a long empty corridor that smells of lemon-sharp toilet cleaner and cheap air freshener. I open the door and slip inside, locking it behind me. For a few moments I stay there, my backpack resting against the door, my arms wrapped around Albie.

I did it. We're here.

It's quiet, the only sound Albie's slow, steady breathing and the rattling wheeze of the air conditioning unit.

The room is dim, a thin strip of sunlight peeking through the gap between the heavy curtains. I insert the key card into the slot on the wall to my right. A few seconds later the lights buzz on one by one, gradually bathing the room in a weak yellow glow. It looks pretty much like the promotional photographs displayed in the foyer, only slightly less glossy – the skirting board a little scuffed, the ghost of handprints on the off-white walls, the duvet significantly less cloud-like than the one promised. I don't care, though. For the next twenty hours, it is mine and that's all that matters.

I set my backpack down on the floor and remove Albie from the carrier. As I cradle him in my arms, he wakes up and regards me with watchful eyes. I perch on the edge of the bed and just look at him. I take my time, methodically studying every perfect millimetre of him. All the while he stares back up at me, his eyes wide and alert.

'Hello, Albie,' I say. 'I'm your mummy.'

As the words leave my lips, I realize it's the first time I've said anything to that effect out loud.

A single tear trickles down my cheek, landing on Albie's. Tenderly, I wipe it away.

'Don't worry,' I say. 'I'm not always like this, I promise.'

He continues to stare up at me, his forehead knitted into a tiny frown. I lean down and kiss him, pausing to inhale deeply. He smells glorious in a way I can't put into words no matter how hard I try.

'We've got a lot of catching up to do,' I say, kissing him again. 'A lot.'

After over an hour of eyeballing one another, he begins to grizzle. I feed him, burp him, then lay his sleepy body in the centre of the bed, surrounding him with pillows so he can't go anywhere, even though, according to the baby book, he's months away from being able to roll over. Content he's comfortable, I move over to the window and push the curtain aside. We're at the back of the hotel, overlooking the car park. Beyond it, I can see an industrial estate, and beyond that, trees and houses.

As I let the curtain fall back into place, it dawns on me that for perhaps the first time in my entire life, no one in the world knows where I am. Apart from the guy on reception perhaps, but he thinks I'm Amelia. As far as he's concerned, Jojo Bright doesn't exist.

A knock at the door makes me jump. Albie stirs but doesn't wake. Cautiously, I slide off the bed and make my way towards the door.

'Who is it?' I call, my voice wavering. Even though I know it's impossible, I can't help but have visions of a furious Mum and Stacey on the other side.

'Housekeeping,' a female voice replies in an Eastern European accent. 'I have your cot.'

I sigh with relief and open the door.

Once she's gone, I place the cardboard do-not-disturb sign on the handle before locking and chaining the door behind me.

I open my bag, unpacking Albie's stuff and lining it up on the little wooden desk. I sort through his clothes, carefully refolding his tiny socks and T-shirts and trousers and babygros. I didn't do such a great job at packing for myself – untangling the mismatched shorts and T-shirts I barely remember grabbing – but I'm pleased with what I managed to get for Albie.

As I rescue my toothbrush and a tube of toothpaste from the bottom of the bag, my fingers graze my phone. I take it out and stare at the blank screen. I know I need to turn it on but I'm afraid of what will greet me when I do – the messages and missed calls and frantic voicemails. Just the thought of my screen filling up with notifications makes my stomach flip-flop and my head swim. I'll do it later. When I've had time to rest and acclimatize and come up with a proper plan.

I place my phone face down on the chest of drawers next to the bed.

Satisfied Albie isn't going anywhere, I go into the bathroom, taking care to leave the door ajar so I'll hear him if he wakes up. I pull back the plastic shower curtain and survey the bathtub. It's spotless apart from a single curling dark hair near the plughole. I turn on the cold tap. The hair appears to cling on for a few seconds before admitting defeat and swirling down the drain.

I haven't had a bath since the birth. I've been avoiding the main bathroom altogether when I can, showering in Mum and Stacey's tiny little en suite instead.

I turn on the shower, the room quickly filling with steam. I undress. In the foggy mirror I can see my hip bones, the gap between my thighs, the outline of my ribs. It doesn't suit me. I've always been slight but there used to be a certain softness with it. Now I just look bony. I'm relieved when the mirror steams up entirely, swallowing up my reflection with it, and I make a mental note to eat the sandwich I bought.

I adjust the temperature of the water and step into the bathtub. I didn't have the space for shower gel or shampoo so I have to use the stuff from the dispenser mounted to the wall, pumping it into my hand. It's bright green, like washing-up liquid. It smells like it too. I close my eyes and wash my body and hair. When I'm finished, I wrap myself in a fluffy white towel, another round my head like a turban and venture back into the main room.

Albie is still fast asleep. He looks so peaceful. I stand over him and am flooded with love. And fear. Because as far as I can tell, when it comes to babies, the two go hand in hand.

I stretch out on the thin available strip of mattress next to Albie and his pillow fort and open my book. It's full of motivational headings like 'You are the expert' and 'You're doing it right' and 'Trust your maternal instincts'. I read chapters on sleeping, feeding, soothing and development. They're packed full of anecdotes from mums who sound just as overwhelmed as me, and even though I doubt the words were written with a sixteen-year-old girl in mind, I can't help but feel reassured.

I finish the chapter on health and glance up. According to the digital clock on the desk, it's nearly seven o'clock. I've been gone for over ten hours now. Swallowing, I set aside the book, knowing I can't put it off any longer. My heartbeat quickening, I turn on my phone before I have the chance to talk myself out of it. The screen glows into life and for a few seconds there's nothing. Then it begins to vibrate in my hand, the screen filling up with notification after notification. The same names and phrases jump out at me over and over again.

Mum.

Stacey.

Frankie.

> Call me.
> We're worried.
> Where are you???

One of Frankie's most recent messages jumps out at me. I open it up so I can read it in full.

> What's going on?? Your mum and Stacey have been round. They're really worried. RING ME!!!! Love you xxx

The idea of the three of them in one room makes my stomach churn. What did they say? What did they give away? From Frankie's message, it looks like they kept their cards fairly close to their chest, but what if they let something slip, something Frankie might figure out on her own later? Whatever words were exchanged, I need to extinguish the situation. More than that though, I just want to hear my best friend's voice.

I was four when I met Frankie. It was the first day of Reception and I was one of a few children clinging to their parent's leg, eyes wet with silent tears. The class teacher, Mrs Percival, had been trying to coax me away for several minutes when a gangly girl with long dark hair in two plaits decided to take matters into her own hands. Mum later admitted she'd assumed she was an older child at first, drafted in to look after the new starters – Frankie was tall for her age and already moved around the classroom like she owned the place.

'Don't be sad,' she said, determinedly peeling my fingers from Mum's leg. 'School is really, really fun, I promise.'

I was so startled I let her lead me away, and by the time I thought to check, Mum had already been ushered out of the classroom.

Frankie stuck by my side all day. At break time, she took my hand and led me out into the playground.

'Let's play a game,' she said.

'What kind of game?' I asked nervously.

'A "Let's Pretend" game.'

'What's that?'

Frankie's mouth hung open. 'You don't know what "Let's Pretend" is?'

I shook my head.

'It's dead easy. We pick something and then we pretend it's real. Like, "Let's Pretend" Weddings and you can be the groom and I'll be the bride. Or "Let's Pretend" Pet Shop and I'll be the shopkeeper and you can be the customer.'

'Or "Let's Pretend" circuses,' I said slowly, getting the hang of things now. 'And you can be the ringmaster man and I'll be the trapeze lady.'

'Yes!' Frankie said, her eyes shining. 'Exactly like that!'

Over the coming years, as our 'Let's Pretend' universe expanded, my friendship with Frankie deepened. It didn't matter that we were different. We just worked, right from the very beginning.

I scroll to Frankie's name and press 'call'.

She answers within three rings. 'Finally!' she cries. 'Where the hell have you been all day? I must have messaged you like twenty times!'

My heart floods with love and guilt. Frankie is my best friend. She's been my everything for most of my life. And I'm about to lie to her – again.

I take a deep breath before speaking. 'Sorry,' I say. 'I only just managed to charge my phone.'

As Frankie quizzes me about the whereabouts of my portable charger and why I haven't been in touch, I sit back down on the bed, my head spinning.

'I had to go to school all by myself, Jojo,' Frankie is saying. 'I looked like a right Billy No-Mates.'

'Sorry,' I say. 'Um, something came up.'

'Something more important than going to collect our GCSE results together?'

I don't know what to say. How can I tell her that the most important thing in my life is something, or rather someone, she doesn't even know exists.

'Listen,' Frankie says. 'My mum's offered to drive us to Ella's. I'm running a bit late but I reckon I could be at yours for about twenty past if my hair decides to dry any time soon. That work for you?'

I pause, rehearsing the lines in my head before speaking them out loud. 'I'm really sorry,' I say. 'But I don't think I'm going to make it tonight.'

'What do you mean?' she cries, wounded. 'This has been in the diary for ever.'

Without invitation, memories of the last party of Theo's I attended nine months ago invade my mind, memories I used to voluntarily replay over and over, supplying material for hours and hours' worth of daydreams. I close my eyes and force them away.

'Are you poorly again or something?' Frankie asks. 'Is that it?'

'No, no, I'm, fine,' I say, my eyes still closed.

'What's going on then?'

Beside me, Albie stirs. I put Frankie on speaker and pick him up, holding him close to my chest.

'I'm at my dad's,' I say.

I feel bad about using my dad's bouts of depression as an excuse but it's the most believable explanation I can come up with right now.

'Is he OK?' Frankie demands. 'He's not done anything, you know, stupid, has he?'

My eyes blink open at what she's insinuating. 'Oh no. No,' I say. 'Nothing like that.'

'He's going to be OK, then?'

'Yes, I think so.'

'Then you can come to the party!'

'I can't just leave him, Frankie!'

'But you literally just said you think he's going to be OK.'

She's getting fed up with me now, I can tell. I know I'm being unfair but I can't help but feel annoyed with her for not accepting my story point blank.

'Exactly. *Going* to be,' I snap.

'But it's results day.'

'I know. And I'm sorry but I . . .' I close my eyes again. Somehow lying seems easier in the dark. 'I just don't feel right leaving him.'

Without warning, Albie lets out an ear-splitting wail. I set him down on the bed and grab my phone, taking it off speaker, and charge towards the bathroom.

'What's that noise? Is that a baby?' Frankie asks.

She sounds almost disgusted at the thought. Frankie has never been into babies. Then again, until three weeks ago, neither was I, particularly.

I'm in the bathroom now, the door closed, Albie's crying just about audible. It makes my heart break, the thought of him marooned on the bed, screaming his little lungs out. But what other choice do I have? I can't risk Frankie hearing him.

'It's the TV,' I say. 'Listen, I have to go. I'll call you tomorrow or something.'

I hang up.

With trembling fingers, I send Mum and Stacey a joint text.

> **We're OK. I'll be in touch x**

Then I turn my phone off and go back into the bedroom where I shove it to the very bottom of my bag.

I pick Albie up, holding him close against my chest as he cries.

OK.

Now what?

For the first time since I left the house this morning, I have absolutely no idea.

Chapter 23

Albie is still crying.

I check his nappy. It looks clean but I change it anyway, just in case. I offer up a bottle but he turns his head away and keeps screaming. Is he too hot? Too cold? I grab Paddington Bear and wiggle him in front of Albie's face. His crying only intensifies. I know babies cry, especially newborns, but even armed with this knowledge, the sound of his screams makes my entire body ache. All I want to do is make it better, but I have no idea what he wants. With one hand, I flick through the pages of my book, searching for a solution I haven't yet thought of. With the other, I turn on the TV and turn to CBeebies.

'*We'll be back at six a.m. tomorrow!*' the written message on the screen cheerfully proclaims.

Eleven whole hours from now.

I flick through the channels until I find an old musical. I sit on the end of the bed and turn Albie around so his body is facing the TV. My chin resting gently on top of his head, I jiggle him on my lap and gradually his crying fades as a man and woman tap-dance across the screen. We lapse into silence, sucked into their magical technicolour world where any problem can be solved with a song and a dance.

I'm sad when it's over. From what I can work out, Albie is too. Within seconds he's crying again. I try the other channels but nothing will distract him.

I stand up and walk back and forth. I sing every song I can think of. I run out of nursery rhymes and lullabies so have to resort to pop songs and musical theatre numbers and TV ad jingles. Not that it matters. Not even my sweetest singing will soothe Albie. I have another go with his bottle. This time he latches on. I sink down on the bed and let out a sigh of relief.

Determined to stick to the rest of his usual bedtime routine, I run him a shallow bath, checking the temperature with my elbow, the way I've seen Stacey do.

As I wash his soft little body, taking care to clean every nook and cranny, I feel myself relaxing once more.

The book is right.

Annie was right.

I can do this.

I can.

Back in the main room, I lower the lights. I put a fresh nappy on Albie and massage lotion into his skin before wrestling his squirming limbs into a white sleepsuit. He smells so clean and sweet and I'm tempted to let him fall asleep in my arms, but I keep remembering what Stacey says about it being a bad idea . . . I kiss him on the head and reluctantly lower him into the travel cot. He lies on his back, his eyes fixed on an invisible spot somewhere above his head. I sit on the edge of the bed and watch as his little body jerks and writhes until eventually he stills and his eyes flicker shut.

I check the time. 7.58 p.m.

My eyes fall on the bed.

What is it they say? Sleep when the baby sleeps?

I go to the bathroom and brush my teeth, then step out of my clothes and crawl under the duvet, falling asleep within seconds.

A knock at the door wrenches me from my slumber.

I stay where I am in the bed, my body rigid, a fistful of duvet in each hand.

It must be a mistake. Someone at the wrong door.

What time even is it? Albie woke up at 10 p.m. wanting a feed, and I feel like I only just got back to sleep. I raise my head a few centimetres so I can see. It's 12.32 a.m. I lie back down and close my eyes.

Whoever it is on the other side of the door knocks again.

I hold my breath.

Silence.

I will them to go away.

Then comes the voice.

A voice I know so well, it's perhaps even more familiar than my own.

'Jojo? It's me, Frankie. Are you in there?'

I freeze.

Frankie is here, on the other side of my hotel room door.

But how? Why?

I feel sick.

She knocks again.

'Jojo, can you hear me? Seriously, open up.'

Everything is racing. My heart, my pulse, my mind.

Still I stay where I am, welded to the mattress, unable to move even if I wanted to.

That's when Albie starts to cry.

Almost immediately, Frankie starts knocking again.

I sit up and turn on the light. Trembling, I get out of bed and pick Albie up.

'I know you're in there, Jojo,' Frankie calls. 'And I know who you've got with you too.'

She knows? But how? Has she spoken to Mum and Stacey? Did she somehow work it out?

'Please, just let me in,' she continues. 'I'm not mad with you, I promise.'

I press my lips together. Mad or not, I can't deal with this right now. I'm not ready to face everything. I need more time. I need her to go away.

She won't, though. This is Frankie Ricci we're talking about, and she doesn't give up. Ever.

Stalling for time, I pace silently, Albie in my arms, his crying quieter now as I try to think.

'Please, Jojo,' Frankie says. 'I'm your best friend. I'm here to help you.'

I keep pacing.

'I love you and I need to know you're OK. I promise you, I've got your back on this.'

I think of all the other times Frankie's had my back. She's never let me down. Ever.

But this is different.

This doesn't even compare.

'Please, Jojo,' she says. 'Just open up. I'm not going anywhere until you do.'

I believe her too. 'Determined' should be Frankie's middle name.

I take a deep breath and creep over to the door. 'Are you alone?' I ask.

'Yes!' Frankie says.

'You promise?'

There's a beat before she answers. 'Of course. It's just me out here, I promise you.'

'You swear?'

'On my life. I'm completely alone.'

I peek through the spyhole. A distorted version of Frankie is standing in the otherwise empty corridor.

'Hang on,' I say.

'OK. I'm not going anywhere.'

Miraculously, Albie has stopped crying, his eyes lolling shut. Carefully, I return him to the cot. Then I straighten up, my heart beating so hard I think my chest might burst, and head towards the door.

Towards Frankie.

Towards my best friend.

Towards the person whose heart I'm pretty sure I'm about to break whether I like it or not.

Chapter 24

The first thing Frankie does is throw her arms around me, and for a moment my terror is replaced by love, pure and simple, and for a few seconds I allow myself to believe everything might just be OK.

'Holy shit, Jojo,' she says, holding me tight. 'I've been so worried. Like you wouldn't believe.'

'Sorry,' I stammer, my voice muffled by her chest.

'Are you OK?' she demands, releasing me from her embrace and standing at arms' length, her hands resting on my shoulders as she looks me up and down.

'I'm . . . I'm fine,' I say.

'You sure about that?'

I don't answer her.

'I mean, what the fuck, Jojo?' she asks. 'This is major, you know that?'

I nod, swallowing hard.

Her gaze shifts to the right.

I know what she's looking at.

The cot.

She removes her hands from my shoulders. 'Is she OK?' she asks.

She?

'Yes,' I say. 'But it's not a she, he's a—'

'Do you mind if I look?' Frankie asks, cutting me off.

'No. Of course not,' I say, standing aside.

I can't believe how cool she's being about all of this. I expected her to shout and scream, to rip my hair out. Instead, she's being almost gentle with me.

I turn and watch as she heads towards the cot, dropping her handbag on the bed en route.

She peers into the cot then looks over at me, her face contorted into a deep frown. 'It's not Olivia,' she says.

'What?'

'The baby. It isn't Olivia.'

'Who's Olivia?' I ask.

'Olivia Sinclair.'

I frown. I have no idea what's she's on about. Should I? I rack my brains but draw a blank. I don't know anyone called Olivia, I'm almost certain.

Frankie crosses over to the bed and grabs her phone from her bag, tapping at the screen for a few seconds before thrusting it at me. I take it from her and scan the news story on the screen, my eyes widening.

'Wait,' I say, my mind whirring. 'You thought I had something to do with this?'

'Of course I did!' Frankie cries.

I blink. What is she saying exactly? That she thought I'd actually kidnapped some baby at random?

'But that's insane,' I say. 'I'd never do something like that.'

'Well, what was I supposed to think?' Frankie splutters. 'You've been acting weird for weeks and then you go AWOL on the very same day a baby goes missing.'

'And from that you worked out I must have stolen her?' I say, shaking my head. 'That's kind of a leap, even for you, Frankie.'

'Even for me?' Frankie says. 'What's that supposed to mean?'

I hesitate.

'I'm not the one in the wrong here,' she says. 'I'm not the one holed up in some hotel with some strange baby. OK, it may not be Olivia, but I'm pretty damn sure it doesn't belong to you.'

I don't know what to say to that.

'Well?' she demands. 'Whose is it? Do they even know you're got it?'

That's when it hits me. Frankie doesn't know a single thing. All that stuff about 'I won't be mad' was based on another scenario entirely – a scenario in which I'd taken off with the blonde baby in the photo, this Olivia Sinclair.

'Well?' she repeats. 'Where did it come from?'

'He,' I say, my voice oddly calm. 'It's not an *it*, it's a *he*.'

She rolls her eyes hard. 'OK, fine. Then where did you get *him*?'

I take a deep breath.

I need to say it quickly. While I still can.

'I didn't get him from anywhere,' I say, my words clipped. 'He's mine.'

For a moment Frankie looks like she's going to burst out laughing. 'What do you mean, he's yours?' she asks after a moment's silence.

'He's mine,' I repeat, standing up a little straighter, my chin raised. 'As in, I'm his mother.'

Frankie shakes her head. 'But that's impossible,' she says. 'To be his mum you'd have had to have given birth to him.'

'I know.' I hold her gaze.

In what feels like slow motion, her face crumples. I roll back my shoulders and try to steady my breathing.

'But you were never pregnant,' she says.

'Yes, I was.'

'No you weren't. I would have known.'

'I was pregnant, Frankie. I just didn't show.'

'What do you mean?'

'I had no bump.'

'So where was the baby?'

'The midwife thinks I must have carried him under my ribs.'

Frankie pulls a face. I don't blame her. When the midwife shared her theory, I shivered with horror.

'But you must have had other symptoms even if there was no bump,' Frankie says. 'What about your periods?'

'You know how irregular they are.'

There's a pause.

'When?' she asks. 'When did you have him?'

Here we go.

'Three weeks ago.'

'So the whole thing about you having a virus . . .'

'It was a lie. I'm so sorry,' I say in a desperate whisper. 'Truly.'

'But why did you lie about it? Three weeks is a long time, Jojo.'

'I know, It's – it's complicated.'

She snorts. 'No shit.'

'I'm sorry,' I repeat.

And even though I mean it with all my heart, out loud my apology somehow sounds flimsy and insincere.

Frankie shakes her head and begins to pace up and down in front of the bed. I stay where I am, standing at the bottom corner. My hands are trembling. I clasp them together in an effort to still them.

'But you're a virgin,' Frankie says, whirling round to face me. 'You've never even had sex, Jojo.'

I don't say anything. I don't need to.

Once more her face sags. I want to look away but I don't dare drop her gaze.

'Why you didn't tell me?' she whispers.

'I told you, I didn't know.'

'What?'

'I didn't know I was pregnant. I had no idea until I was actually giving birth to him.'

'No, Jojo. I meant about losing your virginity.'

I remain silent.

'I told you when I lost mine,' she says.

'I know.'

'I told you practically the second I'd done it.'

She's not exaggerating. I remember her breathless call from Ram's bathroom as if it was yesterday.

Suddenly I feel faint. 'I think I need to sit down,' I say.

'So, sit down,' she mutters.

I lower myself onto the bed.

Frankie stays where she is, her hands planted on her hips. 'Well, who is it then?' she asks. 'Is it someone I know?'

I hesitate before nodding.

'Someone from school?'

'No.'

She frowns. 'OK, then. Someone from Youth Theatre?'

'No.'

'Is he our age?'

'Please don't make me do this, Frankie.'

'I'm not making you do anything,' she says, her eyes flashing. 'I was under the impression we told each other important shit like this.'

'I know. I'm sorry.'

Once more, my apology sounds inadequate, but I don't know what more I can say apart from 'I'm sorry' over and over again.

'I don't want you to be sorry, Jojo,' Frankie snaps. 'I'm sick of sorry. I want you to fucking talk to me.' She sucks in a breath. 'Does he know? The dad, I mean?'

I manage a shake of the head.

'Are you going to tell him?'

I sigh and rake both hands through my hair. 'I don't know what I'm going to do, Frankie.'

I'm exhausted. All I want to do is crawl under the duvet and sleep, but I know Frankie won't let me in a billion years. There are too many unanswered questions.

'So, are you going to tell me who it is or what?' she asks.

'Does it matter?'

She throws her hands up in the air. 'Of course it matters! It's the father of your baby, Jojo.'

I wince.

'What do you think I'm going to do?' she asks. 'Run around telling everyone?'

'Of course not.'

'So, why all the secrecy? We're supposed to be best friends, Jojo. We're supposed to be there for each other.'

'I know.'

'So give me the chance to be there for you!'

I open my mouth, then close it again, my brain trying and failing to come up with the right words.

'Jesus Christ, Jojo!' Frankie cries. 'What is going *on* with you? Seriously, it's like I don't even know you any more!'

That's when I lose it. 'This isn't about you, Frankie!' I shout.

Her eyes bulge in surprise. Answering back and making a scene is normally her department.

'This is about me,' I say, jabbing my chest with my index finger. 'Me and my baby!'

She lets out a splutter of laughter. 'Oh, so I'm the selfish one now, is that it? I'm not asking for the moon, Jojo. I just want you to be honest with me so I can actually try and help you. I would *never* not tell you something like this. Ever.'

'I wanted to!' I cry. 'So badly. Do you have any idea how lonely these past few weeks have been? How scary? I wanted you by my side more than anything!'

'Then why didn't you say something? I was just at the end of the phone. Why didn't you call? I'd have been there in a shot, you know I would. Why let me find out like this?'

'It's not that simple.'

'Then explain it me. At least give me the chance to understand.'

I shut my eyes.

'The father,' I say. 'You know him.'

'I thought we'd already established that.'

'No, you don't understand,' I say. 'You *know* him.'

'Oh my God, it's not Luca's, is it?' she asks, her voice dripping with disgust.

My eyes fly open. 'No! Of course not!' I say, shaking my head frantically.

'Then who?'

Just say it, Jojo. Fast. Like ripping off a plaster.

I can't, though. I'm trying, I swear I am, but the words just won't form.

Another feeble 'I'm sorry,' is the best I can manage.

Frankie swears under her breath and marches back over to the cot. She looks down at Albie, her face in profile.

The longer she looks, the harder my stomach churns.

'Frankie,' I say.

She ignores me and continues to stare, her fingers gripping the edge of the cot, her back and shoulders tensing.

'Frankie.'

Slowly, after what feels like for ever but is probably no more than ten seconds, she looks over at me. Her eyes are full of tears, the realization etched all over her face.

'It only happened once, Frankie, I swear,' I say, wobbling to my feet.

'Shut up, Jojo.'

'But it's true. Please, Frankie, you've got to believe me. I'm sorry, I'm so, so sorry.'

'Shut up,' she says, talking over me. 'Just shut up, Jojo.'

'Please, Frankie,' I say. 'I can explain.'

'I said, SHUT UP!' she shouts.

'But it's not what it seems, I swear to you. Please, if you'd just let me tell you what happened.'

'It's too late, Jojo,' she says, tears running down her cheeks now. 'The damage has already been done. You and me? We're over, OK? Finished.'

She grabs her bag off the bed and storms out of the room, slamming the door shut behind her with such force the entire room seems to tremble.

Chapter 25

Last New Year's Eve

'Happy Almost New Year!' Frankie whoops down the phone.

'Happy Almost New Year,' I reply. 'How's Tenerife?'

'Oh my God, *so* gorgeous,' Frankie says. 'It was twenty-three degrees today. And you know that boy I told you about?'

'The one with the sexy eyes or the one with the sexy hair?' I ask. Over the past three days, I've heard plenty about both of them in a series of emoji-laden messages.

'The one with the sexy eyes,' Frankie says in a dreamy voice.

'What about him?'

'He's asked me if I want to go down to the beach to watch the fireworks with him.'

As she lets out an excited squeal, I can't help but grin. Her break-up with Ram in October hit her hard and from all angles. Listening to her now, giddy and breathless at the prospect of cosying up with a hot boy with eyes so gorgeous she could 'swim laps in them', I'm stupidly delighted to note that the old Frankie is clearly back in business.

'But enough about me. How's Theo's party?' she asks.

'Yeah, OK,' I say. 'Y'know, same old, same old . . .'

'How come it's so quiet?'

I glance across at the closed door, then down at the open book in my lap.

'Jojo,' Frankie says in her very best schoolmarm voice. 'Are you even at the party?'

'Yes, of course I am,' I reply indignantly.

'Then how come I can't hear anything?'

'I'm in the utility room,' I admit.

'The utility room!' Frankie cries. 'What on earth are you doing in there?'

'Just taking a bit of time out.'

'Time out from what?'

'Everyone's really drunk. I just wanted a break from people talking rubbish at me. Seriously, Bex has told me the same anecdote five times now. And it's not even a very good one. I'll go back out in a bit, I promise.'

'Is Toby there?' Frankie asks.

She's talking about Toby Flint. He's in drama club with us and Frankie is convinced he fancies me.

'Yeah, he's about, I think,' I say vaguely.

'And have you spoken to him?'

'No.'

'Why not?'

'We haven't crossed paths.'

'Jojo, I know Theo's house is big but it's not that big. You could easily track Toby down if you put your mind to it.'

'Yeah, yeah.'

'I'm serious. You need to get out of that bloody room and speak to him. Before midnight! You need to lay the groundwork.'

'Groundwork for what?'

'Duh! For a midnight kiss, of course!'

'Ah, but you're assuming I want to kiss him.'

'Well, don't you?'

'No. Not especially.'

'Why not?'

Toby is fairly nice-looking. And he's sweet and interesting and a good actor, and on paper I know I should totally be into him. And yet, I'm just not. I've explained this to Frankie on multiple occasions but she's convinced I'll come around at some point, that my feelings will click into place if I'd only just try a bit harder.

'We've gone through this,' I say. 'I'm just not feeling it. And if Toby likes me as much as you reckon he does, which I don't think is the case for one minute by the way, then I especially don't want to mess him around.'

'OK, fine. So who are you going to kiss?' she asks.

'I don't know. Maybe no one.'

Probably no one.

Almost certainly no one.

'But it's New Year's Eve! Kissing is practically compulsory.'

'Since when?'

'Since . . . I don't know, for ever!'

In the background I can hear someone calling Frankie's name.

'Oh, balls. Jojo, I have to go. Our mains are here.'

'You're still eating? It's nearly eleven.'

'That's how they do it here. Last night we weren't finished until nearly one.'

'Sounds fun,' I say.

'It really is. I bloody miss you, though. I wish you were here so badly.'

'No, you don't. Because if I was there I'd totally get in the way of your sexy walk on the beach with the boy with the sexy eyes.'

She laughs. Mainly because she knows I'm right. Frankie may be boy-crazy, but she's also loyal to a fault. 'Sisters before Misters' is her motto, the girl-power anthem 'Wannabe' by the Spice Girls her theme song.

'Anyone else there miss me?' she asks.

'Uh-huh. Seriously, I've lost count of the number of people who've come up to me asking where you are. Some of them seemed genuinely disturbed by your absence, like the idea of the two of us not being in the same room is personally offensive to them.'

'And they'd be absolutely right,' Frankie says. 'It's not natural, quite frankly. When I get back on Wednesday, I'm coming straight over to yours and I'm going to stay there until we go back to school on Monday, whether you like it or not.'

'I'm gonna hold you to that,' I say happily.

'Excellent.'

'Frankie!' a voice calls.

Frankie groans. 'OK, I really have to go now. Promise me you'll go back to the party the second you hang up.'

'Can I at least finish my chapter first?' I ask.

'You're reading?!?' Frankie splutters.

'How else am I supposed to pass the time?'

'Are you seriously telling me you brought a book along with you to a New Year's Eve party?'

'No. I found it on a bookshelf in the living room.'

'Jojo, I adore you, you know I do, but you really do baffle me sometimes.'

'Have a lovely time with the boy with the eyes. Do all the things I wouldn't do.'

'Ha! Message me if you snog Toby. If you snog anyone.'

I roll my eyes. 'I will. Don't get your hopes up, though.'

'I love you, Joanna Rosalind Bright.'

'And I love you, Francesca Elena Ricci.'

'Happy New Year.'

'Happy New Year.'

I hang up and go back to my book, using the torch on my phone so I can see the tiny print.

I've read maybe another three or so pages when the doorknob begins to turn. My heart sinks. There's still another three whole hours before Bex's dad comes to pick us up. I'd been naively hoping I could commandeer the utility room as my own private hideout until then.

The door creaks open, yellow light from the kitchen leaking in.

A figure – a guy – stands in silhouette.

'Oh, sorry,' he says, noticing me in the gloom. 'I didn't realize anyone was in here.'

'Wait a second. Ram, is that you?' I shine my phone in the direction of his face.

He shields his eyes and squints. 'Jojo?'

'Hello!'

'Oh my God, long time no see. Hello!'

I beam. In the aftermath of the break-up I'd forgotten just how much I enjoyed hanging out with Ram. 'What are you doing here?' I ask.

'I've been asking myself that since I got here.'

'Ah. Not having a great time?'

'Not the best.' He pauses, casually eyeing the space on the tumble-dryer beside me. 'Mind if I join you?'

PART THREE

RAM

Chapter 26

The lift doors slide open and I step out into reception. Reece is nowhere to be seen. A laminated sign proclaiming 'Back Soon!' has been propped on the desk in his absence.

I buy a bottle of water from the vending machine and take a long swig before slumping on the fake leather sofa next to it.

My head is spinning. It has been ever since Reece mentioned the baby. Until then, although aspects of Frankie's so-called evidence were most definitely odd, I never for one second thought Jojo had anything to do with Olivia Sinclair's disappearance. And now? Now, I have no idea what to think. Every time I attempt to visualize Jojo opening that car door and taking Olivia, my brain just seizes up. Jojo is literally one of the kindest, smartest, most sane people I know. True, I haven't seen her since January, but I can't imagine even the most extreme personality transplant would result in her doing something as crazy and downright criminal as this. There has got to be an explanation.

I check the time. Twenty to one. In just over nine hours, I'm supposed to back on the rink for my shift.

Above the desk, a flat-screen TV plays silently, subtitles juddering across the screen. It's one of those *A Place in the Sun* type of programmes that always seem to be on in the background when Mum is bustling around the kitchen making dinner.

I rest my head against the wall behind me and let my eyes fall shut. I'm exhausted. Last night, Roxy had a night terror. It only lasted ten minutes but for ages afterwards I couldn't get back to sleep, her screams echoing in my ears. This morning she had no recollection of it, which was both reassuring and slightly annoying. Then I had a split shift at the rink. The hot weather has resulted in a surge in numbers and the place has been complete mayhem for the past two weeks. Before Frankie turned up, my plan for the rest of the evening was to drive home, fix myself a fish finger sandwich and fall straight into bed.

You could have said no, a voice inside my head reminds me.

I tried, I reply.

Oh, really?

Yes.

Hmmm.

I did!

OK. You just keep telling yourself that . . .

I try to imagine an alternate universe where I told Frankie to get lost and went home as planned. It's pointless, though. The fact is, my fate was sealed the moment Frankie said Jojo was in trouble.

'All sorted?'

I glance up. Reece has emerged from the back office, a Twister ice lolly in his right hand.

'Sorted?' I repeat.

'The baby,' Reece prompts.

I frown.

'The urgent medication?'

Of course. Frankie's cover story.

'Oh, er, yes,' I say. 'Crisis averted. Thanks.'

Reece nods, plonks himself down in his chair and slurps noisily at his ice lolly.

I take another sip of water and pretend to watch the TV. A middle-aged couple is looking around a Spanish villa. He likes it; she's not so keen.

'You can change the channel if you want,' Reece says. 'Here.' He tosses me the remote. I mindlessly flick through the channels, eventually landing on an old episode of *Have I Got News For You?*, but without sound the jokes don't really land. Not that I'm in the mood to laugh anyway.

As the credits are rolling, I text Frankie for an update.

It's been weird, being back in her company after almost a year apart. If I'm honest, it's kind of freaked me out a bit. In so many ways, I feel like a different person to the one Frankie went out with. Being back in close proximity with her almost feels like stepping back in time. I could sense myself slipping into old patterns of behaviour, the familiar dynamic that ultimately led to our downfall rearing its ugly head. Not that things were ever terrible between us. Far from it. In the aftermath of Dad dying, she was the perfect person to have around — bright and funny and silly and energetic — the antidote to grief in human girl form. It was only as time went on that it became clear that something was missing. On both sides.

While I'm awaiting Frankie's reply, I launch WhatsApp.

The message I drafted this morning is still sitting there, unsent.

> Hey! Long time no hear. Good luck today. You'll smash it, I'm sure. I know this is against the rules but coffee sometime? Rx

205

I allow myself to wonder what might have happened if I'd pressed 'send'. Would today have panned out differently? Or is it totally arrogant of me to even think that?

My phone buzzes. It's Maxwell, my best mate.

> M: What's all this about you driving off into the sunset with Frankie? You're not back on, are you??
>
> R: No. I'm just helping her out with something.
>
> M: Oi oi!
>
> R: Nothing like that, you dirty bastard.

Frankie hasn't messaged me back.

I'll give her another fifteen minutes, I decide, then I'll call. I put my phone away and return my attention to the TV, rhythmically clicking through the channels, stopping occasionally to watch something for a minute or two before moving on.

Until something catches my eye.

A red banner scrolling across the bottom of the twenty-four-hour news channel.

A red banner declaring Olivia Sinclair has been found.

My eyes widen as I read the rolling text.

Missing infant Olivia Sinclair found safe and well at a property in Kirkdale . . .

. . . 32-year-old woman in custody . . .

. . . Olivia's parents 'elated' at the news . . .

My body surges with relief. I knew it. I just knew Jojo didn't have anything to do with Olivia's disappearance. I grab my phone to ring Frankie. If we're in the car in the next ten minutes or so, we'll be back in Newfield by 5 a.m. Four hours sleep isn't ideal, but I'm only working until 2 p.m. I can power through, then crash when I get home after my shift.

Frankie doesn't answer. I hang up and am in the middle of composing a text when there's a loud 'ping' and the lift doors open to reveal Frankie, her hands on her hips.

I jump to my feet.

'Look!' I say, pointing at the TV screen. 'They found Olivia! I knew Jojo had nothing to do with it, I knew it!'

But Frankie doesn't even glance at the TV.

She strides straight up to me and, without saying a word, slaps me clean around the face.

Chapter 27

I fall back onto the sofa in shock.

Did that really just happen?

I lift my hand to my cheek. It's stinging like mad. It definitely happened.

But why? All things considered, I thought Frankie and I had been getting on pretty well tonight.

'Someone's not happy.'

I glance up. Reece is smirking at me.

'Lovers' tiff, is it?' he adds a little too eagerly.

I shake my head and stagger to my feet. Frankie is nowhere to be seen.

'Which way did she go?' I ask. 'Did you see?'

'Out the front,' Reece replies, pointing towards the automatic doors.

I run out onto the pavement and look in both directions. The street is deserted.

'Frankie!' I yell. 'Frankie!'

No response.

I walk to the corner and look down the next street. Once more, it's empty. Where are all the people? Then I remember – it's after one in the morning. Anyone sensible is in bed. I jog back, past the hotel entrance, to the road where we parked. No Frankie.

I take out my phone and call her. She picks up after a couple of rings.

'What?' she barks.

She's walking. I can hear the soles of her flip-flops slapping against the pavement.

'Frankie, what the hell was that?' I ask.

She lets out a laugh.

'Seriously,' I say. 'What did I do?'

'What did you do?' she repeats. *'What did you do?'*

'Yeah.'

'Why don't you ask Jojo?' She spits out the words, each one dripping with anger.

'What do you mean?'

She doesn't reply.

'Frankie, what do—?'

She hangs up before I can finish my question.

Why don't you ask Jojo?

What on earth is she talking about?

Unless . . .

Shit.

But Jojo wouldn't tell Frankie about any of that? Would she? She was the one who was adamant Frankie should never ever find out, the one who made me promise never to bring it up.

I try Frankie again. This time it goes straight to voicemail. There's no point in leaving a message. Frankie famously doesn't listen to them.

I swear under my breath and walk back to the hotel. Although it's still boiling, the wind is picking up. It isn't the least bit refreshing, more like having a giant hairdryer blasted at your face. I glance up. Clouds roll overhead. They're moving so fast it almost looks like they're chasing one another.

'You didn't find her, then?' Reece asks as I stride back into the foyer.

'Does it look like it?' I snap.

Reece raises his eyebrows and puffs out his cheeks. 'Listen, I didn't have to help you out before,' he says sulkily.

'I know, I know,' I say, raking my hands through my hair. 'I'm sorry. I'm just . . . under a bit of stress right now.'

'Still. There's no need to take it out on me.'

'I know. Like I said, I'm really sorry.' I head towards the lift. I need to find out what Jojo said to make Frankie fly off the handle like that. 'It was room four-two-six, right?' I say.

Reece doesn't answer.

'Please, mate. I'm sorry I snapped before. It's just that it's important.'

Reece lets out a heavy sigh. 'Yes, it's four-two-six.'

'Thank you, mate,' I say, jabbing at the lift button. 'Thank you.'

As the lift rattles upwards. I study my reflection in the mirrored panel. My cheek is still red from Frankie's powerhouse slap.

Her words keep echoing in my head: *Why don't you ask Jojo?*

Ask Jojo what?

Unless you count the time I saw her sail past me on the number 88 bus a few months back, I haven't actually seen her in the flesh since New Year's Day. A few times I've thought about ringing her or turning up at her house, but every time I've been tempted I've remembered the promise I made and forced myself to keep my distance.

The lift doors stutter open and I step out onto the fourth floor. I take a right and head down the corridor. As I get closer to room 426, my nerves build. It's just Jojo, I remind myself. Even after everything that happened, she's still your mate. There's no need to be nervous.

My pep talk doesn't work. By the time I reach room 426, I'm sweating like mad. I wipe my clammy palms on my shorts and rap on the door. It flies open almost immediately, making me jump.

Jojo's eyes balloon at the sight of me. Her mouth quivers as if attempting to make words, but no sound comes out. I don't need to do much reading between the lines to figure out she wasn't expecting to find me at the door.

She looks pale. Pale and thin.

And beautiful.

After all this time, all I want to do is hold her and make everything OK.

'You thought I was Frankie,' I say.

The horror and confusion in her eyes answers my question. 'What are you doing here, Ram?' she asks, backing away from me into the dimly lit room. Her voice is shaking.

'You mean you didn't know I was here at all?' I ask. 'Frankie didn't say?'

She shakes her head.

'Frankie needed a lift down here,' I explain. 'I was the only person she could think of with a car.'

My words are overlapped out by the high-pitched cry of what sounds like a baby.

I blink.

But Olivia has been found. It was on the news literally a few minutes ago. I saw it with my own eyes.

Then I remember what Reece said about Jojo checking in with a baby. We just assumed it was Olivia, no questions asked. It never dawned on me that there might be another baby in the mix. Why would it? It makes literally no sense.

I look at Jojo. She stares back at me, her eyes full of fear.

'You need to go, Ram,' she says, her voice low.

'Why? What's going on?' I ask.

'Please,' Jojo says, trying to push me out into the corridor.

I stand my ground. I've driven all this way and all I've got for it so far is a slap round the face and a whole lot of confusion and mixed messages. I've had enough of being kept in the dark. It's time for someone to tell me what the hell is going on.

'Please, Ram,' Jojo says, continuing to attempt to push me away. 'I'm begging you. Just wait downstairs.'

'Not until someone explains what's happening.'

The baby is crying louder now.

'I need to see to him,' Jojo says, dropping her hands from my chest. She peels away from me and heads towards the cot by the window, bending over it and scooping up the crying child. As if by magic, it shuts up. Very slowly, she turns to face me.

I blink, my eyes struggling to adjust to the gloom after the harsh brightness of the corridor.

The baby is tiny. Not quite brand-new but close, I reckon. It also has a ton of hair. Thick and inky black. It reminds me of Roxy as a baby. And Laleh before her. And the photo of me as a newborn that sits in a silver frame on Mum's bedside table . . .

Blood rushes to my face.

Frantically, I count back the months. August, July, June, May, April, March, February, January, December . . .

'Is it? It's not. Is it?' The words fall clumsily from my mouth.

Jojo holds my gaze, her chin raised, her lips pressed together.

There's a beat where no one says a word. We just stare at each other, our eyes locked together.

A single tear trickles down Jojo's cheek.

And that's when I know for sure.

The baby in her arms is mine.

Chapter 28

Last New Year's Eve

This was a mistake.

I should have followed my instincts and gone up to my grandma and grandad's house in York with Mum, Laleh and Roxy. They'll be snuggled up in front of a log fire right now, eating crisps and dips and watching some cheesy film or playing Monopoly. Instead, I'm shivering my arse off in the garage of some guy I don't even know, waiting for Maxwell to lose at ping pong so we can go back inside and warm up a bit.

Maxwell is the reason I'm here. It's his cousin's party. I'm not sure why I agreed to come, only that it seemed like a good idea when he suggested it.

I know it probably sounds a bit miserable, but I don't really like parties. On paper, I admit they look kind of fun, but the reality never lives up to the promise. Every party I've ever been to has left me feeling sort of empty and disappointed, and so far this one shows no signs of bucking the trend. It doesn't help that I don't know a soul here apart from Maxwell. I suppose I could make a bit more of an effort and initiate some small talk, but I don't have the energy right now. Christmas was a bit of an emotional slog and I'm not sure I've got much left in the tank.

I take another sip from the warm can of Coke I've been nursing for the past half an hour and watch an increasingly sweaty Maxwell fling himself about the garage, grunting like a Wimbledon finalist with every shot.

'You're Frankie's ex, aren't you?'

I turn to my left. A girl with long, almost aggressively straight blonde hair is smiling up at me. Despite the Baltic temperature out here, she's wearing a little black dress with spaghetti straps, her legs and arms bare.

'How do you know Frankie?' I ask.

'School. She's in my year.'

'Is she here?'

'No. She's in Tenerife, I think. Somewhere like that anyway.'

I nod, simultaneously disappointed and relieved.

'I'm really sorry things didn't work out for you guys,' she says.

'Thanks,' I murmur.

She extends her hand for me to shake. Her arms are puckered with goose pimples and her nails are long and red and glossy. 'I'm Georgia, by the way,' she says, wobbling slightly in her very high heels.

'Ram.'

She shoots me a flirtatious grin. 'Oh, I know who you are.'

I smile tightly and return my attention to the game. It's match point. I will Max to lose so we can go back inside. It's too bright out here. The fluorescent strip lights are making my eyes hurt. Plus, this Georgia girl is looking at me with far more intent than feels comfortable.

Max wins.

Shit.

As he flosses in celebration, I grab his sleeve. 'Mate, I've got to go in,' I say. 'My fingers are about to fall off, it's so cold.'

'Go on then, you pussy,' he says, sweat dripping from his brow. 'I'll come find you in a bit.'

'You're going inside?' Georgia asks as I move towards the door.

'Yeah.'

'You want company?'

'Er, no thanks. I'm just going to the loo.'

'Does that mean you're coming back?' she asks.

'Er, I dunno, maybe.'

Another flirtatious grin. 'Well, I'll be waiting.'

I give her another tight smile, chuck my almost empty Coke can in the black bin bag in the corner and head inside.

In my absence, the house has grown even busier. I squeeze past the people jamming up the hallway and make my way into the kitchen. It's similarly packed, the windows opaque with steam. Someone has written 'Happy New Year, bitches!' in the condensation. I push my way through the warm bodies and open the fridge. There are no cans of Coke left so I have to make do with a glass of flat lemonade from a half-empty bottle on the sideboard.

Over by the patio doors, a bunch of kids have gathered around the kitchen table and are attempting to play beer pong but they don't have the right kind of cups, just those little flimsy clear plastic ones – every shot resulting in a spillage.

Drink in hand, I push my way back the way I came, lemonade

sloshing over the side of my glass. A girl with long black hair flashes me a big smile, I ignore her and keep moving. Girls are the last thing on my mind tonight.

I roam around the house looking for a quiet spot. The living room is clearly the designated make-out zone, loved-up couples everywhere I look.

No thank you.

Maybe I'll just go hang out in the garden for a bit. I'll need my coat, though. I head upstairs to the bedroom where I think Maxwell and I dumped our things earlier, but the second I open the door, a muffled pair of voices scream at me to 'get out' from beneath the pile of coats on the bed. I swear under my breath but do as they've asked.

Sighing, I return to the kitchen.

'Ram! Hey, Ram!' I look up. It's that Georgia girl. She's standing near the patio doors, waving at me. 'Where'd you go?' she calls.

I just shrug.

'Wanna play?' she asks, pointing at the beer pong table. 'We need one more player.'

'No thanks.'

'Oh, go on. You can be on my team.' She tilts her head to one side and bats her eyelashes.

'Really, I'm OK.' I smile apologetically and turn away, pretending to survey the half-hearted buffet. I scoop up a handful of peanuts and shove them in my mouth, all the while trying not to think about the bacteria.

As I wipe my hand on a bit of kitchen roll, something catches my eye. A door tucked away in the corner. I grab a bowl of crisps from the counter and push it open, gutted to discover someone has already beaten me to it.

In the shadows, I can make out a girl sitting cross-legged on top of the washing machine, the torch from her phone trained over the pages of a book.

'Sorry,' I say, 'I didn't realize anyone was in here.' I begin to back away.

'Wait a second. Ram, is that you?'

Hang on, I know that voice. 'Jojo?'

'Hello!' she says.

I break into a grin. 'Oh my God,' I say. 'Long time no see. Hello!'

'What are you doing here?' Jojo asks.

'I've been asking myself that since I got here.'

'Ah. Not having a great time?'

I laugh. 'Not the best.'

Jojo grins and for the first time since I arrived, I find myself relaxing. It's weird, but I don't think I realized how much I missed hanging out with her until this exact moment.

Jojo and I got on from the beginning. To my shame, I don't recall much about our very first meeting. It was at a football match, I know that much. She was there with Frankie apparently, watching from the sidelines. I vaguely remember being introduced, but the memory is hazy, dominated by my nostalgia for seeing Frankie again after all those years.

I met her properly on Frankie's and my second date.

'If you and me are going to go anywhere,' Frankie told me, 'you're going to need the stamp of approval from Jojo.'

It was the end of March and tipping it down with rain. We were all pretty skint so we sat around Frankie's kitchen table, eating round upon round of toast and chatting rubbish.

I liked Jojo right away. She was quiet at first, but she soon warmed up. I liked the way she and Frankie bounced off each other. Frankie was the gregarious one, Jojo her quieter, wittier partner in crime.

The dynamic worked. Jojo reined Frankie in, Frankie set Jojo free. There was something comforting about their shared history, their in-jokes, their intimacy, their ease with one another. When Frankie informed me that she and Jojo told each other everything, I didn't doubt it for one second. I envied their bond in lots of ways. Although I had good mates, by silent unspoken agreement, there were certain subjects we stayed clear of. We stuck to what we knew — football, girls, school, music, telly, general banter. And I'd always been content with that, unaware there was a deeper, more meaningful alternative on offer. Watching Frankie and Jojo interact, I got the feeling there was nothing off limits, a concept I found both terrifying and appealing in equal measure.

At one point, Jojo nipped to the loo.

'Great, isn't she?' Frankie said, her eyes shining.

'She really is,' I agreed, and Frankie beamed with pride.

After that, we spent lots of time together as a threesome. Somewhere along the way, Frankie suggested I try setting Jojo up with Maxwell. I screwed up my face. I loved Maxwell, but I knew him too well to allow him anywhere near sweet, kind Jojo.

'He's still hung up on his ex,' I said instead.

Which was true. Sort of.

'Another one of your friends, then?' Frankie said.

'Have you asked Jojo about this?'

'Uh-huh.'

I raised an eyebrow.

'Oh, you know what Jojo's like,' Frankie said. 'She's shy when it comes to this stuff. We just need to give her a bit of a nudge.'

I went through my friends in turn, trying to picture each of them with Jojo, but every combination made me feel slightly queasy. When I told Frankie this, she laughed.

'It's dead cute how protective you are over her,' she said. 'But Jojo's an independent woman and the smartest person I know. I'm pretty sure she's capable of making up her mind about these boys on her own.'

Still, I resisted, and eventually Frankie stopped pestering me about it, taking matters into her own hands by trying (and failing, as far as I knew) to push Jojo into the arms of some guy from their drama group.

And then my relationship with Frankie ended, terminating (inevitably I guess) my friendship with Jojo along with it.

Until now.

'Mind if I join you?' I ask.

Jojo appears to hesitate for a moment before smiling and patting the tumble-dryer next to her. 'Be my guest.'

Chapter 29

'So, what brings you here?' Jojo asks.

'To the party or to the utility room?'

She smiles. 'Both.'

'Maxwell – you remember my mate Maxwell?'

Jojo nods.

'Well, this is his auntie and uncle's place. Who's the kid having the party? Leo or something?'

'Theo,' Jojo says. 'He's in my year at school.'

'OK. Well, he's Maxwell's cousin.'

'I see. And where's he now? Maxwell, I mean.'

'The garage.' I explain about the ping pong tournament.

'You didn't fancy playing?' Jojo asks.

'Not really. I don't know, I'm just not really in a joining-in kind of mood tonight.'

'Why don't you just go home?'

'You trying to get rid of me or something?'

She laughs. 'Course not. Just why torture yourself if you're not having fun?'

'Says the girl hiding in the utility room with the book.'

'Touché,' she says, playfully swatting me with it.

'I think Maxwell would probably be annoyed if I went home now,' I explain. 'I'll stay until after midnight. That's respectable, right?'

'I'd say so.'

'What about you?' I ask. 'Having fun? Or is that a stupid question?' I nod at the book, on closer inspection a battered Agatha Christie paperback.

'In all honesty, I'm just a bit bored. It was fun at first, but everyone's got to that point of drunk where they don't make any sense and just keep repeating themselves. In fact, you're probably the only sober person I've encountered all night.'

'Same,' I say. 'Maxwell downed a load of tequila on the way here and has been off his face ever since.'

'Is he a nice drunk, at least?' Jojo asks.

'He's a loud drunk. He gets very bellowy.'

'Oh, fun.'

I offer up the bowl of crisps. She takes a handful. I do the same.

As we munch, I sneak a sideways glance at her. Her hair is shorter than I remember, bobbed, like a film star from the 1920s. It suits her.

'I like your hair,' I say.

'My hair?'

'Yeah, you've cut it, right?'

'Oh, yes. Just before Christmas. I'm still getting used to it.'

'It's cool.'

'You reckon?' she says, grabbing a chunk and tugging at it. 'I'm still not sure. I mean, I had it long like for ever so it's kind of a big change.'

'No, it's great. You look really stylish. Like, what's-her-name? Louise something . . . er . . . Brooks! Yeah, Louise Brooks, you look like her.'

Jojo frowns. 'Louise Brooks? I don't think I know her.'

'She was a silent film star,' I say. 'From the 1920s . . . Hang on.' I take out my phone and type 'Louise Brooks' into Google images. 'That's her,' I say, passing the phone to Jojo.

She peers at the rows of photos. 'Her hair's a lot thicker than mine,' Jojo says. 'And much darker.'

'Maybe,' I say. 'You still look like her, though.'

'Thank you. I think you're being overly generous, but it's New Year's Eve and I'm going to start as I mean to go on and take the compliment.' She passes me my phone back. 'I didn't have you down as a film buff,' she adds.

'Oh, I'm not,' I say. 'I'm as low-rent as you can get. Seriously, my favourite film is *Marley and Me*.'

Jojo laughs.

'It's all my mum's doing,' I explain. 'She's really into her old-school Hollywood film history. She's been making us watch all these classic old black and white films since we were little kids.'

'And yet you still prefer *Marley and Me*?'

'Guilty as charged.'

There's a pause.

'So, how have you been?' we ask each other at exactly the same time.

We laugh.

'You go first,' Jojo says.

'No, you. Ladies first and all that.'

She rolls her eyes. 'Fine. Although there's nothing much to tell really. I've just been busy with school and drama club stuff mainly. Frankie and I have just got audition dates through for the Arts Academy so we've started prepping for that.'

'That's the drama school, right?'

'Yeah.'

'You feeling good about it?'

'Oh God, I don't know. It's so competitive.'

'Yeah?'

'Yeah. Thousands of people apply for less than fifty places.'

'Wow. Good luck!'

'Thanks. Frankie's convinced we're both shoo-ins, but you know what Frankie's like . . .'

I smile. 'How is she?' I ask. 'She's away, right?'

'Yes. She's in Tenerife until Wednesday. It's her parents' twentieth wedding anniversary. The whole family have flown out for it.'

'Good old Nino and Angie,' I say with a smile. I always got on well with Frankie's mum and dad, and her older brother, Luca, much to Frankie's annoyance.

'She just called actually,' Jojo adds.

'She all right?'

'Yeah, she's really good. Back on form.'

'Good. That's good.'

I mean it. Frankie and I may have crashed and burned, but I'm glad she's doing well. At the end of the day, she's a good person. No, scratch that, she's a great person. She's just not *my* person. And I'm not hers.

'How about you?' Jojo asks.

'Yeah, I've been OK. Same as you really, school stuff mostly. Thinking about university and UCAS and all that, which seems a bit mad.'

'Wow. That's come around fast.'

I grimace. 'I know. It's all the teachers want to talk about at the moment.'

'Where do you want to go?'

'My first choice is probably Cambridge. But I'm also interested in LSE, UCL, Durham, Glasgow and Nottingham.'

'I'm officially impressed.'

'Well, I haven't got in anywhere yet.'

'You want to study law, right?'

'Yeah,' I say, flattered that she's remembered.

'Sometimes I wish I wanted to do something dignified and respectable,' she says with a sigh.

'Really?'

'A bit, yeah. I mean, even if I do get into the Arts Academy, and that's a big if, and a really good drama school after that, there are still no guarantees I'll have any sort of career.'

'Does that put you off? The uncertainty of it all?' I'm pretty sure *I* couldn't hack it.

'In theory, yes. But the sad fact is, I just can't imagine doing anything else with my life.'

I'm weirdly envious. My choice to study law is largely a practical one. It's a good solid career, one that will enable me to look after Mum and Laleh and Roxy.

I pick up Jojo's book. '*Sparkling Cyanide*,' I read aloud. 'That's quite a title.'

'I know, right?'

'So, whodunnit?'

'Hmmm, it's a bit early to make an educated guess, but if I had to go for anyone at this stage, it'd be Victor.'

'Victor, eh? And what's this Victor like?'

'In the words of Agatha Christie, "a bit of a rotter".' She says this in a flawlessly posh accent.

'Will you read me some?' I ask before I can stop myself.

I've always loved being read to. Before Laleh and Roxy came

along, every night before bed, Dad and I used to snuggle up on the sofa together with a book. He'd do all the voices and sometimes make me laugh so much I thought I was going to be sick. It's one of my very happiest memories of him, which inevitably also makes it one of the saddest.

'Seriously?' Jojo asks. 'You want me to read to you? As in, right now?'

'Yeah. I mean, only if you want to,' I say, my cheeks heating up.

She pauses and I'm about to tell her to forget about it when she says, 'It's a slightly bizarre request, but yeah, OK then. Call it a New Year's Eve treat.'

'Really? You don't have to if you don't want to.'

'No, why not. It'll pass the time if anything else. We'll have to switch the big light on, though. If I keep using the torch, my phone's going to go dead.'

I turn on the light.

'From the beginning?' Jojo asks, opening the book.

'No, no, wherever you've got to will be fine.'

'OK, then. Here goes.'

She clears her throat and begins to read.

And she's brilliant.

I sit there in awe as she jumps from character to character, one second playing the flighty heiress, the next the dowdy secretary, before suddenly transforming into the louche cad who sponges off his aunt.

This is the first time I've ever seen Jojo act and I'm bowled over.

She reaches the end of the chapter and looks up. 'What?' she says, worry clouding her eyes. 'Why are you looking at me like that?'

'You're really good,' I say.

She shakes her head and laughs, clearly embarrassed by my praise.

'No, I mean it,' I say. 'That was insane. Full disclosure, I don't know much about acting, but the way you became all those characters, it was . . . well, it was amazing.'

'Really?' she says, looking doubtful. 'I was just reading out loud.'

'Really. It was so fucking good, Jojo.'

She smiles. 'Well, thank you. That's nice of you to say.'

There's a pause.

'I reckon you're right, by the way,' I add.

'About what?'

'That Victor bloke. He's definitely got something to do with it.'

'Right?'

'Guilty as sin.' My phone buzzes. 'Sorry,' I say, removing it from my pocket.

It's a text from Maxwell.

> **Where you at, man?**

I tap out a quick reply.

> Bumped into an old mate. I'll catch you later.

'Not that I was reading over your shoulder or anything, but you really don't have to keep me company,' Jojo says. 'Honestly, I can entertain myself.'

'I know,' I reply. 'I want to keep hanging out with you. I mean, if that's cool.'

She pauses before answering. 'It's cool,' she says lightly.

'Cool,' I echo.

On the other side of the door, people are chanting and stamping their feet. 'Down it, down it, down it!'

Jojo grimaces. 'I liked parties a lot better when I was younger,' she says.

'Yeah?'

'Absolutely. Pass-the-parcel, jelly and ice cream, party bags . . . And best of all, they always had a strict cut-off time.'

'That's true. If this was a kids' party, it would have been over hours ago.'

'Exactly. Now, speaking of party games . . .' Jojo shuts the book and jumps down from the washing machine. She studies the shelves in front of us. They're rammed with board games – Scrabble and Trivial Pursuit and Monopoly and Kerplunk and Guess Who? and Mousetrap – all of them well played if the faded and falling-apart boxes are anything to go by. She turns back round to face me. 'Wanna play something?' she asks.

'Yeah, go on then,' I say, smiling.

We inspect the games together, rejecting anything with too many pieces or too much setting up involved.

'Cards Against Humanity?' I suggest.

'Minimum of four players,' Jojo says, reading off the box. 'Plus, you really don't want to play that with me.'

'How come?'

'I'd slaughter you,' she replies simply.

I put my hands on my hips. 'Would you now?'

'I'll have you know I'm a demon at Cards Against Humanity.'

'You? I don't believe you for one second.'

'Why not?'

'You're far too sweet and lovely.'

She tuts. 'But that's what makes me so great at it. The element of surprise.'

'OK, now I *really* want to play it with you.'

'Do you want to recruit two more players?'

'Not especially.' The idea of venturing back out into the party holds no appeal whatsoever. 'Why, do you?'

'Nope.'

I'm kind of thrown by just how relieved I am by her answer.

'Back to the drawing board, I guess,' Jojo says.

We end up going for Bananagrams.

As we play, sitting cross-legged on the lino, we relax into being around each other again, laughing and joking and teasing like we were never apart. It's one of the few times I've ever been alone with her and I'm surprised by how natural it feels. We always hung out as a threesome, only really getting one-on-one time if Frankie was in the loo or getting ready. I'd also forgotten how funny Jojo can be, how sharp and witty and observant. Plus there's something extra fun about hiding away from the rest of the party, like we're playing truant from school or something.

'Ten! Nine! Eight!'

The counting is coming from the other side of the door.

'It can't be midnight yet, can it?' Jojo asks.

I remove my phone from my pocket. 23:59. I hold it up so she can see.

'Wow, that hour went by fast,' she says.

'Four! Three!'

We scramble to our feet.

'Two! One!'

In the kitchen, everyone whoops and cheers.

'Happy New Year,' I say.

'Happy New Year.'

I hesitate before leaning down and kissing her on the cheek.

She smells nice.

Really nice.

Jojo raises her eyes to meet mine and for a few seconds we just look at each, our gaze fixed. She has such great eyes. Green with a circle of hazel around the pupil. How have I never noticed how cool they are before? The air feels thick with something I can't quite put my finger on. An energy. A force invisible to the naked eye.

Jojo looks away first, pulling out her mobile phone.

In the kitchen, someone has started a clumsy rendition of 'Auld Lang Syne'. Within seconds, the entire party seems to be singing.

'I should probably go find Bex,' Jojo says, not looking up from her phone. 'Make sure she's OK.'

I clear my throat. 'And I should probably hunt down Maxwell.'

Together we silently pack away the Bananagram tiles and put the yellow case back where we found it.

By the time we emerge from the utility room, 'Auld Lang Syne' has petered out, replaced with a slow, sexy R&B number. We squeeze past snogging couples and make our way into the living room.

Jojo stands on her tiptoes as she looks around for Bex. 'Ah,' she says.

'What?'

She points through the tangle of entwined bodies. 'Over there,' she says. 'The blonde girl in the green dress.'

'You mean the one with her tongue halfway down my mate Maxwell's throat?'

'Wait, that's Maxwell?'

'Yep.'

'Oh my God.'

We both laugh, Jojo's amazing eyes sparkling as she shakes her head.

'So, you gonna head?' Jojo asks.

'Head?'

'It's after midnight. And, call me presumptuous, but I have a feeling Maxwell isn't exactly going to mind if you skip off without him.'

'Ha. Yeah, maybe you're right. What about you? You going to hang out for a bit longer?'

'I dunno. I was supposed to be getting a lift home with Bex, but that's not going to be until two . . .'

'In that case, look, I don't know about you but I'm kind of partied out. You wanna hang out at my house for a bit?'

'At your house?' Jojo asks slowly.

'Yeah,' I say, shifting my weight from one foot to the other. 'I mean, if you want to. It's not that far. I have Bananagrams and loads of other board games. And a fridge full of food left over from Christmas. Do you like chicken drumsticks? We have like a million of them.'

'I'm a vegetarian.'

Shit. I knew that.

'Er, crisps then? We have a shitload of crisps. And biscuits. And pickled onions, weirdly. Like five jars. They must have been on offer at Aldi or something . . .'

Jojo smiles. 'I'm not doing to deny it, the promise of unlimited pickled onions does sound extremely tempting.'

'I'm sensing a "but" coming.'

'I don't know, I just . . .' Her voice trails off.

'What is it?'

'I don't know,' she says, fiddling with the hem of her top. 'Frankie, I guess.'

'Frankie?'

'Yeah.'

'What about Frankie?'

'I just don't know how she'd feel about it.'

'It's just two mates hanging out,' I say. Even as the words leave my mouth, I'm not entirely sure I believe them. I wonder if Jojo does.

'I know,' she says. 'I just . . . I don't know.'

'OK. Well, I don't want you to do anything you're not comfortable with.'

There's a pause.

'Maybe if I called her,' Jojo says.

'Called her?'

'Yeah. Just to run it by her.'

'Oh. OK.'

'I'll be back in a sec.'

While she's gone, I retrieve my coat, then sit on the stairs to wait. I'm scrolling through my Instagram feed when Jojo returns, her own coat draped over her arm.

'Frankie says "hi".'

'It's OK then?' I ask, scrambling to my feet.

'Yeah. She was totally cool about it. Overwhelmingly so, actually.'

'That's great. You ready to go then?'

'Ready.'

Chapter 30

We chat the entire way back to mine, fireworks exploding above our heads as we amble through the streets, filling the sky with glitter. Drunken groups pass us, pausing their garbled renditions of 'Auld Lang Syne' to wish us a 'Happy New Year'. We smile and return their wishes. I wonder if they assume Jojo and I are a couple. It's weird but I sort of want them to.

In spite of the cold, we take the long way home, through the park, the ground littered with beer cans and burned-out sparklers from the earlier fireworks display. As we weave amongst the debris, we talk.

We talk about everything: our earliest memories (mine: getting stung by a wasp on a family holiday in Spain, Jojo's: being propped on the back of her grandad's motorbike for a photo); which super-hero power we would choose (mine: flying, Jojo's: time travel); which food we couldn't live without (mine: pizza, Jojo's: her mum's aubergine parmigiana); the film that made us cry the most (we both agree on *Dumbo*). We debate the death penalty, flat earth conspiracy theories, old age and free speech.

And it's great. Like, I have a laugh with Maxwell, but our friendship is built almost entirely on banter and Marvel references. It's rare we really talk like this. I'm struck by how easy it is, how energising. I love the way Jojo takes her time before answering and how carefully she listens when it's my turn to respond. I love that she has opinions, but equally isn't afraid to say 'I don't know'. I love that she isn't trying to show off or look cool in front of me.

As we turn into my street, we fall silent for the first time since we left the party. I suddenly feel nervous but don't have a clue why. I glance across at Jojo to try and work out where she's at but she's too bundled up for me to gauge anything, just her eyes and the tip of her nose peeking out over the top of her bulky grey scarf.

'Er, this is me,' I say, pointing at my house. I push open the gate and gesture for her to go first.

On the doorstep, I fiddle with my keys, dropping them on the concrete step with a loud clatter. Why am I being so clumsy?

'Sorry,' I say. 'Cold hands.'

'No problem,' Jojo replies.

I usher her inside. The house, usually noisy and tropically hot, is cold and silent in Mum's absence. 'I'll put the heating on,' I say. I push open the living-room door and turn on the light. 'Make yourself at home. I'll be right back.'

'Shoes on or off?' Jojo calls after me.

'On is fine.'

I dash into the kitchen and turn on the boiler. 'Would you like a drink?' I holler.

'Just water, please.'

I pour us each a glass of water, and fill up a tray with crisps, biscuits and the promised jar of pickled onions before returning to the living room. Jojo is perched on the edge of the sofa with her coat still on. Her phone in her hands. I set the tray down on the coffee table and switch off the main light, turning on the Christmas tree lights instead.

'Your house is really nice,' Jojo says.

She's kind of got a point. Mum has always been pretty OTT when it comes to Christmas decorations but she's really outdone herself this year, cramming every available surface with tacky ornaments and hanging so many paper chains it looks like that scene from *Elf.*

'I wasn't completely sure you celebrated it,' Jojo adds. 'Christmas, I mean.'

'Oh, yeah. So my dad never went in for any of the religious stuff, but he was always happy for my mum to go to town with the decorations and presents and things.'

I kneel down and turn on the gas fire, the fake coals glowing orange. 'Sorry it's so cold,' I say. 'It'll warm up soon, I promise.'

'It's fine,' Jojo says, smiling.

I join her on the sofa.

'I was just texting Bex,' she explains, putting her phone down on the mosaic coffee table. 'In case she comes up for air and wonders where I've disappeared to.'

'Good idea. I should probably text Maxwell too.'

I take my phone out of my pocket. There's a message from Mum.

> Happy New Year, my darling boy. I'm so ruddy proud of you. Hope you're having fun at your party. We'll be back around teatime xxxx

I quickly reply, then compose a message to Maxwell.

'Done,' I say, laying my phone face down next to Jojo's.

There's an awkward silence.

'Er, Happy New Year,' I say, picking up my glass of water. 'Again.'

'Happy New Year,' Jojo echoes, reaching for her own glass.

We clink them together.

'There's alcohol if you want it,' I say. 'I think there's some Prosecco in the fridge I could open. Or Baileys?' I'm pretty certain there's still half a bottle left over from Christmas.

'No, thank you,' Jojo says. 'I don't actually drink.'

'What, ever?'

'No.'

'Me neither.'

We sip our water.

'Why don't you?' I say. 'I mean, if you don't mind me asking.'

'Oh, no sinister reason. I just don't like the way it tastes. Or the way it makes people act sometimes.'

I nod.

'How about you?' she asks.

I hesitate. I usually keep things simple by saying I'm allergic, but for some reason lying to Jojo just doesn't feel like an option. 'My dad was using a zebra crossing when he was hit by a car and killed,' I say. 'The driver was five times over the limit.'

Jojo's hand flies to her mouth. 'Oh my God, I'm so sorry,' she says. 'I knew your dad had passed away, but I had no idea that was what happened.'

'Yeah. I don't tend to talk about it very much.'

'Did the driver go to prison?'

'He did. Not for long, though. He was out after eighteen months. Good behaviour, apparently.' I give her a grim smile.

'God, that's awful. I'm so, so sorry, Ram.'

I shrug. 'It is what it is . . .'

'When did it happen? The accident, I mean.'

'Two Christmases ago. I was fourteen.'

'It happened at Christmas?'

'The day before Christmas Eve.'

'Oh, Ram.'

'Mum was up late finishing off the Christmas cake. She ran out of icing sugar so Dad nipped out to get some more from the twenty-four-hour Co-op. He was on his way back when he got hit. The driver was returning from a Christmas party. Reckons he didn't even see my dad, that was how out of it he was.'

I still remember the doorbell ringing; looking out my window and seeing a police car parked on the kerb, its blue light flashing; Mum's cry of anguish; the sight of her at the bottom of the stairs, collapsed into the policewoman's arms.

'Anyway,' I continue, shoving the images to the back of my mind where I do my best to keep them. 'I haven't had a drink since. Not that I was a prolific drinker before that or anything, just a few cans down the park every now and again . . .'

'Do you ever feel tempted?' Jojo asks.

'Never,' I say firmly. 'I mean, alcohol is the reason my dad's not here, and even though I know loads of people drink and wouldn't ever dream of getting behind the wheel, I just can't get my head around letting myself get in the headspace where I might even contemplate it, you know?'

Jojo nods. 'Is that him?' she asks, pointing to the collection of photos on the mantelpiece.

'Yeah.'

'Can I take a closer look?'

'Course.'

I join her in front of the fireplace. The shrine has grown over the years and now takes up the entire chimney breast, Dad's name — Albanaz (although Mum usually just called him Al) — spelled out in lumpy papier-mâché letters made by Laleh. There are photos of him throughout the ages, from a chubby baby on my gran's lap back in Tehran, to the final photo ever taken of him — blowing out the birthday candles on his fifty-fourth birthday, just three weeks before he died.

'You look like him,' Jojo says, studying the photos one by one.

'Do you reckon?' I ask, cocking my head to one side.

'Yeah. Especially in this one.' She points out a photograph of my dad as a young teenager, back in Iran. He's leaning against a wall with his arms folded, a relaxed smile on his face. 'How old is he here?' she asks.

'I'm not sure. Fifteen at the most,' I reply. 'He left Tehran in 1978, just before the revolution.'

'He looks older.'

'I think it's the leather jacket.'

'Maybe. Whatever it is, he looks like a real cool dude.'

I smile. 'Yeah, he really was.'

I know it must be easy to romanticize a dead parent, but when it comes to remembering my dad there's nothing rose-tinted about it. He was the best. End of. Kind and funny and clever and interesting, but most of all interested — in his family, in politics, in art and film and literature and science, in the people around him. He was always reading books and magazines and newspapers and Googling facts and asking our opinions on current affairs or posing philosophical questions at the dinner table. As a younger kid, I found it tiring and kind of annoying to be quizzed on a nightly basis, but as I got older, I found myself looking forward to our debates, planning out what I was going to say on certain topics, eager to impress.

'Christmas must be a really difficult time for you all,' Jojo says.

'You could say that.'

That first year we all just sat around in shock, traditions like stockings and crackers falling by the wayside. Last year, we had a go at celebrating, but it felt like we were going through the motions. This year, Mum's approach had been to throw as much food and tinsel and Michael Bublé tunes at the situation as possible. Christmas is barely over and I'm already exhausted by just the thought of next year.

'Mum invited the entire family and half the street round,' I add. 'And, I don't know, no matter how busy the house is, and how much music and laughter and Christmas pudding there is, there's still this gaping hole . . .'

Jojo nods, her eyes soft.

I swallow, self-conscious suddenly. I'm not used to talking about Dad so openly, at least not with people outside the immediate family unit. 'How about you?' I ask, clearing my throat. 'How was your Christmas?'

'Oh, it was fine,' Jojo says with a flick of her hand. 'It was my year to be with my dad this Christmas Day.'

'And how was that?'

'It was . . . OK,' she says. 'Just very quiet. It was just me and him for most of it.'

'He hasn't remarried or anything?'

'No.'

'Would you like him to?'

She thinks for a moment. 'If he met the right person, definitely. I hate the idea of him being all by himself. Not that it's not possible to be perfectly happy on your own; it is, of course it is. But that's the problem – I don't think he's even close to being happy. I just don't think he knows how to move on.'

'Do you think he still misses your mum?'

'Big time. Not that he'd ever admit it.'

'That's sad.'

'I know. I've tried suggesting he go on a dating app or something, but he won't even entertain the idea.'

'Maybe he just needs a bit more time.'

'Yeah, maybe,' Jojo says, trailing her finger along the edge of the mantelpiece. 'What about your mum?' she asks, studying a photo of my mum and dad on their wedding day, laughing under a shower of confetti. 'Can you imagine her meeting someone else?'

'I might be wrong,' I say. 'But I can't imagine it happening any time soon. She was in her late twenties when she met my dad, and although she'd had boyfriends before that and had even been engaged once, she always says she didn't know what love was until he walked into her life. Lightning doesn't strike in the same spot twice and all that . . .'

'Wow,' Jojo says softly. 'It sounds like they were seriously in love.'

'They really were.'

When I was younger, their public displays of affection used to make me squirm with embarrassment. Now I'd do anything to see them kissing and cuddling just one more time.

Jojo and I drift into silence, the only real sound the ticking of the sunburst clock that hangs on the opposite wall. We're standing very close together, our shoulders touching, fingers almost grazing and I get this sudden weird urge to reach for her hand. It's the same energy force I felt in the utility room earlier. It scares me a little.

'Shall I put some music on?' I suggest.

I don't wait for Jojo's answer, striding over to Dad's old record player.

'Er, yeah, sure,' Jojo says, following me.

I kneel down and lift up the cream leather lid.

'Is this vintage?' Jojo asks, crouching down next to me.

'Uh-huh. It's from the sixties. Dad bought it at a car boot sale.'

'It's gorgeous,' she says, stroking the maroon trim.

'Yeah, he was pretty proud of it.'

Dad used to play his records every Friday night, dimming the lights before settling into his favourite chair for the duration of the evening. As a little kid I loved falling asleep to the sound of music floating up the stairs.

'Do you want to pick something?' I ask, nodding towards the shelves that house Dad's epic collection.

'Are they in order?' Jojo asks.

'Not really.'

She pulls out sleeves at random, inspecting the covers before slotting them back. It's an eclectic selection – Motown and soul mingling with folk and country.

'It's quite a mix,' Jojo says.

I laugh. 'Yeah, I know. What can I say? My dad just really loved music. All kinds.'

'There are so many. Where did he get them all?'

'Second-hand record shops, eBay, car boot sales. He loved a car boot sale.'

She passes me 'Meet the Beatles'. 'Basic, I know,' she says.

'Nothing basic about the Beatles,' I reply. 'What track do you want?'

'Er, number one?'

'Coming right up.'

Carefully, I slide the record from its sleeve and drop it onto the turntable, before gently lowering the needle. There's a crackle before the jangling guitars kick in and the Beatles start singing 'I Want to Hold Your Hand'. Jojo shrugs out of her coat, draping it over the arm of Dad's chair before plopping on the floor in front of the record player. I like the way she moves in time to the music, her shoulders popping, her head swaying, a serene smile on her face. I like that she's not self-conscious with me. She catches my eye on the second chorus and grins. I grin back. It's that kind of song: smiling is practically compulsory.

'OK, your turn,' she says, as the song ends.

I pull out an album at random. Luckily it's a good one – 'Easter' by the Patti Smith Group. I put on track three – 'Because the Night'.

Jojo sings along.

'You've got a good voice,' I comment as the song fades out.

'Nah,' she says. 'Not really. I mean, I can hit the notes, but only just. Frankie's the one with the pipes.'

The mention of Frankie jars. I'm not sure why. I push it away and retrieve our tray of snacks, setting it down between us on the carpet. 'Your turn,' I say.

We keep going like this, lurching from disco to euro-pop, R&B to heavy metal. We play A-ha, Bowie, Grace Jones, The Strokes, Shirley Bassey, Le Chic, Nirvana, Van Morrison, Stevie Wonder, Elvis, Dolly Parton, Dr Dre, Lady Gaga, Guns 'n' Roses, Kate Bush, Aretha Franklin. As the music plays, we eat biscuits and exchange anecdotes – the first music we ever spent money on, the best gig we've ever been to, the song we wished we'd written.

And it's fun.

It's the most fun I've had in ages.

'Yes!' I say. It's my turn to pick and I've just found one of my child-hood favourites.

'What? What is it?' Jojo asks, kneeling up.

I hold up the record.

'Superman, Black Lace,' she reads aloud, her forehead scrunched.

'It reminds me so much of being a kid,' I say. 'We always used to play this at family parties, without fail.' I remember my dad leaping about the living room, teaching all the kids the actions.

I place the record on the turntable and wait for the familiar introduction to kick in. And just like that, I'm catapulted back in time.

'Do you know it?' I ask, scrambling to my feet.

Jojo shakes her head.

'Seriously?'

'No. I've literally never heard of it.'

'What? You'll be telling me you don't know Agadoo next.'

'Aga-what?'

'Oh my God, Bright, you've got some urgent catching up to do. C'mon, the actions are really easy to pick up.'

'Actions?' she says, her face flooding with alarm.

I hold out my hands and pull her to her feet.

'What are we doing?' she asks.

'Just copy me.'

Even though I haven't danced to this song in years, the moves are second nature.

'Spray!' I yell, miming applying deodorant to my underarms.

'Ski!' I bellow, crouching down and pretending to ski down a mountain.

'Macho Man!' I shout, parading back and forth, flexing my biceps.

The entire time, Jojo is too busy giggling to properly join in.

At the end of the song, she collapses onto the sofa, breathless from laughing so much.

'Oh my God,' she says, wiping her eyes. 'That was . . . something else.'

'Want to go again?' I ask. 'I swear you'll get it the second time around.'

'I don't think I can handle it,' she says.

'Was it that sexy?' I ask, flopping on the sofa beside her, the word 'sexy' and all its complications hanging invisibly between us.

'You flatter yourself, Ramin Jandu,' she says, prodding me on my forearm.

I like the way she says my name. I like the way she says stuff full stop.

Shit.

'My turn,' she says, jumping up and pulling out an album at random. She peers at the cover.

'What is it?' I ask.

She turns it towards me so I can see the sleeve.

'I'm Wide Awake, It's Morning,' I read. 'Bright Eyes.'

'Do you know it?' Jojo asks.

'Nope. You?'

She shakes her head. 'Pick a number from one to ten,' she instructs.

'Er, six.'

She consults the track listing on the back of the sleeve. 'First Day of My Life,' she reads.

She puts it on and we settle back on the floor. Jojo curls up in a ball, her chin resting on her bent knees while I lean with my back against the armchair, my legs loosely crossed at the ankle.

The introduction is instrumental – just an acoustic guitar – a complete contrast to the in-your-face silliness of 'Superman'. I let my head drop back and listen to the lyrics, really listen to them. They're stupidly romantic. Not in a cheesy or overblown way. They're sweet and gentle and heartfelt and intimate and quietly revelatory.

I swallow hard and sneak a glance at Jojo. She's peering at me over the top of her knees, her beautiful eyes wide and unblinking.

They lock with mine for a touch longer than feels natural. I want to look away. I know I should look away. And yet I don't. I can't.

I hold her gaze until the end of the song.

And she holds mine.

'Good choice,' I say, my voice cracking slightly.

'Thanks,' she murmurs.

The silence is deafening.

We're still looking at each other.

There's maybe a metre and a half max between us. I want it to be less. I want to kiss her, hold her.

Wait, what am I doing? This makes no sense.

Since when do I want to kiss Jojo?

She's my ex-girlfriend's best mate. A friend, nothing more.

So why can't I stop thinking about it?

The next track begins.

'I should probably go,' Jojo says, getting to her feet.

'Please don't,' I blurt.

She looks down at me, her eyes foggy with confusion.

I stand up to face her. 'I mean, you don't have to,' I backtrack. 'Not yet anyway.'

She hesitates. 'It's late.'

I glance at the clock. It's 4.15 in the morning. We've been playing records for over three hours.

'Can I use your bathroom before I go?' she asks.

'Er, yeah, of course. There's one downstairs. Go through the kitchen and it's on your left.'

She thanks me and leaves the room.

I remove the record from the turntable, return it to its sleeve and turn off the record player. Slowly, I pick up the records scattered across the carpet and return them to the shelves, inserting them in the gaps at random. I hear the toilet flush in the distance. I leave my task and intercept Jojo in the shadowy hallway.

'Find it OK?' I ask.

It's a stupid question but I'm not ready to say goodbye.

'Yeah, fine thanks,' she says.

I want to ask her to stay.

You already did, a voice inside my head reminds me. *She said no.*

We stand facing each other at the foot of the stairs. It's dim, the only light source the faint rainbow glow produced by the Christmas lights in the living room.

'Do you have the number for a local cab company?'

'Er, yeah, I think we've got some cards in the kitchen.'

'Cool.'

'I'll, er, be right back.' I head into the kitchen and pluck a taxi card from the notice board. I picture the cab arriving outside, Jojo putting on her coat, the door falling shut behind her as she leaves.

I hate every frame.

I return to the hallway.

'It might be expensive,' I say, handing over the card. 'New Year's Eve and all that.'

'That's OK.'

Jojo dials.

Please be engaged, please be engaged.

They answer almost straightaway. I listen as Jojo recites my address.

'Five minutes,' she says, hanging up.

'Great.'

'I should get my coat.'

She disappears into the living room, returning a few seconds later, her coat draped over her arm. I help her put it on. She turns around to face me.

'I've had a really good night,' she says, not quite meeting my eye as she pulls up the zip.

'Me too,' I reply, my voice soft.

I move in a little closer. Jojo does the same. My right index finger catches on her left one. Slowly, one by one, the rest of our fingers entwine. For a few seconds we just stand there, our spare arms hanging limply at our sides, our chests rising and falling in time.

And I swear, I've never wanted to kiss someone so much in my entire life.

Slowly, carefully, I place my left hand on the small of Jojo's back.

In response, Jojo puts her spare hand on my neck, sending a bolt of electricity whizzing down my spine.

There's a beat where no one says or does anything. It's almost like someone has pressed 'pause', freezing us in this weird pre-kiss limbo.

And then they hit 'play' and Jojo and I are kissing like it's the last night on earth.

Chapter 31

I wake up early, dawn seeping through the gap in my curtains. I don't know what time we dropped off, but I can't have got much sleep – an hour or two at the very most. Jojo is curled up next to me, her hair fanned out across the pillow. I study her face as she sleeps, noting the sprinkling of freckles across her nose and cheeks, the softness of her lips, the tiny scar in the gap between her eyebrows. She's wearing one of my favourite T-shirts – the grey Rolling Stones one I inherited from my dad, the logo patchy and faded. I like the way she looks in it. I imagine her wearing other items from my wardrobe – my olive-green hoodie, my grey beanie, a pair of my joggers, the drawstring pulled extra tight so they won't fall down. I want to touch her, hold her, make her sigh and gasp the way I did last night, but at the same time I'm afraid of waking her up and somehow breaking the spell. While she's still asleep, anything is possible and I'm not quite ready to let go of that.

I start to feel a bit creepy just staring at her, so I roll onto my back and think about last night instead. It comes back to me in snapshots

— kissing on the stairs, kissing on the landing, kissing in the doorway to my room, kissing as we made our way towards the bed. We didn't speak. We just kissed. In fact, I'm pretty certain I've never kissed anyone for that long and that continuously before. Not that it felt like a chore. It felt the opposite. It felt as natural as breathing, as thrilling as a bungee jump. My lips feel sore and slightly swollen. I like it. I don't want them ever to return to normal. I want 'recently kissed by Jojo Bright' to be my default state from this moment on.

I imagine the day ahead. I'll let Jojo doze a bit longer and then I'll make her breakfast. If it's a nice day, maybe we can go for a walk, down to the river perhaps. And if it's not, we can hang out here. Maybe we can watch a film, or listen to some more records. If I'm honest, I don't care what we do. I just want to be with her.

I must fall back to sleep because the next thing I know, the light is brighter and Jojo is sitting on the edge of my desk chair pulling on her socks. She's back in her own clothes, the Rolling Stones T-shirt folded neatly and placed at the end of the bed.

'Hi,' she says, biting her lip.

'Hey,' I say, sitting up and rubbing my eyes.

'I should get going,' she says.

'Now?' I grope for my phone so I can check the time. It's just gone nine. 'It's still early.'

'I know. I just . . .' Her voice trails off.

'What about breakfast?' I ask.

'Breakfast?'

'Yeah. Do you like eggs, then?' I say. 'I'm a demon scrambler.'

A 'demon scrambler'? What am I even on about?

'No, thanks.'

'Toast then? Or cereal? We've got cornflakes, Coco Pops, Crunchy Nut, granola, some thing Ruby's into that's like 50% marshmallows . . .'

'Honestly, it's fine,' Jojo says. 'I'm actually not all that hungry.'

'Well, at least let me get you a tea or coffee then.'

Jojo hesitates.

'Please,' I add.

'OK.'

I jump out of bed and pull on a T-shirt and pair of tracksuit bottoms over my boxers.

Down in the kitchen, Jojo sits at the breakfast bar as I make her tea (not too strong, milky, half a sugar). I commit her preferences to memory. Just in case.

There are so many things I want to say.

Last night was incredible.

I don't want you to go home after you've drunk your tea.

You look really fucking beautiful when you sleep.

But I can't seem to pluck up the courage to say any of them.

'Is it OK?' I ask instead, nodding at the steaming mug in her hands.

'Spot-on,' she says.

I take a deep breath. 'About last night,' I begin.

'Please don't,' Jojo says.

'Please don't what?' I ask, blinking.

'Say . . . stuff.'

I'm opening my mouth to ask her what on earth she means when I hear the lock in the front door. I enter the hallway just in time for Mum, Laleh and Roxy to tumble in, Roxy in Mum's arms.

'Hey, sweetheart,' Mum says. They all look knackered.

'What are you guys doing here?' I ask. 'I thought you weren't due back until teatime.'

'We think Roxy might be allergic to Mum and Dad's new cat,' Mum says, sighing. 'She's been up all night coughing and sneezing, poor baby.' She kisses a miserable-looking Roxy on the head. 'Come on, you,' she adds. 'Let's get you a drink of water, then straight to bed.'

In the kitchen, Jojo is standing next to the fridge, her face bright red.

'Oh, hello,' Mum says, setting Roxy down.

'Mum, you remember Jojo,' I say.

'Of course I do,' Mum says. 'You're Frankie's friend.'

'Yes.'

'Are you?' Roxy says, her face visibly brightening.

'Er, yes,' Jojo says.

'Is she here too?' Roxy asks eagerly.

'Er, no,' Jojo stammers. 'She's in Tenerife.'

'Awwwwwww,' Roxy says, pouting.

'Sorry,' Jojo says, her face growing redder by the second.

Mum looks from me to Jojo and back to me again.

'Jojo and I were at the same party last night,' I say.

'And I forgot my house keys,' Jojo blurts. 'So, er, Ram said I could stay here.'

'Yeah,' I say, following her lead. 'She, er, slept in Laleh's bed.'

'I hope that's OK,' Jojo adds quickly.

'Sure,' Laleh says, shrugging and prising the lid off the biscuit tin.

'I was just going actually,' Jojo says, tipping her unfinished tea in the sink and rinsing out her mug.

'Oh, don't rush away on our account,' Mum says. 'Please.'

'No, no, I need to get back,' Jojo says.

She wishes Mum, Laleh and Roxy a stilted 'Happy New Year' and heads for the door.

I follow her.

'What are you doing today?' I ask in a low voice as she sits on the

251

bottom step – the exact same step we collapsed onto kissing less than five hours ago – and laces up her trainers.

'I have plans with my mum and stepmum,' she says.

Only she doesn't. They were at a party in the Peak District last night and aren't due back until the evening. She told me so last night. Last night, when everything was different. When the world was alight with possibility. I want to go back in time and hold onto it somehow, bottle it, keep it safe from harm.

Jojo stands up and pulls on her coat. I watch her, chewing my lip.

'Thanks for having me,' she says, not quite meeting my eye as she yanks her jade-green bobble hat down over her hair. The colour makes her eyes look even more striking.

'You're welcome,' I murmur.

As I sleepwalk towards the door and unlock it, there are a million things I want to say but I don't manage any of them, my tongue in knots.

'Happy New Year,' Jojo says, stepping onto the path. It's pearly white with frost.

'Happy New Year,' I echo.

I stand in the open doorway and watch her walk down the path and turn left onto the pavement.

I will her to look back.

She doesn't.

Go after her, a voice at the back of my head whispers as she walks down the street.

She doesn't want me to, I hiss back.

How do you know that?

'Jojo!' I yell. 'Wait!'

I slip my feet into a pair of old wellies and run after her, the cold air nipping my bare arms. As I plant myself in front of her, I realize

I have no idea what I'm about to say. All I know is, I have to say something.

'What is it?' Jojo asks.

'I want to see you again.'

'Ram, we can't.'

'At least think about it.'

'It was a one-off.'

Despite her words, the tremor in her voice gives me a sliver of hope.

'But why?' I say. 'I mean, do you want it to be? I don't think I do.'

'It's not about what we want, Ram.'

'Of course it is.'

'What about Frankie?'

'But you called her. She said it was OK.'

'There's a pretty big difference between just hanging out and what ended up happening, Ram.'

'She'd understand.'

'Would she?'

'Well, maybe not right away, but give her a bit of time . . .'

Jojo shakes her head. 'No. It's not fair.'

'But last night. It was . . . damn, it was amazing, Jojo. Are you honestly prepared to turn your back on that?'

Jojo hesitates before answering. 'We have to.'

'But Jojo—'

'Frankie's my best friend,' she says, talking over me. 'And you were her first love.'

I wince.

'But that's all in the past now,' I say. 'We broke up.'

'Yeah, like barely two months ago.'

'She was the one who dumped me, remember?'

'It doesn't matter. This would crush her.'

'How do you know that?'

'Because I know Frankie. And I know how her heart works. Any other girl, she might be able to cope with. But me?' Jojo shakes her head hard. 'No way.'

'What about further down the line? Once there's a bit more water under the bridge? I mean, I'll wait, if that's what you're asking.'

Jojo takes a deep breath. 'Ram. I like you. I like you a lot. And last night was . . . amazing.' Her cheeks flush. 'But Frankie cannot ever know about it.'

'What, never?'

'Never.'

'But things might change. Maybe if she starts seeing someone else . . . ?'

Jojo doesn't say anything, just chews her bottom lip, her face tense with worry. All I want to do is hug her and tell her it'll all be OK and take her back inside.

'Can I text you at least?' I ask.

'I think it's best if you don't. I'm sorry, Ram. I just can't risk hurting her. She's my best friend. She's too precious to me.'

I let out a long exhalation. 'You're a really fucking good person, Jojo.' *And right now, I wish you weren't*, I add silently.

Jojo laughs a hollow laugh. 'No, I'm not, Ram.'

'Yeah, you are. Frankie's lucky to have you.'

She presses her lips together and for a second I think she might cry. 'I should go,' she says.

'Can I at least check in, in like, I dunno, the spring or something?' I ask. 'See how the land lies then.'

She shakes her head sadly. 'I don't think so.'

'But—'

'Please, Ram. Promise me you won't make this harder than it already is.'

I hesitate.

'Please,' she repeats.

'I promise.'

'I'm sorry,' she says.

And I can tell she means it. Not that it makes any of this feel any less shit.

'Happy New Year,' she adds one final time, her voice almost a whisper.

'Happy New Year,' I murmur.

There's a beat, then she turns on her heel and walks briskly away from me.

This time I let her go.

When I return inside, I head into the kitchen where Mum and Laleh are eating crumpets slathered with peanut butter.

'Laleh,' Mum says. 'Would you mind going into the living room?'

'Why?' Laleh asks.

'I just want to have a private word with your brother.'

'Can I watch telly?'

'Yes. But make sure you close the door. I don't want you to wake Roxy.'

Satisfied with this arrangement, Laleh picks up her plate and leaves the room.

'So, what's up?' I ask, peeling a sticker off a sad-looking apple from the fruit bowl.

'You tell me,' Mum says, cocking her head to one side.

I shrug.

'Where did you say Jojo slept again?'

'In Laleh's bed.'

'I thought that was what you said. It's just that I put Roxy to bed just now, and, call me crazy, but Laleh's bunk didn't look all that slept in to me.'

I hesitate.

Mum smiles. 'Ram, it's fine. You're sixteen. I'm OK with girls in your bed. It's just a bit of a surprise – I didn't realize you and Jojo were an item.'

'We're not,' I say.

Mum blinks. 'Oh. I assumed . . .'

I shake my head and take a bite of the apple. It's too soft, the flesh all woolly.

'Want to talk about it?'

'Not right now, thanks.'

'OK, sweetheart. But know that I'm here if you change your mind.'

I nod. 'I might just head upstairs actually, have a lie-down. It was kind of a late one.'

She gives my shoulder a squeeze and lets me go.

Up in my room, the twin indentations from mine and Jojo's heads are still visible on the pillows. I chuck the apple in the bin and pick up the T-shirt she wore, lifting it to my nose. It smells of us both, our scents mingling together. It works. It makes me want to chase after her and wave it under her nose as proof, but I get the feeling it wouldn't change anything. At least, not right now.

I flop on to the bed, open Spotify on my phone and type 'First Day of My Life, Bright Eyes' into the search bar. I close my eyes and listen to the song five times in a row like the lovesick fool that I've become.

Chapter 32

Was that all really only nine months ago? It feels like a lifetime has passed. In the gap, it's taken on a hazy dreamlike quality, my memories of the night reduced to a series of flickering snapshots. – Jojo reading from *Sparkling Cyanide*; Jojo creasing up with laughter as I danced around to 'Superman'; the look in her eyes before we kissed for the first time; the way her skin felt against mine . . .

'But we used protection,' I say.

Another one of my memories – retrieving a condom from the box I keep at the back of my sock drawer, my fingers trembling as I ripped open the packet.

'I know,' Jojo says. 'I was there too, remember?'

'Did you realize it had split?'

'Of course not. I would have done something about it if I had.'

'Sorry,' I say. 'I didn't mean it like that.'

There's a pause.

'When?' I ask.

'What do you mean?'

'When did you, er, give birth?'

'The first of August.'

I begin to do the maths in my head.

'He was early,' Jojo says, cutting off my calculations.

He. It's a little boy. I have a little boy.

Wait.

The first of August. That's three weeks ago.

Three whole weeks.

Twenty-one entire days.

He's existed all this time and I had no idea. Jesus, I didn't even know Jojo was pregnant. Why didn't Frankie say anything? She must have known. There's no way she couldn't have. We just spent three hours stuck in a car together. Did it not dawn on her to mention it? To think it was relevant somehow? Unless this was all just some elaborate ruse to get me down here. But that makes no sense either.

My head is spinning.

'When were you going to tell me?' I ask.

Jojo doesn't answer.

'OK, let me rephrase that. Were you ever going to tell me?'

Jojo's eyes flash. 'I didn't know what I was going to do, OK?' she says. 'I still don't know!'

'You're talking like you're the only one who gets a say.'

She doesn't answer, just continues to rock the baby, *our* baby, in her arms.

'Why didn't you tell me you were pregnant in the first place?' I ask. 'I know we're not a couple or anything, but surely I was entitled to at least know. Whatever you'd have wanted to do, I've have supported you.'

'I didn't know,' Jojo says, her voice flat.

'About what?'

'I didn't know I was pregnant. And before you say, "that's impossible", let me assure you that it isn't.'

'But how could you not know?' I ask. 'Didn't you put on weight and stuff?'

I picture my mum when she was pregnant with Laleh and then Roxy. Both times, she was huge, so huge I remember my dad wrapping his arms around her bump from behind and his fingers only just managing to interlace at the front.

'I feel like a walrus,' she used to sigh.

'A very sexy walrus,' Dad would say, kissing her on the neck and I'd groan, outwardly mortified by their affection for each other, at the same time as being secretly delighted by it.

'I didn't show,' Jojo says. 'I was carrying him up behind my ribs apparently.' She relays what the doctors told her. From her slightly weary delivery, I get the feeling this isn't the first time tonight she's had to explain this.

I nod, trying to take it in.

'So when did you find out?' I ask. 'How late on was it?'

'The first of August.'

'Wait, you didn't realize you were pregnant until you were, what, in labour?'

'Yes.'

'Where were you?'

'The bathroom.'

'You had him at home?'

She nods.

'Was someone with you?'

She shakes her head.

'You were all alone?'

She nods once more.

259

'But that must have been terrifying.'

'Ha. That's one word for it.'

She's trying to make light of it, but I can see the darkness in her eyes.

'Did it last long?' I ask instead. 'The birth, I mean.'

'Honestly? I have no idea . . .'

'You should have called me,' I say.

Jojo lets out a hollow laugh.

'I'm serious,' I say.

'And said what? Oh, hi, I know we haven't spoken in eight months, but just so you know, I'm in labour, oh, and guess what, I'm pretty certain it's yours.'

'I wouldn't have cared!' I insist. 'Do you know how many times I've wanted to call or text you? Probably hundreds. The only reason I never actually pressed "call" or "send" was because of that promise you made me make on New Year's Day.'

She bites her lip.

'I'd have been there for you, Jojo. Every step of the way.'

'It's not that simple, Ram.'

'I didn't say it was. But that's no reason to keep me out of everything. I mean, Jesus, Jojo, I'm his *dad*.'

Saying it out loud is one of the most surreal moments of my life. I'm his dad.

I, Ramin Jandu, aged seventeen years and four months, am someone's father.

I always assumed I'd be a dad one day, but I always figured I'd be older, in my thirties at least, married with a good job and a mortgage – all the grown-up stuff already in place – and that the baby would be planned, the product of a series of mature conversations and careful planning – spreadsheets and budgets and a fully decorated nursery and all the proper gear. I never for one second dreamed it would be like this.

I sink down on the bed and let out a long deep exhale. *I'm a dad. I'm a dad. I'm a dad.* No matter how many times I say it to myself, it doesn't seem real.

I look up. Jojo is watching me, her lips pressed together, her eyes wide. I lower my gaze to the baby.

'Can I hold him?' I ask.

She blinks, as if thrown by my question.

'Please,' I add.

'OK,' she says.

Slowly, carefully, she lowers the baby into my arms. 'You got him OK?' she asks.

'I've got him.'

He's warm and smells like Laleh and Roxy did when they were babies – sort of sweet and milky.

'What's his name?' I ask. I can't believe I haven't thought to ask until now.

'Albie,' Jojo says.

'Albie,' I repeat. 'Albie what? What's his surname?'

Jojo's face pales. 'I, I don't know yet. He hasn't been registered.'

'Right.'

There's a long pause. My head is swimming. Jojo and I have made a baby. Together. Fuck.

'I'm going to use the loo if that's OK,' she says.

I nod.

'Will you be all right with him?'

'Of course.'

She hovers for a moment, chewing on her thumbnail before padding towards the bathroom, closing the door behind her with a soft click. I look down at the baby nestled in my arms. Albie. My son. I take in his features one by one – his button nose, his long sooty black lashes, his plump lips, his squished ears, his masses of thick dark hair. As I make my inspection, about a billion different emotions fly around my head and body, bashing and colliding, fizzing and exploding.

Fear and anger and hurt and confusion and frustration.

And love.

Love like I've never known.

Jesus, I've only know this baby exists for a few minutes and already I'm drunk on love for him. I'm dizzy with it.

And it's fucking terrifying.

How could Jojo not tell me about him? I know we haven't been in touch but it's not like I'm some stranger to her. I thought she liked me. No, scratch that, I *know* she liked me, and I'm pretty sure she thought I was a decent guy too. How did she think I was going to react? Did she think I was going to kick off or something? Shout and scream and throw stuff around? Or start making crazy demands? That makes literally no sense.

Then it hits me.

I know exactly why she didn't tell me. It's the exact same reason why she bolted from my house on New Year's Day and begged me to pretend it never happened.

'Frankie,' I say, as Jojo returns to the room, wiping her hands on a towel.

'What?' she says.

'That's why you didn't tell me. Because of Frankie.'

Jojo doesn't say anything.

'Jesus, Jojo. I know she's your best friend but were you really prepared to keep Albie a secret from me just to protect her?'

'It's not just about Frankie.'

'But she's a big part of it, right?'

Jojo doesn't answer, instead pushing her hands through her hair. It's longer than it was at New Year, brushing her collarbone, her grown-out fringe just about long enough to tuck behind her ears.

'Listen,' I say. 'I know Frankie's upset and I get why, but she can't stay mad at us for ever.'

'Can't she?' Jojo whispers.

'Of course not.'

'But we completely betrayed her.'

'Not on purpose.'

'It's doesn't matter. She's hurting and it's all our fault.'

'She'll come around.'

'You didn't see the look on her face when she figured it all out, Ram. She hates me.'

'Well, for what it's worth, I don't think she's my number one fan right now either.'

'What time is it?' Jojo asks.

I check my phone. 'One thirty.'

'She's been gone for over half an hour now.'

'She'll be OK.'

'What makes you so sure?'

'Frankie's not stupid. Once she's had her strop, she'll come back.'

'How do you know that?' Jojo snaps.

I blink. 'What?'

'How do you know what she's going to do?'

'I did go out with her for seven months.'

'Yeah well, I've been best friends with her for twelve years, and I think this is a bit more serious than a "strop".'

I sigh. Everything is coming out all wrong.

'I didn't mean it like that,' I say. 'But this is Frankie Ricci we're talking about, remember? She's all about making a big splash, then moving on. It's her signature move. Once she's made her point, she'll come back, I'm certain of it.'

'And until then?'

'We wait.' *It's not like we haven't got stuff to talk about*, I add silently.

Jojo responds by grabbing a long-sleeved T-shirt from her bag. She pulls it on over her camisole and slips her feet into a pair of flip-flops. She then reaches for what looks like a baby carrier, yanking it on over her head and fastening the straps around her torso.

'What are you doing?' I ask.

'What does it look like I'm doing?' she says, holding her arms out for Albie. 'I'm going to look for her.'

PART FOUR

FRANKIE, JOJO

AND RAM

Chapter 33

Frankie

I stumble out onto the pavement and turn left, half running, half walking to the end of the street, where I take a right, then a left, then another left. I have no idea where I'm going, no plan. All I know is that I need to get as far away from the hotel and Jojo and Ram and the baby (their baby) as possible.

I shake out my hand. It's tingling like mad. I've never hit anyone before. Not properly, anyway. Luca and I used to play-fight when we were kids but that was more pushing and shoving than anything. Until tonight, I'd always assumed that face slapping was a habit reserved for characters in soap operas or Victorian melodramas.

My sweaty feet slide about in my flip-flops, the bit that goes between my toes rubbing. I don't stop, though. I need to keep moving. Because I'm afraid if I don't, I'll fall apart.

My phone buzzes against my hip. I still haven't saved Ram's

number but I know it's him. Just seeing the familiar digits makes me hot and furious. I jab at the screen to accept the call.

'What?' I snarl.

I like how fierce I sound. If only my hand wasn't shaking quite so badly.

'Frankie, what the hell was that?' Ram demands.

He actually has the nerve to sound pissed off. If I wasn't so angry, I'd probably laugh.

'Seriously,' he says. 'What the fuck did I do?'

What did I do? *What did I do?* Is he actually kidding me? No wonder he volunteered to drive me down here. It all makes complete sense now.

'Why don't you ask Jojo?' I snap.

'What do you mean?'

But Jojo's got another thing coming if she thinks I'm going to do her dirty work for her. If Ram wants to know what's going on, he can go up there and figure it out for himself.

'Frankie, what do—?'

I hang up before he can finish his sentence.

He calls back straightaway. I press 'cancel' and drop my phone to the bottom of my bag. The whole time I keep walking, changing direction at random, letting my instincts guide me.

The wind is gathering, the air hot and heavy. Sweat trickles down the back of my neck and the insides of my thighs.

I take a left, then a right, then another right.

Jojo and Ram.

Ram and Jojo.

Then it hits me.

New Year's Eve.

Jojo called me. It was just after midnight and I was on the beach watching the fireworks with that boy, the one with the gorgeous eyes who never emailed back. She said she'd bumped into Ram and was it OK if she went to his to hang out. And I said yes . . .

I feel sick.

No matter how hard I try, I can't stop picturing them together.

I hate how clearly I can see it.

Them talking. Smiling. Holding hands. Kissing . . .

I hate that they make sense as a couple. More than Ram and I ever did.

It makes me feel so stupid.

Why didn't I see it before now? How could I have been so bloody blind? Was stuff going on between them while Ram and I were still together? Have they been laughing behind my back this entire time?

Jojo insisted it was a one-off, but of course she's going to say that – anything to cushion the already mighty bombshell. Plus, isn't that what people always claim?

It was just the once.

I don't know what came over me.

It was a mistake.

It'll never happen again.

If this were a TV drama, I'd be yelling at the screen right now, begging the heroine to wake up and smell the coffee, to stop being so bloody naive.

I find myself on the high street. It's pretty quiet apart from a small crowd spilling out of a chicken shop about ten doors away from me. I head towards it. The heady smell of fried food reminds me how hungry I am. Apart from a few sweets in the car, I haven't eaten anything since I was at home. I check my purse. There are two one-pound coins, a fifty-pence piece and a collection of smaller coins. Enough for some chips at least.

I head inside and join the back of the queue. The place is packed, mainly with kids around my age, most of them drunk, their faces shiny beneath the unforgiving fluorescent lights. What are they all doing out so late? Then I remember. It's GCSE results night. They're celebrating, just like I was supposed to.

I reach the front of the queue and order a portion of chips.

'That'll be one pound ninety,' the guy behind the counter says.

I give him the coins.

He studies them in his palm before handing back one of the coins. 'That's a euro,' he says.

'Really?' I peer down at the coin in my hand. He's right. Shit. 'OK, hang on,' I say, opening my purse. I count the remaining coins out onto the shiny metal counter. I'm 13p short. 'I don't have enough.'

The guy shrugs as if to say 'what do you expect me to do?' and looks over my shoulder to serve the person behind me.

'How much do you need?' a husky voice asks.

I turn in its direction.

A girl with candyfloss-pink hair and a silver nose stud is leaning against the counter, slurping what looks like a strawberry milkshake through a straw.

'Sorry?' I say.

'To pay for your food. How short are you?'

'Oh. Er, 13p.'

She digs into her pocket and flips me a twenty-pence piece. Miraculously, I manage to catch it.

'Wow, thanks,' I say.

She smiles, shrugs and saunters away.

Chips in hand, I grab a couple of ketchup sachets and look around for my Good Samaritan, eventually spotting her at a crowded table by the window. Judging by the amount of fast-food debris strewn across the table, her group has been here for a while. They're all talking at once, their animated conversations overlapping.

The girl notices me hovering. 'All right?' she says, cocking her head to one side.

'Yeah,' I say. 'I just wanted to say thanks again.'

'No problem.'

'Here's your change.' I place the leftover coins on the table and push them towards her.

'Cheers,' she says, scooping them up and dropping them into her metallic bum bag. 'Wanna sit down?'

Where? There are no free seats. I'm about to point this out when the girl gets up and plops herself on the lap of the boy sitting next to her.

'Thanks,' I say, sliding into her vacant seat.

'I'm Lily by the way,' she says.

I hesitate before answering. 'Kristin.'

I wonder if I should offer to share my chips, but in the end, everyone just helps themselves anyway and within about twenty seconds flat, the carton is empty.

'Lost your mates or something?' Lily asks as I wipe my salty hands on a napkin.

'Er, yeah,' I reply. 'Something like that.'

'Can't you ring them? See where they are?'

'No battery.'

'Oh shit.'

'Yeah.'

'Listen,' the girl opposite me interrupts, clearly unmoved by my plight. 'Are we going to the club or what?'

'What time's last entry again?' one of the boys asks.

'Two,' Lily supplies.

'Exactly,' the girl says, flipping her swishy Ariana Grande-style ponytail from one shoulder to the other. 'So if we're doing this, we need to get a serious move on.'

'I'm not sure I can be arsed,' another girl chimes in. 'It's gonna be rammed.'

'Oh, don't be such a melt,' Lily says. 'It's results night. Don't you wanna have a dance?'

'Lil's right,' the boy she's sitting on drawls. 'Plus, where else are we going to go? It's way too early to go home and I doubt anywhere else will let us in at this time.'

'Fine,' the girl who can't be arsed says. 'I'm not queuing, though.'

'Oh my God, you are such a princess,' Lily says, rolling her eyes. She stands up, the others following.

I scramble to my feet to get out of their way.

Lily turns to me. 'Coming?' she asks.

'Where to?'

'Where do you think? The club.'

I hesitate. Ram and Jojo will be wondering where I've got to. I should go back to the hotel. Talk to them. Hear their point of view. Try to be mature about things.

And yet the idea of facing them right now makes me want to throw up in my mouth.

'I don't have any money,' I say.

'It's only three quid to get in,' Lily replies. 'I'll cover you.'

'Really?'

'Sure.'

I make up my mind there and then. I'll go to the club. Just for a bit. I'll have a dance. Clear my head. Dancing always relaxes me. Let Ram and Jojo stew for a bit. It's the very least they deserve. If they're even stewing in the first place. God knows what they're up to right now . . .

I shudder, push the thought away.

'Well,' Lily says. 'You in or what?'

'You sure that's OK?'

'Course. The more the merrier. And, hey, maybe your friends will be there.'

'Yeah, maybe,' I murmur.

I follow Lily and her crew out onto the pavement.

'It's gonna storm,' one of the boys announces, jerking his head upwards.

'You reckon?' the girl with the ponytail asks, twirling it round her index finger.

'Deffo. You can smell it.'

'In that case, let's get our arses in gear,' Lily says, picking up the pace. 'Getting soaked tonight is not part of my plan.'

As we walk to the club, Lily introduces her mates in turn. The girl with the sulky face is called Annalise. The tall boy with the curly quiff, Harrison. They're the only two names that stick, though. The rest I forget almost immediately.

'You're not from round here, are you, Kristin?' Lily says, falling into step with me.

'What makes you say that?'

'Your accent.'

'What about it?'

'It's proper Northern.'

I laugh. 'No it's not. I'm from the Midlands.'

'Well, it sounds northern to me. That's a compliment by the way. I wish I had an accent.'

'What are you talking about? You totally have an accent.'

'No, I don't.'

'Er, yeah, you do.'

I do an impression of her offering to pay for my chips in her West Country lilt. She bursts out laughing before calling out to the others. 'Oh my God, guys, listen to Kristin pretending to be me! It's so fucking funny.'

I repeat my impression for the group. They squeal with laughter and beg me to do each of them. I oblige, taking them off in turn. I've always been good at impressions, ever since I was a little kid playing epic games of 'Let's Pretend' with Jojo. I used to make her laugh so hard sometimes she'd be gasping for breath, begging me to stop.

The memory stings. I shove it away and try to bask in my new audience's howling laughter and applause instead.

'That's fucking hilarious, Kristin,' Lily tells me, linking her arm through mine. 'Seriously, you should do that for a living.'

I smile faintly.

'So, how'd you wind up in Swindon?' she asks. 'You just move down here or something?'

'Er, no, just visiting.'

She pulls a face. 'What? Like a holiday or something?'

'Sort of. It was my friend's idea.'

'Weird.'

'Yeah, I know . . .'

The club, Aphrodite's, is down a dingy side street.

'What kind of music do they play?' I ask, as we approach the garish neon sign.

Annalise laughs.

'What?' I ask. 'What's so funny?'

She rolls her eyes hard. 'No one goes to Aphrodite's for the music.'

'Oh,' I say.

'And if they do, they're a moron.'

'Are they going to want to see IDs or anything?' I ask Lily.

'Not tonight,' she replies. 'GCSE results is literally the one night of the year they turn a blind eye.'

The club is down a set of narrow stairs.

'I'll pay you back,' I promise Lily as a stocky man dressed all in black stamps a palm tree on the back of my hand.

'It's only a few quid,' Lily replies with a wave of her hand. 'Seriously, Kristin, don't worry about it.'

Inside the club, it smells of stale sweat and Red Bull. 'What Makes You Beautiful' by One Direction is blasting through the speakers.

'Kill me now,' Annalise mutters, pretending to shoot herself in her head with her index and middle fingers.

'Drinks?' Harrison suggests.

En masse, the group heads for the crush at the bar. I tug on Lily's arm.

'I'm just going to the loo,' I say.

'OK. Come find us when you're done.'

Even by usual manky club standards, the loos at Aphrodite's are especially gross – doors hanging off their hinges and puddles on the floor. I squeeze into the farthest cubicle and have a wee, squatting so my bum doesn't touch the seat. As I'm hovering, I get my phone out.

There are no more missed calls.

Not one.

I picture Ram and Jojo in the hotel room, sitting side by side on the bed, their fingers interlaced. They're talking about serious stuff. Grown-up stuff that doesn't concern me. The baby. Their baby. They don't have time to come running after me – Frankie the silly drama queen. Well, good. Because I don't want them to.

I open the cubicle door and make my way towards the sinks. The attendant, a woman with weary eyes, pumps liquid soap into my hand then passes me a paper towel to dry them with.

'I'm really sorry, I don't have any money,' I say.

She tuts and wanders back to her stool by the door.

I can't find Lily at the bar so I do a circuit of the club. Its name is reflected in the decor – fibreglass Greek-style pillars adorned with fake ivy – and the bar staff's uniform – togas and plastic headdresses sprayed gold. It's not especially big, just one long room with a sunken rectangular dance floor at one end, the bar and loos at the other, but it's rammed with people my age, talking and dancing. I finally spot Lily and her mates at the far end of the dance floor, near the DJ booth, and make my way towards them, the bass line of 'Call Me Maybe' thumping through my body and making my ears ring as I squeeze through the dozens of sweaty bodies. When I arrive, they let out a rowdy cheer. I smile, stupidly grateful for these strangers who have adopted me for the evening. Lily pushes a plastic cup filled with dark liquid into my hand.

'Got you a drink,' she says.

'You didn't have to.'

She rolls her eyes. 'I know. I just figured you might need one.'

I take a sip. It's vodka and Coke. The Coke is flat, the vodka strong. I try to dance but it's tricky with a drink in my hand, the contents sloshing over the side.

'Oh, just down it!' Lily says, laughing.

I do as I'm told, chugging the lot in three seconds flat. Lily and her friends cheer as I place the empty cup on the edge of the DJ booth and raise both my arms in the air in triumph.

I dance to song after song, yelling along with the lyrics I know, making up the ones I don't. For all of Annalise's complaints about the quality of the music, she's dancing pretty hard too, twerking like there's no tomorrow and tossing her blonde hair back and forth in time with the beat. Sweat pours down my face and neck and legs, my hair sticking to my forehead and upper back and cheeks. I must look a proper fright. I don't care, though. All I want to do is forget, let the music take over. The alcohol helps. It makes me feel like as long as I just keep dancing, everything might just be OK.

At one point, another one of Lily's friends, a skinny boy with a mop of bleached white hair presses a sticky shot glass into my hand.

'I'm sorry,' I shout over the throbbing music. 'I can't get you one back.'

'It's just a shot,' he yells back. 'I ordered one too many by accident.'

I take a sniff. It smells like liquorice. I hesitate. I don't usually drink very much, and I never do shots. Despite my height, I'm a complete lightweight, and I know from experience that my line between tipsy and flat-out drunk is almost non-existent.

I'll just have this one, I decide. After that, I'll stop.

I gulp it down. It's horrible, burning the back of my throat.

'Ugh, what was that?' I ask the boy.

'Sambuca,' he says, grinning. 'Why? Want another?'

I shake my head hard and he laughs.

The Sambuca takes effect a few songs later, making my head spin and turning my legs to jelly. Lily grabs my hand to steady me.

'You OK?' she asks.

'Yeah, fine,' I say, struggling to focus on her face properly.

'You wanna sit down?'

'Yeah, yeah, maybe.'

She takes my arm and leads me to an empty booth overlooking the dance floor. A laminated sign that says 'reserved for Suzie' is propped on the table. Lily chucks it aside and we sit down. The seating is plastic and sticks to the back of my thighs.

'You OK?' Lily asks again. 'You're not going to be sick, are you?'

I shake my head.

'Wait here,' she says. 'I'll get you some water.'

While she's gone, I take out my phone. No missed calls, no messages. Nothing. I can't believe they haven't even tried to get in contact with me.

'I thought you didn't have any battery,' Lily says on her return, a plastic pint glass of water in each hand.

She doesn't sound annoyed or cross. More curious than anything.

I place the glowing phone face down on the seat next to me and reach for one of the waters, taking a big gulp.

'What happened tonight?' Lily asks, flopping down next to me. 'Did you and your mates fall out or something?'

'It's complicated,' I say.

'Isn't everything?'

'No, but this really is.'

'Go on then. Tell me. I'm good at complicated.'

I suppose I've got nothing to lose. Lily doesn't know me. Or Jojo. Or Ram. Maybe it'll be good to get someone else's take on the whole stupid thing. Someone unbiased. Someone who won't be swayed by Ram and Jojo's squeaky-clean reputations.

'What would you do,' I ask slowly, 'if you found out your ex-boyfriend and your best friend had had sex behind your back?'

'Depends,' Lily says. 'How long had you and your boyfriend been broken up for when it happened?'

'Two and a half months.'

'And was it a long relationship?'

'Seven months.'

'And how did you find out? Did they tell you?'

'Not exactly. I kind of figured it out for myself.'

'Ouch.'

'Yeah.'

'Was it a one-off?'

'Apparently . . .'

'Did they say why they didn't tell you?'

My spinning head stops me from answering right away. I put down the water and drop my head between my knees. I really shouldn't have had that shot.

'Kristin?'

Kristin? Who's Kristin? Then I remember, *I'm* Kristin.

'Yeah,' I say.

'Are you sure you're not going to be sick?'

I nod and slowly sit back up.

'Here, drink the rest of this.'

Lily hands me my water. Diligently, I take a sip.

'This best friend,' she says. 'Have you been mates with her for long?'

'Since Reception.'

'And has she done anything like this before?'

'No. I mean, I don't think so . . .'

'What you doing, bitches?'

I glance up as Annalise and one of the other girls (Farah? Zara? Sara?) plonk themselves opposite us.

'Well?' Annalise demands.

'I'm counselling Kristin,' Lily replies. She turns to me. 'You don't mind if I fill them in, do you?'

Before I have the chance to answer, she goes ahead and tells them about Ram and Jojo.

'What a slut!' Annalise exclaims.

'Excuse me, what about him?' Farah/Zara/Sara demands. 'It takes two to tango, you know.'

'Yeah, but this girl is meant to be her best friend. Where's the loyalty? Seriously, Kristin, you need to ditch this bitch.'

'It's not that straightforward,' I say. 'We've been friends for ever.'

'Exactly. And how does she repay you? By shagging your ex.'

'Plus,' Lily chimes in, 'it sounds like she only 'fessed up to that because she got found out. Who knows what other shady stuff she's been up to behind your back.'

'She's not like that,' I insist.

But Lily and her friends aren't listening, continuing the debate like I'm not even in the room.

'Lily's right,' Annalise is saying. 'As if this is a one-off.'

'It might be,' Farah/Zara/Sara offers.

'Bullshit!' Annalise and Lily proclaim in unison.

They burst into giggles, high fiving one another.

'You need to get real, Zara,' Annalise says.

'Yeah, try putting yourself in Kristin's position,' Lily adds. 'Imagine how you'd feel if Annalise shagged Ryan and then lied about it.'

Zara hesitates.

'See!' Lily cries gleefully.

'OK, maybe I'd be a bit mad,' Zara admits.

'No maybe about it. You'd want to tear Annalise's hair out and you know it.'

But Annalise isn't Jojo. Not by a long shot.

And this isn't a hypothetical situation; this is my life.

And these girls aren't my friends.

They don't know me. Or Jojo. Or a single thing about our friendship. Suddenly I wish I'd never said anything.

'OK, let's turn the tables then,' Annalise continues. 'If you had sex with Jimbo behind my back, I wouldn't speak to you again.'

'What, ever?' Zara asks, her eyes wide.

'Never,' Annalise confirms, folding her arms across her chest. 'You'd be dead to me, Zara. Dead.'

'I believe her too,' Lily says, laughing.

I try to imagine a world in which I never speak to Jojo ever again. I picture us passing in the street and not saying a word, looking through each other like we're a pair of ghosts.

Tears spring in my eyes.

But I can't cry in front of these people. I refuse to.

I need to get out of here.

Now.

I wobble to my feet.

'Where you going?' Lily asks, frowning.

'The loo,' I reply.

'You going to be sick?'

I shake my head, pull my bag over my shoulder and push my way through the crowds of people, back towards the bar area. Only instead of going to the loo, I head for the exit, staggering up the stairs and out into the street.

'Night then,' the bouncer calls after me.

I ignore him and turn left, back towards the high street. The wind is gathering, and I have to hold my dress down with both hands to stop it from flying up.

I reach into my bag for my phone so I can find out the time.

It's not there.

I check again, turning everything out on the pavement.

No phone.

Shit.

'Sorry, we're not letting anyone else in,' the bouncer says when I return to Aphrodite's just a few minutes later.

'But I was literally just here,' I say. 'Look.' I thrust out my hand, but the palm tree has already been reduced to a grey smudge.

The bouncer gives me a sceptical look.

'But I was,' I yelp. 'You said good night!'

'Sorry, love. No admission after half one.'

'But I need to get my phone. I left it in one of the booths. I'll be straight in and out, I promise.'

'Sorry, sweetheart, you'll have to come back tomorrow.'

'But I need it now!'

'I'm sure you do, but those are the rules.'

'Well, can you go get it for me, then?' I ask desperately. 'I can tell you exactly where it is.'

'I don't think so, darlin'. Look, ring up tomorrow. If you're lucky, it'll have been handed in.'

'Seriously? That's the best you can do?'

'That's the best I can do.'

'Well, thanks a lot.'

He shrugs. 'Just doing my job.'

I swear under my breath and wander back up the street. I take a left, then a right, then another right. I walk down street after street, each time thinking I must nearly be back at the hotel, each time winding up disappointed.

If only I had my phone. I could *kill* that stupid bouncer. But to do that I'd have to find my way back to the club and right now I have no idea what direction that is.

A drop of rain bounces off my scalp, making me flinch.

I look up at the sky. It's thick with clouds, the moon nowhere in sight.

Another drop of rain. This time it gets me right in the eye. Then another. And another. And another.

Until it's raining so hard I can barely see across the street.

Chapter 34

Jojo

'Maybe we should try ringing her again before we do anything,' Ram says as I gently guide Albie's legs into the carrier.

I still can't believe he's here. In my hotel room. Standing just a metre or so away from me. I've spent the entire year trying to convince myself that New Year's Eve was just a blip, a moment of madness masquerading as romance. To make doubly sure, I removed Ram's number from my phone, unfollowed him on Instagram and steered clear of his usual haunts. Any time he wriggled his way into my thoughts, I shoved him back before he could take hold. On the rare occasions Frankie brought him up in conversation, I did my best to gloss over it, although the guilt often made my attempts to change the subject a little clumsy. Not that Frankie noticed. That was perhaps almost the worst part – her complete lack of suspicion.

To an extent, my approach worked. As the months went on, it

got easier to separate myself from the events of New Year's Eve. It helped that I had other things to focus on – school work, *A Midsummer Night's Dream*, the Arts Academy audition. My focus shifted. The memory of New Year's Eve became hazy. I dreamed of Ram sometimes and it'd leave me in a strange mood all day, wistful and sad, but I'd do my best not to dwell, to stop my mind from going back there, and by and large I succeeded.

It's only now he's standing in front of me I realize how pointless my efforts were. Nothing has changed.

After everything that's happened, I still want him.

My stomach performs an involuntary somersault. I try to ignore it. I *have* to ignore it. Now is simply not the time for going down this road. I need to focus. I need to prioritize.

I *need* to talk to Frankie.

'Why is she suddenly going to pick up now?' I ask, trying not to meet Ram's eye.

'It's at least worth a try. She's had a bit of time to calm down.'

'I don't know . . .'

Frankie and I are best face to face. We always have been. I just need her in front of me. So I can explain, make her understand. Over the phone just isn't going to cut it.

'Maybe you should try from your phone,' Ram suggests.

But just the thought of turning my phone on after all this time makes me want to be sick.

'I can't,' I stammer.

'How come?' he asks.

'No battery.'

'OK, I'll try then.'

Ram takes out his phone, scrolling to Frankie's name.

I count the rings.

One, two, three, four, five . . .

The voicemail will kick in any second.

'Hello?' Ram says. 'Frankie?'

My eyes widen. She's answered?

'Who is this please? Where's Frankie?' Ram asks. 'Is she there?'

'Put it on speaker,' I say.

Ram does as I've asked.

It sounds like the call is coming from inside some sort of bar or nightclub.

'Frankie?' a girl's voice says. 'Who the hell is Frankie? This is Kristin's phone.'

'Kristin?' Ram mouths at me, his forehead knotted in confusion. 'Who's Kristin?'

'OK, Kristin then,' I say, grabbing the phone from Ram and bringing it closer to my face. 'Is she there?'

'No, she's chucking up in the loo.'

'Is she OK?' I ask.

'How should I know? She's been in there a while, though. Listen, who are you exactly?'

'I'm her best friend,' I say, my shoulders automatically rolling back. 'Who are you?'

There's a muffled silence on the other end of the line.

'Have they hung up?' Ram asks.

'I don't know. Hello? Hello? Is anyone there?'

After about ten seconds, the sound of the club or bar returns.

'Hello?' I repeat.

'If you know what's good for you, you'll leave Kristin alone,' the girl says.

'What?'

'You heard me. Slut.' This time she does hang up.

Blinking, I hand the phone back to Ram.

'What the fuck was that?' he asks. 'And who's Kristin?'

'Kristin is Frankie. It's a stage name she came up with years ago. Kristin Winters.'

Kristin Winters and Amelia Wylde.

'And who was that?'

'I haven't a clue. She didn't sound very nice, though.'

'No, she didn't.'

I bite down on my lip. 'We need to go get Frankie, Ram.'

'But we don't know where she is.'

'There can't be that many clubs or bars in walking distance that are still open at this time.'

'Yeah, but we can't just rock up at every late-night venue in town on the off-chance she'll be there.'

'Well, we can't just stay here. She might be in trouble. You know she can't handle her alcohol very well. What if she has an accident and hurts herself? Or someone takes advantage of her?' Panic rises in my voice.

'It's OK,' Ram says, the flicker of worry in his eyes betraying his confident delivery. 'We'll find her. I just don't think hitting clubs at random is our best option here . . .'

I sit down on the bed and Google clubs and bars in Swindon. There are literally dozens of listings. Ram is right, it'd be like finding a needle in a haystack.

'This is all my fault. This is all my fault,' I repeat, as I scroll through the listings, hoping intuition will kick in and I'll somehow just magically know where she is.

'No it isn't,' Ram says, his voice firm. 'Yes, this is a crazy situation, but it was Frankie's choice to storm off.'

'It doesn't matter. She would never have run off if it wasn't for me. I'm supposed to be her best friend . . .'

'That's it,' Ram says, cutting me off.

'What?'

'*Find Your Friends.*'

'What are you talking about?'

'The app. That's how Frankie knew where to find you. Do you still have it installed on your phone?'

'I don't know. I think so.' I retrieve my phone from where I shoved it to the very bottom of my bag and turn it on.

'I thought you said you were out of battery,' Ram says.

I ignore him, my hand trembling as the screen glows into life. Within seconds, notification after notification fills up the screen – missed calls and voicemails and messages. I minimize them all, scrolling through my apps until I find the *Find Your Friends* icon. I log in.

Within seconds, we have a location.

We're nearly at the club, Aphrodite's, when it begins to rain. It's just a few spots at first, but within less than a minute it's a deluge and we're forced to shelter in a shop doorway.

'We're wasting time,' I say, my body jangling with nerves as the rain falls down in sheets in front of us. 'The club's going to be closing soon.'

'But we'll get drenched,' Ram points out. 'I don't mind, but what about Albie?'

A crash of lightning makes Ram and I jump. Miraculously Albie, fast asleep against my chest, doesn't even stir.

'But what if she leaves before we get there?' I ask, my words almost drowned out by a menacing roll of thunder. 'She's all by herself, drunk and upset in a town she doesn't know . . .'

'Hang on,' Ram says.

He pulls off his T-shirt and slips it over my head so it covers Albie. The T-shirt smells of New Year's Eve. I shove the thought away. This is not the time for nostalgia. 'How's that?' he asks, his hands resting gently on my shoulders. 'It won't protect him completely but it might stop him from getting completely soaked.'

'It's perfect,' I say, trying not to look at Ram's bare torso, trying not to remember what it felt like against mine, skin on skin.

For a moment we stay like that, his hands on my shoulders, our eyes locked together.

'We should go,' I say.

Ram nods and removes his hands. 'Ready to make a run for it?' he asks.

'Ready.'

'No chance, last entry was at half one,' the bouncer tells us when we turn up at the entrance to the club a few minutes later, out of breath from our mad dash through the rain.

'But we have to come in,' I say, panting. 'My best friend is in there.'

The bouncer rolls his eyes. 'As sob stories go, I've heard better.'

'But we're really worried about her. Please, we won't be long.'

'Sorry, love. Even if it wasn't way past last admission, I couldn't let you in anyway.'

'Why not?'

'Mr Universe here,' he says, nodding at Ram's naked torso. 'Call us old-fashioned, but we prefer our punters fully dressed.'

'Hang on,' I say, pulling off the damp T-shirt and handing it back to Ram.

He tugs it on.

'Wait a second,' the bouncer says, squinting down at my chest. 'Is that a bleedin' baby?'

'Oh,' I say, taking a tiny step backwards and wrapping my arms protectively around the still-sleeping Albie. 'Yes.'

He throws back his head and laughs. 'I've seen it all now!' he says. 'You'll be wanting a family discount next.'

'Please,' Ram says. 'We just need to get to our friend. We called her phone and a stranger answered and we're worried she might be in some kind of trouble.'

The bouncer pauses. 'Hang on a second,' he says. 'This friend of yours, she got an accent like yours?'

'Yes,' Ram and I say in unison.

'Why?' I ask. 'Do you remember her coming in?'

'Maybe. It's just that a bit ago, some girl was trying to get back in the club, banging on about needing to get her phone or something.'

'A bit ago? Can you be more specific?'

'God, I dunno,' he says, pushing his hands through his thinning hair. 'Ten minutes ago, fifteen.'

'And what did she look like?' I demand. 'The girl?'

'How am I supposed to remember? Do you know how many people come through these doors? They all look the bloody same after a while.'

'Tall? Short? Dark? Fair?' Ram asks.

'Tall, I think. And dark . . .' The bouncer furrows his brow. 'Yeah. Dark. Bit exotic-looking maybe?'

'Italian?' I suggest.

'Yeah, now that I come to think of it, she might have had a touch of the Med about her.'

'OK, I'm pretty sure that's her,' I say.

'Oh. Well, in that case, you're not going to find her here.'

'What do you mean?'

'I sent her on her way.'

'What? Why?'

He taps the framed sign on the wall. 'No readmission after one thirty a.m.,' he says, rolling his eyes. 'It's not bleedin' rocket science.'

'But she's all by herself in a town she doesn't know,' I say.

The bouncer sighs a long weary sigh. 'Look, I know it sounds harsh, but that's not my problem. Once you're on the other side of this line' – he pauses to motion behind him – 'then you're my problem, but until then . . .'

I turn to Ram. 'Where do you think she's gone?'

'Back to the hotel?'

'I hope so. She's terrified of thunderstorms.'

Ram peers out into the street. The rain shows no absolutely no signs of stopping anytime soon. 'OK, how's this for a plan?' he asks. 'You wait here where it's dry. I'll go back to the hotel, pick up the car, and hopefully Frankie, then come back and get you and Albie. I should be fifteen minutes tops.'

A woman comes up the stairs. Like the bouncer, she's dressed all in black, a walkie-talkie clipped to her belt. She zones in on Albie immediately, her stern face melting into a wide smile. 'And who's this little stunner?' she asks.

'Er, Albie,' I say.

''Ello, Albie,' the woman says, stooping down so her face is level with his. 'I'm your auntie Kaz. Now, aren't you a cutie?' She straightens up and turns to the bouncer. 'What's going on?' she asks.

'Ask them two.'

'Our friend left here about ten minutes ago,' Ram explains. 'She's all by herself and we're worried about her. Would it be OK if my friend waited here while I go get her?'

'You must be joking,' the bouncer says. 'This is a nightclub, not a bleedin' crèche.'

'Oh, Alex,' Kaz says. 'You really are a miserable git sometimes.' She turns to me. 'Come with me, sweetheart. Auntie Kaz will sort you out.'

The cloakroom is down the stairs, just before the double doors leading into the club. On the other side I can hear the thump of music. The cloakroom attendant, a girl of around nineteen or twenty dressed in a toga, her hair a mass of thick black braids, is sitting in the kiosk window, hunched over a textbook. The rails behind her are largely empty.

'All right, Aisha,' Kaz says.

Aisha looks up, her forehead wrinkling with confusion at the sight of me and Albie at Kaz's side.

'This is . . .' Kaz pauses. 'Sorry, sweetheart, I never asked your name.'

'It's Jojo,' I say.

'Aisha, this is Jojo. Jojo and Albie. They need somewhere to hang out until this storm dies down. They OK to sit with you for a bit?'

'I guess so,' Aisha says, pulling a face. 'Hang on a sec, I'll just grab the door.' She abandons her textbook and disappears from view, reappearing a few seconds later in the door to the left of the kiosk window.

'Thanks, Aish,' Kaz says. 'You're a star. I'll be back in a bit.' She jogs back up the stairs, leaving Aisha and me facing one another.

'He yours?' she asks, nodding at Albie.

'Er, yeah.'

'How old are you?'

'Sixteen.'

'Sixteen?'

I nod.

'Mental.'

I don't really know what to say to that.

'You'd better come in,' Aisha says, standing aside, a wry expression on her face.

I smile tightly and squeeze past her into the cloakroom.

Chapter 35

Frankie

OK, I'm officially lost now. Not to mention soaked. It felt good at first. Refreshing. But now it just feels itchy and uncomfortable. I've always had a crap sense of direction but it's never failed me this badly before. Another flash of lightning slices across the sky, making me jump. I hate thunderstorms. I have ever since I was little and Luca told me that our dog Lola didn't die from a stroke like Mum and Dad said but had been struck by lightning. I had nightmares featuring an electrified Lola for months afterwards, no matter how many times Mum and Dad tried to reassure me that Luca had made the whole thing up.

I haven't seen another person for a while now, Every so often a car sails past but I've listened to far too many episodes of *My Favorite Murder* to even think about flagging one down. I make the executive decision to turn round and retrace my steps back towards the town centre. At least there'll be people around. And I know the name of the hotel. There must be someone who can direct me back there.

I don't see the step. Obviously. If I had, I wouldn't be sprawled chest down on the pavement right now. For a moment I just lie there, too shocked to do anything. I let out a moan and pull myself up onto all fours before staggering to my feet. Both knees are bleeding and my hands are grazed from where I put them out to break my fall. My chin hurts too. I touch it. It's wet. Is it bleeding? In the rain and the dark, it's hard to be sure.

'For fuck's sake!' I scream.

My words are swallowed up by the storm, which only increases my irritation.

I try again. Louder this time. And with my eyes shut and my arms outstretched to the sky. I must look like a mad woman but I don't care. It just feels good to let out everything out.

'Frankie!' My eyes spring open. 'Frankie!'

There it is again. My name. I squint through the driving rain.

I see his T-shirt first. Bright white. Then his distinctive walk. Confident (but never cocky), grown-up, the oldest teenager in town.

Ram.

My heart in my mouth, I limp towards him.

We stop a couple of metres apart from one another. For a few seconds we just stand there, separated by a thick sheet of rain.

'I'm sorry,' he shouts.

'What for?' I shout back. I want him to spell it out.

'For everything.'

I shake my head. 'Not good enough.' Nowhere near.

'For what happened with Jojo,' he says. 'And for not telling you about it. I didn't want to hurt you.'

Then why does it feel like it's ripping me apart right now?

'Do you love her?'

'What?'

'You heard me. Jojo. Do you love her?'

'No. I – I don't know.'

So, yes then.

Fuck. I feel like I've been punched in the stomach.

'Listen,' he says. 'I need you to know I didn't develop feelings for her until after we'd broken up. I swear to you, Frankie. It was New Year's Eve. We hung out and I dunno, something just switched—'

'It just switched?'

'Yeah. We were just talking and, I don't know, one second she was just Jojo and the next—'

You were falling for her.

Oh God, oh God.

'It was just that one time, that one night. This is the first time I've seen her since I—'

'Since you impregnated her?'

Ram visibly winces.

Good.

'Please don't do that,' he says.

'Do what?'

'Make it sound like that.'

'Like what?'

'Like it was something sordid.'

'Oh, I'm sorry,' I snap. 'Rose petals and candles, was it? Actually, don't answer that.'

'I'm sorry, Frankie.'

'Yeah, you said that already.' I can't have this conversation any more. It hurts too much.

'Come on,' Ram says. 'I'll walk you back to the club.'

'The club? What club?'

'Aphrodite's. Jojo's waiting there. I'll go get the car, then come pick you up.'

'No way.'

'Frankie.'

'I said no!' I yell.

'Please, Frankie. Jojo's worried about you.' He reaches for my arm.

'Well, tell her I'm fine,' I snarl, shaking him off.

'Only you're not, are you?' He gestures at my bleeding knees.

'What do you care?'

'I care a lot, Frankie. I know we're not together any more, but I still fucking care about what happens to you.'

'You had sex with my best friend,' I spit. 'And now she's had your baby and I just don't know if I can live with that, OK?'

'I know. And I'm sorry. But it happened and I can't change it. Any of it. It's all very new. To all of us. We need time to process things and—'

'Stop it!' I cry.

'What? Stop what?'

'Being so grown-up and reasonable.'

'How else do you want me to be?'

'Like a fucking human being!'

'I don't know what you mean, Frankie.'

'Yes, you do! It's the entire reason we didn't work out. Do

you know how hard it is? To constantly feel like the crazy one in almost every situation? Just because I have emotional reactions to things, just because I let myself actually *feel* stuff.' I smack my palm against my chest.

'I don't think you're crazy, Frankie.'

'Oh yeah? What about earlier then? At the rink? You pretty much laughed in my face.'

'That was different.'

'No, it wasn't. You were all "Frankie the drama queen, at it again".'

'But what you were saying, it sounded so . . . mad.'

'Madder than what we actually found?'

Ram opens his mouth then closes it again.

'Exactly!' I cry. 'You just don't get it, Ram. You make out I'm crazy, but has it ever dawned on you that I might be the normal one? Huh? You're so obsessed with being the good guy and fulfilling your dad's legacy or whatever, you're incapable of just letting go and having a genuine emotional reaction to anything. Everything's so measured and contained and *fucking sensible*.'

He lets out a laugh. 'Measured? Sensible? Do you seriously think I feel any of those things right now? Frankie, I just found out I have a three-week-old son. I'm fucking freaking out.'

'Then show it!'

'How?'

'I don't know! It's not up to me, is it? Scream! Shout! Do something! Just stop putting on this act all the time. Stop thinking you have to be so bloody perfect. You don't have to do that. Not in front of me, Jesus.'

There's a beat when Ram doesn't do anything.

'Go on then,' I yell, using both hands to push against his chest. 'Do it! I dare you!'

He flinches, and for a second I think he might actually allow himself to lose control for once.

'Do it!' I repeat. 'Do it!'

Another pause. I hold my breath. Ram opens his mouth.

'I'm taking you back to the club,' he says.

I almost burst out laughing.

'Oh my God, you can't, can you?' I say. 'You literally don't know how to let go. Even now, even after everything that's happened tonight.'

He sighs. It reminds me of the way teachers sigh at school when we're being too noisy or too slow to settle down – impatient and somehow above it all.

'I don't know what you want me to say, Frankie.'

But that's the whole point. I shouldn't have to tell him how to react. If he isn't going to get it now, he's never going to get it.

'Forget it,' I mutter, pushing past him. 'Seriously, just forget it, Ram.'

Chapter 36

Frankie

I walk back to the club in silence, my arms folded firmly across my chest. Ram doesn't try to initiate conversation and I'm glad. I'm sick of talking. I'm sick of being the only one to say what I'm thinking. I'm sick of going round in circles and being made to feel like the mad one, the out-of-order one, just because I have actual feelings and dare to express them. All I want to do is crawl into bed and wake up to discover this was all some weird-ass dream.

When we arrive back at Aphrodite's, the bouncer is leaning against the entrance, looking at his phone.

'The wanderer returns, eh?' he says when he sees us approaching. He slides his phone back into his pocket, his piggy eyes glinting with amusement.

'No thanks to you,' I mutter.

Luckily he doesn't seem to hear me. 'Your little mate and her kid are down in the cloakroom,' he says.

Ram turns to me. 'I won't be long.'

'What? What do you mean?'

He's leaving me here? Alone? With Jojo and the baby?

'Why don't I just come with you?' I ask.

Not that I especially want to hang out with Ram any more tonight. I'm just not sure I can handle seeing Jojo right now, never mind be stuck in a confined space with her.

'I'll be quick, I promise.'

Before I can argue, he's gone, sprinting back down the wet street.

'Cloakroom's at the bottom of the stairs,' the bouncer says.

'Thanks,' I murmur.

A pretty girl with braids is in charge of the cloakroom. She clocks my soaking dress and hair and pulls a face. I'm guessing I'm not exactly looking my best right now.

'Got your ticket?' she asks, holding out her hand.

'Ticket?'

'Don't worry, she's with me.' Jojo emerges from the gloom of the back of the cloakroom, the baby cuddled to her chest. The sight cuts through me like a knife.

My best friend and my ex-boyfriend had sex and now they have a baby together.

The cloakroom attendant looks from me to Jojo and back again.

'Can she come in?' Jojo asks.

The girl rolls her eyes but opens the door to the left of her little window.

I go inside, closing it behind me.

Jojo takes a step in my direction. She's chewing on her bottom lip, the way she always does when she's nervous. Under any other circumstances I'd give her a cuddle and a stern/inspiring pep talk – a 'Frankie special', she used to call them.

'Are you OK?' Jojo asks.

I shrug. 'Wet?'

'But apart from that?' she asks, her eyes bulging with concern.

I sigh and look away. 'I'm fine.'

She hovers in front of me, shifting the baby to the crook of her left arm, and I get the feeling she wants to hug me. I'm glad when she doesn't. I'm not ready for that. Not by a long shot.

'Where's Ram?' she asks.

It's clear she feels uncomfortable saying his name out loud. Or at least in front of me.

'Getting the car,' I reply. 'He shouldn't be long.'

'Is it still raining?'

I gesture at my soaking dress. 'What do you think?'

She presses her lips together and hands me a towel. 'Here, take this. Get dry.'

'Sorry, it's a bit damp,' she adds. 'I used it on Albie.'

'Albie?'

Her face flushes. 'Sorry, the baby.'

'Oh, right.'

Albie Bright? Albie Jandu? Albie Bright-Jandu? Albie Jandu-Bright? I half-heartedly rub at the lengths of my hair and stare into space.

The baby, Albie, starts crying. Jojo lifts him up so he's level with her face and sniffs his bottom. 'Sorry,' she says. 'I have to change him. Is it OK to do it in here, Aisha?'

'Whatever,' Aisha replies with a wave of her hand.

Jojo heads to the back of the cloakroom. Instinctively,

I follow her. She crouches down on the dingy carpet; Albie howls his lungs out, as she opens her backpack with her free arm. She pulls out a plastic changing mat, unfolding it and spreading it out in front of her. Carefully, she lays Albie on it and removes his nappy. It stinks. I can't help it; I purse my lips together and turn my face away. I watch out of the corner of my eye as Jojo reaches for a wipe, getting into all the nooks and crannies until Albie's bum is clean. She then wraps up the soiled nappy and slips it into a thin plastic bag, neatly knotting the ties and tossing it aside. Next comes a thick layer of nappy rash cream, then a fresh nappy, by which time Albie has stopped crying. It's weirdly mesmerizing. She makes it look so easy. Natural, even. Like she was born to do it.

I remove my hand from my face. 'You're good at this,' I say as she does up the poppers on Albie's sleepsuit.

'Am I?' she asks without looking up.

'Yeah. Like you've been doing it for ever.' Despite the compliment, my voice is flat.

She doesn't say anything, just sits back on her haunches as Albie stretches and wriggles on the mat, his movements jerky.

Man, he looks like Ram. How is that even possible? He's just a little baby. And yet, every feature screams his dad. Apart from his eyes. Alert and watchful, even at just three weeks old, they're pure Jojo.

I still can't get my head around the fact that he grew in Jojo's belly. I think of all those hours we spent together, oblivious to his presence inside her. I picture us on stage in *A Midsummer Night's Dream*, tearing about the set as Helena and Hermia, Albie tucked beneath Jojo's ribs the entire time, growing silently, stealthily.

'Did it hurt?' I blurt out.

'What?'

'Giving birth. Did it hurt? Or is that a ridiculous question?'

'Yes, it hurt.'

'A lot?'

I think of the play we did in Year Ten – *Be My Baby*. It was set in the 1960s, in a home for unmarried mothers. I played Queenie, the mouthy one. Jojo was Mary, the posh new girl. At the end of the play, Mary gives birth. In preparation, Jojo and I watched loads of episodes of *One Born Every Minute* as research. I remember hiding behind my fingers while Jojo made careful notes, filling up page after page with her neat handwriting.

She pauses before answering. 'It was like no pain I've ever experienced before.'

I know she means it too. I've witnessed Jojo trap her fingers in the car door and barely make a whimper. If she says giving birth hurt, then it must have been agony.

'Didn't they give you anything for it?'

'They?'

'At the hospital. Don't they have drugs they can give you?'

'I didn't have him at hospital. I had him at home.'

'What?'

'Remember those period pains I was having?'

I do. I remember coming out of Lidl with my grandma and reading her texts.

'Was anyone with you? Your mum or anything?'

Jojo shakes her head.

'So you were all on your own?' I ask, my voice almost a whisper.

She nods.

'Shit.'

Her lips curl into an almost-smile. 'Yeah, it kind of was.' She reaches for her bag and begins to pack Albie's nappy stuff away. Even though she looks like the same old Jojo on the outside, something has shifted, something I can't quite put my finger on. That's when it properly hits me – she's someone's mum now and no matter how many questions I ask, I'm never going to understand what that feels like or how that might change a person. The realization makes me feel stupid and childish.

'Am I the reason you ran away?' I ask. I hate how small my voice sounds.

Jojo blinks in surprise. 'What? No. Why would you think that?'

'I don't know. I just . . . All this massive stuff has happened to you, Jojo, and I feel like I'm the last one to know.'

'It's not you, Frankie.'

'Then who is it? Ram?'

She shakes her head.

'Who then?'

She hesitates.

'Who, Jojo?'

She swallows hard before speaking. 'Mum and Stacey,' she says. 'I ran away from Mum and Stacey.'

Chapter 37

Jojo

I don't know how long it takes me to explain everything to Frankie, only that she doesn't interrupt once. She just lets me talk, the two frown lines between her eyes deepening with every new detail I reveal.

When I've finished speaking, she doesn't say anything for ages.

'They can't force you to give him up, you know that, don't you?' she says finally.

'Maybe it's for the best,' I say automatically.

'Says who?' Frankie demands.

I hesitate.

'Your mum and Stacey?' she says. 'Well, of course they're gonna say that.'

'But what if they're right?' I say. 'I'm sixteen. I don't have a clue how to raise a baby, not really. I certainly can't do it and be an actor at the same time.'

'Why not? Loads of people juggle kids and careers. Why does it have to be one or the other?'

'Who would look after him all day?'

'Couldn't your mum and Stacey do it?'

'They have jobs.'

'I know they do. But from what you're saying, they're perfectly willing to shift things around so *they* can raise him, which means they're also capable of helping you out.'

'But that's the thing. They're prepared to make all these sacrifices for their own baby. Can I really expect them to give up so much for a baby that's not even theirs?'

'It's not like they're not related. He's their grandkid, remember?'

'But they don't want a grandson. They want a child of their own.'

'That might be the case, but the fact is, he isn't theirs, he's yours.'

I shake my head. 'It's too late. I agreed.'

'Jojo, you'd literally just given birth. You'd barely had time to get your head around the fact you had a baby full stop, never mind agree to something as huge as giving him away. It wasn't fair for them to ambush you like that. You had no idea what you were signing up for.'

I frown. It hadn't felt like an ambush. It had felt well-meaning and loving. *That doesn't make it right*, a voice at the back of my head whispers.

'And all that "let's keep it between the three of us" stuff,' Frankie continues. 'They had no right to say that. No right at all.'

'It's too late,' I say. 'I've had three weeks to pull out of the arrangement and I haven't. I can't just take him away from them, not after all this time.'

Stacey has already cleared out the spare room (formerly the office) for Albie's nursery – painting the walls a soft powder blue and installing a mobile over his cot.

'Yes, you can!' Frankie cries. *'He's your baby*, Jojo, and if you want him, if you want to be his mum, you need to stand up and say so. Now is not the time to be bloody polite.'

'It's not that easy. You haven't seen them with him. They're besotted. I swear, I've never seen Stacey look so happy.' She's been floating around with a smile a mile wide on her face ever since we got home from hospital.

Frankie takes a deep breath. 'Jojo, listen to me. I like Stacey. I've always liked Stacey, but you are not responsible for her happiness. Or your mum's. Especially not at the cost of your own.'

'But they'd be devastated, Frankie,' I whisper.

She shrugs. 'Maybe they will, maybe they won't, but however they feel, it won't be your fault, Jojo.'

'How can it not be? I'm the reason they couldn't have a baby together in the first place, and now I'm thinking about taking one away from them.'

'First of all, Albie is not their baby; he never was. Second of all, you are not the reason they couldn't have a baby.'

'Yes, I am, Frankie,' I say. 'If I hadn't been such a difficult birth, Mum would have been able to have more kids, and I'm the reason they couldn't get IVF on the NHS.'

Frankie shakes her head hard. 'No, Jojo,' she says fiercely. 'I'm not having that. You are not to blame for any of this.'

So why can't I escape the guilt pushing down on me? Whichever way I look at it, Mum's and Stacey's happiness is within my control.

'Is that why you agreed to it?' Frankie asks, her voice a little gentler now. 'Did you think letting them have Albie would make up for things somehow?'

'Partly,' I admit.

Frankie sighs, pushing her fingers through her still damp hair. 'Jojo, it sucks that your mum and Stacey can't have kids of their own, but it's not up to you to put that right.'

I close my eyes. I know she's talking sense. But where does that leave me? Everything is such a jumble. The only thing I'm entirely sure of right now is my unwavering love for the tiny human being currently nestled against my chest.

'There's a reason you ran away, Jojo,' Frankie says. 'If you were as hunky-dory with this plan as it sounds like your mum and Stacey have convinced themselves you are, you would be home right now, happily playing big sister and getting on with your life. You certainly wouldn't be holed up in a nightclub cloakroom in Swindon.'

I hesitate. Because once again she's right.

'Does your dad know?' Frankie asks.

'No.'

'Would he be able to help out?'

'I don't know. I doubt it. He's on the road half the time . . .'

'But if you told him, he'd step up, surely.'

'I don't know.'

'Ram's mum, then?'

I don't understand why she's trying to help. Two hours ago she stormed out of the hotel room saying she never wanted to see me again. 'Why are you being so kind to me?' I ask.

She wrinkles up her nose. 'What kind of stupid-ass question is that?'

I'm asking because I'm afraid you might hate me.

I don't say this, though – I'm too afraid of her response – so I just shake my head.

We sit in silence for a few moments. On the other side of the wall, the music has stopped and the clubbers are beginning to leave, stumbling past the cloakroom and up the stairs, laughing and singing and shouting.

'What happened to us?' Frankie asks quietly as Aisha distributes the last few jackets.

'What do you mean?'

'We used to tell each other everything.'

'I know.'

'So what went wrong? Why did you stop?'

I hesitate. Because I know exactly why I stopped. And when. On the first of January. 'I didn't want to hurt you,' I say.

'I'm not just talking about what happened with Ram.'

'Oh.'

'There's the whole thing with the Arts Academy too.'

'What about it?' I ask carefully.

'After the letters came through, we never really talked about it. Not properly. Why?'

'I – I don't know.'

'Did you ever even consider turning your place down?'

For a moment I consider bending the truth, before dismissing the idea. I've had enough of lying.

'No,' I admit. 'Not seriously.'

Frankie blinks and I get the feeling she's surprised by the frankness of my answer.

'Sorry,' I add quickly.

'I asked,' she says with a shrug.

She's styling it out, but I know Frankie and I'm not buying her nonchalance. 'It's not like I didn't think about the implications,' I say. 'Or worry about how you'd feel about me taking up the place. I did. Loads. It's just that just every time I thought about turning it down, I knew I'd regret it for ever.' I pause, adjusting my grip on Albie. 'The truth is, I genuinely didn't think I'd get in,' I say. 'Not in a trillion years.'

I remember coming out of my audition, all those months ago, so sure I'd messed up. When Frankie bounced out of hers an hour or so later, she tried to downplay how well it had clearly gone for my benefit and I'd loved her for it. Never for one minute did I consider the possibility that I was the one who had shone in there.

'I was so shocked, I called them up to make sure,' I add.

'What?'

'The day after I got my letter, I rang to double-check there hadn't been some sort of mistake, that they hadn't mixed me up with someone else.'

'You're joking me?'

I shake my head. 'It wasn't until I spoke to someone who'd actually been on the audition panel and remembered me that I started to believe I'd got the place fair and square, and even then it took ages to properly sink in. Once it did, I knew there was no way I could turn my back on the place. You're a star, Frankie. Everyone says so. I know this probably sounds like bullshit but you don't need the Arts Academy.'

'And you do?'

'I think so, yeah. The thing is, they saw something in me, some-thing they could work with. They saw past my nerves and decided I was worth taking a chance on. And that meant everything to me . . .' I let my voice trail off. It feels almost perverse talking about the Arts Academy when literally everything else in my life is so up in the air.

'You never said any of this,' Frankie says quietly.

'I know.'

'Why not?'

'I felt weird about it. Like I'd be rubbing your nose in it or something. The Arts Academy was our thing, this shared dream for such a long time. After I got in, I just didn't know how to talk about it with you, and you never brought it up so I decided it would be best if I just kept quiet.'

In the months since we'd received our letters, by silent mutual agreement, the Arts Academy had become our very own 'Voldemort'. I'd hidden my excitement, and in exchange Frankie had hidden her own feelings about it so well I'd conveniently been able to trick myself into believing she couldn't have cared all that much about it in the first place.

'Jojo,' Frankie says.

'Yeah?'

'Will you promise me something?'

'What?'

'I want you to promise me that you'll always tell me what's on your mind, even if it might hurt me or piss me off.'

'OK,' I say slowly.

'I mean it, Jojo. You've got to promise me. And I'll do the same. Starting right now. She takes a deep breath. 'I'm gutted I didn't get into the Arts Academy, Jojo, and I don't know when I'll stop feeling gutted about it. Maybe never.'

I bite down hard on my lip.

'And that's not all. It kills me that you and Ram have this baby together. Because it tethers you to each other for ever and there's no way I can compete with that. And I know it's stupid to feel that way. Ram and I didn't work as a couple, and that's a fact. For fuck's sake, I was the one who suggested we break up, but just knowing all this doesn't magically stop me from feeling jealous, from feeling like whatever we had, even though it's most definitely over, is tarnished somehow. And it doesn't stop me from wanting him to still want me. It's idiotic, I know, but it's how I feel.'

'It's not idiotic,' I say. 'It makes complete sense. He was a big part of your life for a proper chunk of time. The memory of that doesn't just disappear.'

'But it'll fade. It already has. But thanks to Albie, you and Ram, you have a bond for life now. And I'm not part of that, and it hurts. And I need you to know that I don't have a clue how I'm going to process all of this. It might not be pretty. In fact, it might get really bloody ugly. But I'm going to promise you that I'll always be honest going forward.'

Her eyes meet mine. They're full of tears. All I want to do is hug her and make everything all right. I know I can't, though, at least not the second bit.

'OK,' I say.

'And I want you do to the same. No more secrets.'

'I promise.'

'Pinky promise?' She holds out her little finger. I lock it with mine. Just like old times.

'Pinky promise,' I confirm.

Chapter 38

Ram

As I walk back to the hotel, the rain beating down on my back, frag-
ments of my conversation with Frankie keep playing on loop inside
my head.

What was it she said?

That I was incapable of letting go? Of having an emotional
reaction to anything?

What a joke. In fact, she's so far off the mark, it's unbelievable.
Just because I know how to hold myself together doesn't mean I
don't know how to express emotion.

You haven't cried since the night your dad died, a voice inside my
head says.

That isn't relevant, I hiss back. I had a job to do. I had to look after
Mum and Laleh and Rox. Be strong for them. Make Dad proud. I
didn't have time to cry, OK? I didn't have that luxury.

No one told me this was what I had to do. No one took me

aside and gave me a pep talk about how I was the 'man of the house' now and that my mum and sisters would be relying on me. The opposite. Every day in those first few weeks after Dad died, people went out of their way to reassure me. They told me it was OK to cry, to mourn, to let things slide if I needed to, to go easy on myself. It was me who decided to ignore every bit of their advice, me who decided what was and wasn't an appropriate way to behave. And my instincts were right. Nearly three years on, there's a reason Mum and Laleh and Rox are thriving. And no, I don't for even one second think that's all down to me, but the way I've handled things must count for some of it, right?

As I approach the car, I reach into the right-hand pocket of my shorts for my keys. They're not there. I check the other pockets, patting them in turn. No keys.

That's when I remember. They're in the front pocket of my bag, up in the hotel room.

I sprint back into the hotel.

In the foyer, Reece is nowhere to be seen. A woman is sitting in his place, her white-blonde hair pulled back into an aggressively tight ponytail.

'Sorry, we're full,' she says, barely glancing at me.

'I'm not after somewhere to stay,' I say. 'I need a spare key card for room four-two-six.'

She consults her computer. 'And you are?'

'Er, Ram. Ramin Jandu.'

'Are you on the booking?'

'No. My friend is. Jojo Bright. Wait, no, sorry, it's Amelia, er, Amelia . . . someone.'

The woman frowns.

'Amelia someone?' she repeats.

'Amelia's not her real name,' I say. 'Jojo Bright is. Please, I need to get into the room. My car keys are in there.'

'No can do,' the woman replies. 'I can only deal with the person named on the booking and that is plainly not you.'

'But I need my keys.'

'In that case, I suggest you ask your friend, this "Amelia Someone", to help you.'

'I can't. She's not here. I need my car so I can pick her up.'

The woman sighs. 'I'm sorry, young man, but there's nothing I can do. Now, if you'd kindly step outside, you're dripping all over the tiles.'

I think about arguing my case, but something in the woman's demeanour tells me I'd be wasting my time. I mutter my thanks and head back out into the rain.

I return to the car, on the off-chance I acted totally out of character earlier and forgot to lock it. I didn't, though. Of course I didn't.

I sigh and give the front wheel a half-hearted kick. Almost immediately I realize my mistake. It's too late, though; the alarm has already gone off, its ear-splitting squeal filling the street.

Fuck.

Fuck, fuck, fuck.

How could I be such an idiot? I lectured Frankie about how sensitive the alarm is literally just a few hours ago.

If I had the key, I could turn it off in seconds. Without it, I don't have the foggiest how to get the noise to stop.

I let out a howl of frustration and kick the wheel again. Harder this time.

How about that, Frankie? That enough of a reaction for you?

I picture her watching me, her arms folded across her chest, her head cocked to one side, unmoved and unimpressed.

Well, I'll show her.

I kick the wheel again, booting my foot against the tyre with as much power as I can muster.

What about that then? 'Emotional' enough for your super-high standards, Ms Ricci?

Panting, I pace back and forth on the pavement, my heart hammering in my chest, anger bubbling in my belly.

I want it out of me.

I take a few steps back before chucking my entire body against the side of the car.

Slam.

It hurts.

I like that it hurts.

I stagger back and do it again, hitting the car with such force I almost bounce back off it, the soles of my trainers skidding against the wet paving slabs.

More. I want more.

I do it again.

And again and again and again.

I keep doing it until my body is aching and I can't see straight.

I don't care, though. I couldn't stop now even if I wanted to. It's like I've been possessed, the anger and frustration and hurt I've been bottling up for God knows how long spurting out of me with every howl, every swear word, every kick, every body slam.

I don't see the blue flashing lights.

I don't hear the shouts or footsteps.

I don't even properly register the hands on my body until I'm being dragged from the screeching car and shoved up against the brick wall, the rough clay scraping my right cheek and ear.

'Calm down,' a voice says as I continue to thrash.

Calm down? Is he joking me?

Then comes the sensation of cool metal as a pair of handcuffs is snapped onto my wrists.

'You are under arrest on suspicion of criminal damage. You do not have to say anything, but it may harm your defence if you do not mention when questioned something which you later rely on in court. Anything you do say may be given in evidence.'

Finally, my brain catches up with what's happening.

'Wait,' I cry. 'Stop! It's *my* car!'

The police officer's grip on me loosens slightly. My hands still cuffed behind my back, I shuffle around to face him. He's tall and broad with a closely shaven head.

'If it's your car, then why were you throwing yourself at it like a maniac?' he asks, folding his arms across his chest.

'I'm locked out.'

He laughs. 'Well, that's certainly convenient.'

'I'm telling the truth, I swear. I'm supposed to be picking my friends up.'

He sighs. 'Got any ID?'

'Er, yeah. In my wallet. Back pocket.'

'OK if I grab it?'

'Yeah.'

He reaches into my pocket and pulls out my wallet, flipping it open. I see a flash of the photo of me, Mum, Dad, Laleh and Roxy I keep in the front. What would they think if they could see me now? I don't even want to think about it.

'Ramin Jandu, eh?' the police officer says, studying my driving licence.

'Yes.'

'I'm going to need to run a check on this.'

'Fine.'

He unclips his radio from his belt and turns away from me. 'Control room, can you run a PNC for me? Licence plate is . . .'

While I wait, I stare at my car. My beloved car, the one I've been saving up for since I was about ten years old, all covered in dents. Dents that I made. What the hell was I thinking? But I suppose that was the whole point. For maybe the first time in years, I wasn't.

After a few minutes, the police officer slides his radio back onto his belt. Without saying anything, he gestures for me to turn around and removes the handcuffs. 'The details matched up,' he says as I shake out my wrists. 'You're free to go.'

'That's it?' I say. 'I'm not arrested any more?'

'You're not arrested any more,' he confirms.

I nod, flexing my wrists. It's a curious anti-climax.

'You're bleeding,' the policeman says.

'What?'

'Your hand. It's bleeding.'

I look down. The knuckles on my left hand are covered with blood.

'It needs bandaging,' he says.

'It's fine,' I murmur. 'Really.'

He shakes his head but walks back to his car.

I sink down on the kerb. It's only then I realize the alarm has stopped. I stare at my feet. My Converse, box-fresh and brilliant white at the beginning of the evening, are soaked and streaked with dirt.

'Hey,' a voice calls out.

I look up.

It's the police officer, the passenger door of his patrol car flung open. 'Let me bandage up your hand.'

'Seriously, I'm OK.'

'No, you're not. Now, just get in. Please.'

I look back down at my hand. Even with the rain pelting down and washing it away, the blood keeps oozing. The scary part is, I don't even remember doing it.

'It might save you a visit to A&E,' the police officer adds.

That does the trick. A long wait at the hospital is the last thing I need tonight.

I push myself to my feet and get in the car. 'I'm going to get the seat all wet,' I say, shutting the door behind me.

'Don't worry about it. I'm Andy, by the way.'

'Er, hi.'

'And you're Ramin, right?'

'Yeah. Most people just call me Ram, though.'

'Ram it is, then. Now hold out your hand.'

I do as I'm told.

Andy starts by cleaning my knuckles with an antiseptic wipe. 'That sting?' he asks.

It does but I shake my head. The last time I had any sort of interaction with a police officer was the night my dad died. I can still conjure up his face – craggy yet kind, with pale blue eyes and flecks of white in his reddish beard. I saw him again about a year later, laughing with a female colleague in the street. It was weird to see him smiling and sharing a joke, weird to see that he existed outside the realms of my grief-stricken house. Without really thinking about it, I raised my hand in greeting, and he responded with the bland blank smile of someone who doesn't have a clue who you are. I didn't mind, though. He was kind when it mattered and that would do for me.

'Now, here's a question,' Andy says as he begins to bandage my hand. 'What's a decent-seeming kid like you doing bashing up his car, and a pretty nice car at that?'

'I don't know.'

Andy raises an eyebrow. 'You don't know?'

'No,' I murmur, tracking the progress of three separate raindrops as they slide down the windscreen.

'So you just started chucking yourself at your car for no reason?' Andy says.

'Pretty much.'

'Right.'

He's clearly not buying it and I don't blame him. Nothing about my explanation adds up.

'Did something happen tonight?' he asks. 'Something to make you kick off like that?'

I don't say anything.

'Look, Ram, you're under no obligation to talk to me, but you never know, getting whatever's gone on tonight off your chest might just help. I mean, it's not going to make things worse, is it?'

'I found out I was a dad tonight,' I say, before I can talk myself out of it.

'Congratulations.'

I don't say anything.

'I'm taking it, it came as a surprise,' Andy says.

'You could say that.'

'It's been a lot to get your head round, huh?'

I nod. 'Do you have kids?' I ask.

'I do. Two. Samuel and Kiera. What have you got? A boy? A girl?'

'A boy,' I say. 'Albie.'

'Nice.' He finishes bandaging my hand. 'That OK?' he asks. 'Tight enough?'

'Yeah, great. Thank you.'

He's done a good job.

'So, what's the story?' he asks, putting the lid back on the first aid kit.

'The story?'

'I'm assuming there's a story here. There generally is where kids are involved.'

'Yeah, there's a story.'

'Want to tell it to me?'

I hesitate. I wouldn't even know where to begin.

'How about you start by telling me what you're doing in Swindon,' Andy says, like he's reading my mind. 'And we can go from there.'

And so I do. I tell him about Frankie turning up at the rink with her crazy theory about Jojo and Olivia Sinclair; I tell him about our journey down here and the moment Frankie emerged from the lift and slapped me; I tell him about New Year's Eve and how I've spent most of this year trying (and failing) not to think about it; I tell him about going up to Jojo's hotel room and the moment everything clicked into place; I tell him about Albie, about how amazing he is and how my brain is still trying to wrap itself around the fact that he's mine, that Jojo and I made him together; I tell him about my argument with Frankie in the street; I tell him about Dad, about what a great bloke he was, and how I miss him every single day but hardly ever admit it out loud; I tell him about Mum and Laleh and Roxy and my hopes and dreams for them.

At first I'm self-conscious and hesitant, relying on Andy's questions and prompts, but soon the words are pouring out of me and Andy is able to just sit back and listen. And when I cry for the first time in over two and a half years, he just places his hand on my shoulder and lets me, not saying a word.

Chapter 39

Jojo

I wake up nose to nose with Frankie. I'd forgotten how peaceful she looks when she sleeps, even with smudged eyeliner and a big fat graze on her chin. Her face is soft and serene, her eyelids smooth, her lips gently parted, her hair curly from the rain.

The room is silent. The storm must have finally passed.

I wonder what time it is. I sit up. Ram's makeshift bed on the floor is empty.

'Over here,' a voice says.

I look to my right.

Ram is sitting on the floor next to Albie's cot.

It was gone 3 a.m. when he turned up at the club, full of apologies, his hand in a bandage. His car keys locked in the hotel, we ended up getting a cab, all four of us stuffed in the back seat, silent with exhaustion.

Back at the hotel, I'd fallen asleep the moment my head hit

the pillow, all the sleepless nights of the past few weeks finally catching up with me.

'Hey,' I say softly.

'Hey.'

'How long have you been up?' I ask.

'A while,' he replies. 'I couldn't really sleep.'

'What time is it?'

He checks his phone. 'Just before seven.'

'He'll be awake soon,' I say, nodding at Albie.

'Yeah?'

'Yeah. For his feed. He'll go back down after it, though.'

Ram nods.

We sit in silence for a few moments, our eyes trained on Albie as his chest rises and falls. I glance at Ram. He's transfixed.

I have so much I want to express but no idea what to say first. It all feels too huge to even consider putting into words.

'Look at his eyes,' Ram says. 'The way they're flickering. Do you think he's dreaming?'

'Yeah, maybe,' I say, drawing my knees up under my chin and wrapping my arms around my legs.

'What about, do you reckon?'

'Milk,' I say decisively.

Ram smiles and looks back down at Albie, wonder in his eyes. 'He's amazing,' he says.

'I know.'

'I can't stop looking at him.'

I smile. I'm familiar with that feeling.

'I'm serious,' Ram says. 'I've been staring at him for like an hour now and I legit haven't got bored.'

I tell him about the night I went up to the Special Care Baby Unit, how I held Albie for so long my arm went dead.

'He was poorly when he was born?' Ram asks, his eyes soft with concern.

'Low blood sugar,' I explain. 'It was easy to fix, though. He was on the ward with me within a day.'

'There's so much I don't know,' Ram says.

'I know. I'm sorry. And I'm sorry you had to find out like this,' I add.

He considers this for a moment. 'At least I know now,' he says. 'That's the important thing, right?'

'I guess.'

There's a pause.

'Frankie told me about your mum and stepmum.'

'She did?' I ask, swallowing hard.

'Yeah. Last night. You were asleep.'

'You must think I'm the worst person in the world,' I say.

He frowns. 'Don't be stupid. I mean, the idea of you going through with it is awful, but I get why you were tempted.'

'You do?'

'Yeah. A baby is a big deal and what they were suggesting must have sounded appealing, especially at first, when everything was brand-new and extra-scary.'

'I wouldn't have gone through with it,' I say. I think I knew this all along, deep down, but it feels a relief to admit it out loud.

Ram smiles up at me. 'I know. And I'm glad. We're in this together.'

'Are you sure?'

He looks confused. 'Of course. Why do you ask?'

'But what about uni and stuff? What about becoming a lawyer?'

I remember our conversation back in the utility room on New Year's Eve – the way Ram's chest puffed out and his voice glittered with pride when he talked about his career plans.

'I can still go to uni and be a dad at the same time. Just like you can still go to the Arts Academy and be a mum.'

He makes it sound so simple, so manageable, like it's just a matter of sorting out a few logistics.

'You really think we can make it work?' I ask.

'Why? Don't you?'

'I don't know,' I admit. 'I like to think I can do anything but . . .' My voice trails off.

'I know it's not going to be easy,' Ram says. 'It's going to be really fucking hard work and we're not going to be able to do it alone, but we're smart people, Jojo. Surely we can make this work if we put our minds to it.'

'You know,' I say slowly, 'I didn't realize it at the time, but I think part of the reason I took off with Albie yesterday was to test myself.'

Ram cocks his head to one side. 'How do you mean?'

'To see if I could do it – if I could look after Albie all by myself. Mum and Stacey have spent the last three weeks telling me it's impossible, that I'd be hopeless without them. I guess I wanted to prove them wrong, prove myself wrong.'

'And? Have you?'

'I think I've done an OK job.'

Ram glances at Albie then looks back up at me. 'I think you've done more than an OK job, Jojo.'

I shrug, embarrassed by his praise.

'I mean it,' he says. 'You've been really brave.'

'I don't feel brave. If I'm honest, I feel like I've spent the last three weeks in a near-constant state of terror.'

'Isn't that kind of the point, though? It only counts as bravery if it scares the shit out of you.'

I smile gratefully.

'Can I ask you a question?' he adds.

'Sure.'

'If you'd found out you were pregnant earlier, say within the first few months or something, what would you have done, do you think? Would you have gone through with it?'

I hesitate. Mainly because this is something I've thought about a lot since Albie was born.

'You don't have to answer if you don't want to,' Ram says when I don't respond right away.

'No, no, it's fine,' I say. 'Honestly? No, I don't think I would have gone through with it. In fact, scrap that, I know I wouldn't. And that's been kind of hard to get my head around, because right now I can't imagine life without Albie in it, but the fact is, I never planned on getting pregnant at sixteen. And I think that's OK, you know? For both those things to be true at the same time; for both paths to be right.'

He nods.

'I would have told you,' I add. 'Whatever I decided to do, I would have wanted you to be a part of it.'

'And I would have supported you,' he replies.

'I know.'

'Can I ask you another question?' he adds.

'OK.'

'It's about his name. Why did you choose Albie? Don't get me wrong, I like it, it really suits him, I'm just curious as to why you picked it. I mean, it's not like it's really common or anything.'

Picking the name was one of the few things Mum and Stacey

let me have ownership of. In hindsight, part of me wonders if it was compensation, a little something to keep me sweet.

'After all,' Stacey said when I revealed I'd already come up with a name, 'lots of older siblings help pick their little brother or sister's names.' Just the memory of her saying this makes me wince.

'Jojo?' Ram prompts. 'You OK?'

'Sorry,' I say. 'In my own world for a second there.'

'That's all right.'

'The truth is,' I say slowly, 'I named him after your dad.'

'My dad? What do you mean?'

'Albie. It's short for Albanaz.'

Ram's entire face slackens and for a moment I'm worried I've made a terrible mistake. 'Seriously?' he says.

I nod, my cheeks heating up once more. 'Is that . . . OK?'

He pumps his head up and down. 'Jojo, it's . . . it's perfect.'

Right on time, Albie begins to stir. I let Ram go ahead and pick him up, sitting on the bed and watching as Ram cuddles him to his chest. Together, we prepare his bottle and change his nappy. And it feels nice to have him by my side. More than nice.

For maybe the first time since Albie was born, I don't feel like I'm doing this alone.

Chapter 40

Frankie

We've been on the road for about half an hour. Jojo and Albie are asleep in the back – Albie and his cuddly Paddington Bear snuggled in a hastily purchased baby seat from the local branch of Mothercare, Jojo next to him, her head resting against the window.

Ram and I are up front. I'm back on navigational duties, Ram's phone nestled in the palm of my hand. I never did get my phone back. I'd hoped it would get handed in at the club, but no such luck. Mum's going to go mad. It'll be the third time she's had to make an insurance claim because of me 'being careless'. I can't bring myself to get too stressed about her reaction, though, not when Jojo has her mum and Stacey to face.

'Mind if I wind my window down a bit?' I ask.

'Go for it,' Ram replies.

It's the sort of day Mum would describe as 'fresh'. The sky

is clear and there's a slight chill in the air following last night's almighty storm. I let down my ponytail and allow the breeze to air-dry my slightly damp hair.

I down the dregs of my takeaway coffee and lean back in my seat. I can't believe it's barely twelve hours since I was last sitting here, convinced my best friend had kidnapped Olivia Sinclair. It seems ridiculous now, of course. Not that I'm about to admit this to Ram.

When I woke up this morning, he and Jojo were cooing over Albie together, their shoulders touching – Mummy and Daddy in action. I'm not going to lie, seeing that hurt. When they realized I was awake, they broke apart straightaway, which somehow only made things worse, like I was interrupting something private, intimate, something I have no chance of ever truly being a part of. Ram jumped up and volunteered to go on a coffee and pastries run, leaving Jojo and me alone.

'Seeing the two of you doing the whole parenting thing is going to take a lot of getting used to,' I told her as she began packing up Albie's things.

'I know. I'm sorry.'

'Don't be. It's not about being sorry any more. It's about being honest, remember?'

She nodded.

'What about you?' I asked, hugging a pillow to my chest. 'How are you feeling about seeing your mum and Stacey later?'

She stopped folding. 'Terrified,' she said.

'You're doing the right thing.'

'I know I am. It still feels terrifying, though.'

'But they love you.'

'I know. But they love Albie too.'

'It's not like they're never going to see him.'

'I know, I—' She looked away and I got the sense she was finding the prospect of returning to Newfield even scarier than she was letting on. 'I might get a shower if that's OK,' she said, standing up.

'OK.'

'Do you want to hold Albie while I'm in there?'

At that point, he was on the floor, lying on his changing mat.

I leaned backwards. 'Er, I dunno. You know how crap I am with babies.'

'You'll be fine.'

She ordered me to sit on the bed with my back against the headboard, before gently lowering Albie into my arms, his head nestled in the crook of my right arm.

'He's really warm,' I exclaimed.

'I know. Like a human hot water bottle,' Jojo said, grabbing a towel and heading towards the bathroom.

'What if he cries while you're in there?' I called after her.

'He won't,' she replied.

And she was right. He didn't make a peep the entire time I was holding him.

I glance over at Ram. He looks shattered. Handsome (as always) but utterly shattered.

'What are you going to do about your shift at the rink?' I ask.

'I've pulled a sickie.'

'Let me guess, your first ever?'

'How did you know?'

I roll my eyes. 'Once a goodie-two-shoes, always a goodie-two-shoes.'

He smiles.

It feels good to be joking around with each other again, even if it does feel a little forced. 'I'm sorry,' I say. 'About what I said last night in the street. I was angry and upset and I took it out on you. You're not incapable of expressing emotion or whatever I said. You were right. We're just different. We always were.'

'No, you were speaking the truth,' Ram replies.

I raise an eyebrow. 'What do you mean?'

He takes a deep breath. 'You know the damage to the car?'

'Yeah.' We'd returned to Ram's car this morning to discover it covered with dents.

'I know who did it.'

My eyes widen. 'Who?'

'Me.'

'What?'

'I'm the one who damaged the car.'

'But that makes literally no sense.'

'I know. It's the truth, though. How do you think I got this?' He holds up his bandaged hand.

'But I thought that was an accident.' He'd told us he'd slipped in the rain.

'Nope. All self-inflicted.'

'But why? Why would you do that?' I just can't imagine it. After Jojo, Ram is one of the most self-disciplined people I know.

He sighs. 'Like I said, you were right. OK, so maybe I'm not totally incapable of expressing emotion but I do keep stuff bottled up to save face or to protect other people and, I dunno, last night, everything kind of hit me all at once and I just . . . lost it for a bit.'

'Shit, Ram,' I murmur, unable to remove the utterly bizarre image of him trashing his car from my head.

'I know. Stupid, right? I mean, what kind of idiot attacks their own car?'

'No,' I say. 'It's not stupid at all. I think . . . I think it's . . . great!'

He frowns. 'Great? You think it's great that I wrecked my car?'

'Yes! I mean, if it helped you in some way. Did it?'

He thinks for a moment. 'Yeah,' he says slowly. 'Yeah, I think maybe it did.'

'But that's amazing!' I say.

And in that brief moment, I don't exactly know why but I'm so happy for him I could burst.

Ram doesn't look quite so enthused. 'Is it amazing, though?' he asks. 'It's going to cost hundreds to fix all those dents. And it's not like I don't have other things to spend my money on right now.' He pauses to glance at Albie in the rear-view mirror.

'Yeah, well maybe it was worth it,' I say.

A hint of a smile tugs at the corners of Ram's mouth. 'Maybe,' he murmurs.

The news comes on the radio. The arrest of Olivia Sinclair's kidnapper is the lead story. We listen to the details in silence.

'Say it, then,' I say.

'What?'

'You know what.'

Ram shakes his head.

I tut. '*I told you so?*'

He doesn't say anything.

'Oh, come on,' I say. 'You must be dying to come out with it. Go on. Get it out of your system.'

'No.'

'No?'

'No. I don't want to. You drew a conclusion based on the information you had available to you at the time.'

I snort. 'You've changed your tune.'

'Look, I shouldn't have given you such a hard time about the Olivia thing.'

'But I was wrong.'

'So? At the end of the day, you were just looking out for your friend. And you were right to. She really did need you.'

No one says anything for a moment.

'I wonder if she fits the profile,' I say.

'Who?'

'The woman who took Olivia. You know, all those articles I looked at.'

'Oh, I don't know. Maybe.'

'It's weird, but I almost feel sorry for her. Like, I'm not saying what she did was right but, I don't know, you must be in a pretty bad place to take someone else's baby.'

'I guess so.'

'I hope they're being kind to her. The police, I mean.'

Ram reaches across and gives my hand a squeeze. 'I'm sure they are,' he says.

We turn off the radio and sit in silence for a while.

'What's that noise?' I ask. A gentle rumbling sound is coming from the back seat.

'I think it might be Albie,' Ram says.

'What?' I twist round to look. Sure enough, the noise is emanating from Albie. I laugh. 'Oh my God, like father, like son.'

'I don't snore!' Ram exclaims.

'Er, yeah, you do.'

'Well, only when I'm really tired.'

'OK, sure. Keep telling yourself that.'

'Do you want to walk home? I can pull over right here.'

'Like you'd dare.'

We grin at each other.

'I meant what I said last night, Frankie,' Ram says.

'About what?'

'About how much I care about you. No matter what happens, you'll always be one of my special people.'

I look down at my lap. My dress is creased from sleeping in it.

'And I meant what I told you about Jojo as well,' Ram continues. 'I honestly didn't look at her as anything more than a friend until that night. I swear, when we were going out, Frankie, there was never anyone else. It was all about you.'

I bite the inside of my cheek.

'You believe me, don't you?' Ram says.

I nod. Because deep down I know Ram wouldn't lie to me, not about something so important.

'Good,' he says. 'Because it's true and I want you to know that.'

'OK. Thanks.'

There's a long pause.

'Are you going to try to make a go of it?' I ask, pulling at a bit of loose skin on my right thumb. 'You and Jojo.'

'God, I don't know,' Ram says, his cheeks reddening a little.

'Would you like to?'

'It's not about what I want,' he begins.

I roll my eyes. 'Oh, just answer the question, Ram. It's not hard. Do you want give things a go with Jojo or not?'

He looks in his rear-view mirror before replying in a low voice. 'Yes. I think I would. If she wanted to, that is. And if the time was right.'

It hurts to hear him say this out loud but a lot less than I thought it would.

'Then you should try,' I say.

'What?'

'You should give it a go, see what happens. I mean, if Jojo is on board, of course.'

'Seriously?'

I shrug. 'Yeah.'

'And you'd be OK with that?'

I take a deep breath before answering. 'Eventually.' And I mean it.

'You're a really good person, Frankie.'

'Tell me something I don't know.'

Ram laughs.

'Another thing,' I say.

'What's that?'

'Don't you dare hurt her, OK?'

'I won't. You have my word.'

'Good. Because if you do, I will hunt you down and make you wish you'd never been born.'

I mean that too.

Chapter 41

Jojo

We stop at a service station for an early lunch. The smell of fried food makes me feel a little queasy, but I manage to force down a cheese and pickle sandwich from Marks and Spencer while Frankie and Ram wolf down Big Macs and fries. While we eat, Ram holds Albie. I still can't get over the sight of the two of them together – father and son. From the wonder in his eyes every time he looks down at Albie, neither can Ram.

'I should change him,' I say, when everyone has finished eating. I hold out my arms so Ram can pass Albie over to me.

'I can do it,' Ram says.

'On your own?'

'Yeah.'

'Are you sure?'

'Jojo, I've changed a nappy before. In fact, I've changed multiple nappies.'

'I know, I just—'

'What?' he asks.

Aside from trips to the bathroom, it'll be the first time I've been apart from Albie in over twenty-four hours, and even though I know it's stupid, and that Albie will be perfectly safe with Ram, I can't help but feel a flutter of fear at the thought of being separated from him, even for just a few minutes.

'Nothing's going to happen, Jojo,' Ram says, his voice gentle.

'I know,' I murmur.

'Listen, if we're going to make this work, we're both going to have to get really good at delegating. Starting right now. You go get some fresh air. I'll take care of this.' He pats Albie's bottom.

I take a deep breath and hand him my backpack. 'Everything's in there,' I say. 'Nappies, wipes. If he's sore, put some nappy rash cream on. Oh, and warm up your hands up before you get him undressed. He cries if they're too cold.'

'Noted,' Ram says, swinging the backpack over his left shoulder. He kisses Albie on the top of his head. 'C'mon, kiddo, let's get you cleaned up.'

'I'll come find you when I'm done,' he adds.

Frankie wants something from the shop, so I head outside on my own. After the stifling heat of the last few weeks, it feels chilly. I zip up my hoodie and walk round the side of the building where I find a cluster of mostly empty wooden picnic tables. I sit down. Without Albie or my backpack, I feel almost naked.

I take my phone out of my pocket and stare at the blank screen. My thumb strokes the 'power on' button but I can't quite bring myself to press it.

'Dessert?'

I look up. Frankie is standing on the other side of the picnic table, holding up a paper bag.

'Dessert?' I repeat numbly.

She sits down opposite me and carefully rips open the bag, revealing two Krispy Kreme doughnuts – an original glazed and a chocolate-iced custard-filled, just like old times. I'm hit with the familiar scent of sweet dough, and with it the collective memory of dozens of Friday afternoons spent licking our sugary fingers on the last lingering leg of the journey home from school.

'Do you want the original glazed all to yourself or do you want a bit of each?' Frankie asks.

'A bit of each, please,' I say. 'I mean, if that's OK.'

Frankie roughly divides the two doughnuts. I insist she takes the bigger half of the chocolate-iced custard-filled. She agrees on the basis that I take the bigger half of the original glazed.

Despite our promise, we're still being overly polite with each other and I get the feeling we're just at the beginning of a long adjustment process.

We munch in silence for a few moments. As usual Frankie gets chocolate icing all around her mouth. And as usual she tries (and fails) to lick it clean with her tongue.

'So,' she says, finally giving in and using a napkin. 'You gonna call them or what?' She nods down at my phone.

'Oh,' I say, ripping my remaining piece of doughnut in half. 'I don't know.'

'I'm not saying you need to have a massive conversation or anything like that. You could even just send a text. I'm just thinking it might be a good idea to let them know you're on your way back. Give them a bit of time to calm down and prepare.'

She's right. Mum and Stacey must be frantic. And yet the

idea of turning on my phone, of facing reality, makes my stomach flip.

'When were you last in contact with them?' Frankie asks.

'Yesterday. Just after I spoke to you on the phone. I texted to let them know Albie and I were OK, and then I turned it off.'

'Jojo, they're going to be going crazy with worry.'

'Do you think I don't know that?'

'Hey, I'm not having a go,' Frankie says. 'I'm just saying maybe it wouldn't be a terrible idea to put their minds at rest a bit.'

'At rest? I'm about to rock up and tell them I'm not going to let them have Albie for themselves after all.'

'Jojo, this isn't just about Albie. They're going to be worried about you too. They're going to want to know you're *both* OK.'

I want to believe her but I can't. I know how much Mum and Stacey love Albie. I know how badly they wanted a baby. No matter how much they care about me, I can't see those feelings trumping the ones they have for Albie.

'Look at it this way,' Frankie says. 'If you turn it on, at least you know what you're walking back into.' She has a point. 'After three,' she commands. 'One, two, three.'

Before I can chicken out, I pick up the phone and turn it on. It seems like for ever before the screen glows into life, my stomach churning as it fills with notification after notification, just as I predicted.

'Whoa,' Frankie murmurs as the messages pile up.

A massive part of me wants to shove the phone into her hands and ask her to delete every last text and voicemail before giving it back to me, all trace of the drama and upset I've caused over the last twenty-four hours wiped clean away. I know I can't, though. Once more, Frankie's right. I need to know what I'm walking back into.

I unlock the home screen.

I have forty-seven missed calls and fifty-eight messages. I show Frankie.

'I have voicemails too,' I say.

'I don't know if this helps, but at least three of them are from me,' Frankie offers.

I'm too anxious to acknowledge her quip. 'They're going to be so angry,' I whisper.

'Maybe,' Frankie says, scrunching up her napkin in her fist. 'But maybe they've had time to think too. Wherever they're at, you won't know unless you listen.'

With newly trembling fingers, I dial voicemail.

'*You have nineteen new messages,*' the robotic voice informs me.

Nineteen. Shit.

'I feel stupid asking this, but if I put it on speaker, will you listen with me?' I ask.

Somehow the idea of listening as a pair seems that bit less scary.

Frankie doesn't answer right away and for a second I'm worried she's about to tell me to get lost. After everything that's happened, I suppose I couldn't really blame her. Instead, she reaches across and takes my hand in hers.

'Course I will,' she says.

The first message was left at 9.35 a.m. yesterday. Already, it feels like a lifetime ago.

'Jojo, it's Stacey. I've just got back from my mum's. Where are you? Can you call me the moment you get this, please?' The stress in her voice is clear. Stacey wears her emotions on her sleeve and this is no exception. I glance up at Frankie.

'It's OK,' she says. 'Just keep going.'

The next message was left twenty minutes later. It's Mum. In the background, I can hear the buzz of the office – phones ringing and photocopiers whirring: 'Jojo, it's Mum,' she says briskly. 'Can you give me a ring back as soon as you get this?'

Stacey left her next message less than half an hour later: 'Jojo, it's Stacey again. Listen, I'm sorry if what I said last night upset you, but running off with Albie is not the answer to things, OK? Come home and we can talk about it. I'm not mad, I promise. I just . . . just call me, please and I'll come get you.'

Then it's Mum's turn again. From what I can work out, she's walking, the click of her high heels clearly audible on the line: 'Jojo, it's me again. I mean it, you need to ring me the second you get this message, OK? Stacey's in such a state I've had to leave work to be with her. I don't know what you're trying to achieve here but running off like this is not helping anyone. Just call us, Jojo, please.'

The next voice I hear is Frankie's: 'Jojo, it's me. Where the flip are you? I've got to be at the salon by midday, remember? If you're not here by eleven, I'm going without you, OK?'

'Sorry,' I say.

Frankie raises an eyebrow.

'I never asked how you did,' I add.

'I did OK,' she says. 'You know, as expected.'

I want to ask for more details but the next message is kicking in. It's Mum again: 'Jojo, I don't know what you think you're playing at but this isn't funny any more. Albie is three weeks old. He needs to be at home, where he belongs.'

'She sounds mad,' I say, biting my thumbnail.

'She sounds worried,' Frankie says. 'Just keep listening.'

The next few messages are of a similar ilk – Mum and Stacey taking it in turns to beg me to come home. In one of the messages, Stacey is crying.

I'm relieved when I hear Frankie's voice again: 'Jojo, it's me. Listen, I hadn't finished talking to you. Can you call me back, please?' And then: 'Jojo, it's me again. I know you're not at your dad's. You really need to ring me.' She sounds especially pissed off in that one.

'Sorry,' I say again.

She waves away my apology.

The next message is from Dad: 'Hey, Jojo, it's your old man. Listen, I don't suppose you could give me a call when you get the chance? It'd be good to chat. It's been a while. Love you.'

The sound of his voice makes my heart ache. In the aftermath of the birth, I fobbed him off over and over again, desperate to avoid having to lie to him.

Frankie gives my hand a squeeze. 'You can call him back later,' she says.

I nod.

Mum continues to leave messages. Sometimes it's just her, sometimes Stacey is in the background, tearfully chipping in.

'We're begging you now, Jojo,' Mum says. 'Just come home. Whatever it is that made you run off like this, we can sort it out. We just want you both home. Please, sweetheart. Just call us back. We love you.'

And then: 'Darling, please, we're going out of our minds here. We just want to know that you're both safe. That's all we care about, OK? That you're both all right.'

She's just saying that, though.

Right?

I look up at Frankie. She nods encouragingly.

There's then a gap of a few hours where Mum and Stacey must have attempted to grab some sleep before leaving a voicemail, their fourteenth, at 6.35 a.m.

'Jojo, it's me,' Mum says. She sounds exhausted. 'Stacey and I have been talking and we . . . we wonder if we might have put a bit too much pressure on you. I don't know, when we suggested the two of us taking Albie on, genuinely we were doing what was best, darling. And yes, I admit it wasn't an entirely selfless act. You know how badly we've longed for a baby. But please believe me when I say we always had your best interests at heart, yours and Albie's.' She pauses and sighs. I can imagine her raking both hands through her hair the way she does when she's tired or stressed. 'But, well, you running off like this, it's forced us to acknowledge that perhaps we've got a bit carried away. The past few weeks, they've been such a blur but if I'm really honest with myself, I knew you were unhappy with the arrangement from the very beginning. I just managed to convince myself that all you needed was a bit of time; that once term started up again and things were official, everything would get easier and you'd get on board . . .' She sighs again. 'Like I said, I knew you were unsure about things but I never for one second thought you'd do something like this. Why didn't you just talk to us, darling?'

'I tried to,' I whisper, a tear rolling determinedly down my cheek. 'So many times.'

'Or maybe you tried to,' Mum continues. 'And we just blocked it out because it wasn't what we wanted to hear . . . What I'm trying to say is, I'm sorry. Stacey and I shouldn't have pushed you the way we did. We were naive to think we could raise Albie as our own without there being serious implications for you. We

344

realize that now. We just want you home, sweetheart. Both of you. Then we can talk. And this time, I promise we will listen. I promise, darling. Just come home. That's all we care about now. I love you, Jojo. So much.'

I raise my eyes to meet Frankie's. She's been holding my hand this entire time. Right now, she's studying me carefully, her head cocked to one side. I wipe away the tear tracks on my cheeks and look back down at my phone.

There's one voicemail left.

There's a pause before I hear Stacey's voice, hoarse and trembling on the line: 'Jojo, I – I just want you do know that I was by your mum's side when she left that message right now and I echo everything she said. We just want you home. Please, Jojo. Just come home.'

'*You have no new messages,*' a robotic voice informs me.

I remove my hand from Frankie's and hang up.

'You OK?' Frankie asks.

I manage a nod.

'They just want you home, Jojo.'

'But what if they're just saying that?' I ask.

'I really don't think they are. In any case, you won't know unless you speak to them.'

I nod again and pick up my phone, turning it over in my hands.

'Thank you,' I say. 'For doing that. You being there just then, it meant a lot.'

For a moment I imagine a universe in which I'd told Frankie the truth from the very beginning. I'd been so afraid of hurting her, of damaging our friendship, that I hadn't even considered the possibility.

'What are friends for, eh?' she says, shrugging.

'I love you, Frankie,' I say.

She blinks, clearly surprised by the suddenness of my declaration.

'You don't have to say it back,' I say quickly. 'I mean, I get it, after everything that's gone down . . .'

She shakes her head and smiles a sad sort of smile. 'I love you too, Jojo. Now, are you going to text your mum back or what?'

With shaking hands, I pick up my phone and compose a message to Mum and Stacey.

> On my way home. We're both fine. I'm sorry I worried you. See you in a couple of hours. Jojo xxx

'We good to go?'

Frankie and I look up in unison. Ram is heading across the grass towards us, Albie in his arms.

'What do you reckon, Jojo?' Frankie asks. 'Ready to go home?'

I take a deep breath and press 'send'.

'Ready,' I reply, sliding my phone back in my pocket.

By the time we get back to Newfield, it's early afternoon.

Ram kills the engine and for a moment no one moves. I catch sight of my reflection in the rear-view mirror. I look terrified, my cheeks drained of colour.

Frankie twists around in her seat. 'It's OK,' she says, reaching for her hand. 'We've got you. Right, Ram?'

'Right,' Ram says.

I nod, count to five in my head, then unclip my seat belt before leaning over to attend to Albie.

We assemble at the bottom of the driveway, Frankie on my right-hand side, Ram on my left, holding Albie, still sleeping in his car seat.

Stacey's face appears at the living-room window. 'Helen!' she calls, her voice just about audible through the glass. *'Helen!'* She moves away from the window.

Frankie's left hand finds my right one. 'I've got you, remember,' she says, as the door opens and Mum and Stacey come down the driveway towards us, barefoot, their arms outstretched. 'I've got you.'

'I know,' I reply, squeezing her hand hard. 'You always did.'

She squeezes back.

'Always will.'

EPILOGUE

Jojo

'Happy birthday to you, happy birthday to you, happy birthday, dear Albie, happy birthday to you!'

Frankie's mum places the sparkler-festooned cake in front of a slightly bewildered-looking Albie, currently installed on Ram's lap, as everyone applauds and snaps photos.

Ram leans in and blows out the oversized number one candle on Albie's behalf. Cue more applause, more photos and Albie's chubby fist reaching for one of the still-burning sparklers.

'Oh no you don't, little man,' Ram says, laughing and hoisting him up and away from the cake.

Albie lets out a yowl of protest.

Frankie leans in to whisper in my ear. 'Poor kid,' she says with a sigh, 'He's gotta be so confused right now.'

'He'll be fine once he's got his hands on some cake,' I reply.

Cake, along with buses, horses, swings, drums and, weirdly, an ancient kids' TV programme from the 1980s called *Button Moon*, is firmly amongst Albie's very favourite things. I should probably add Frankie to that list. I don't know what it is about her, but without fail Albie's face lights up the second she enters the room. He was especially delighted to see her today, whooping with delight when she appeared at the front door with a massive number one balloon tied round her wrist and a bundle of wrapped gifts in her arms. She's been in London for the past few weeks, having won a place on the National Youth Theatre's summer course. She returned to Newfield late last night, the boy she's seeing (someone else from the course), a softly spoken Londoner with cheekbones to die for called Malachai, in tow. He's over by the buffet at the moment, having an impassioned discussion about arts funding with Stacey.

'Does he need rescuing?' I ask, nodding in their direction.

'Nah,' Frankie says. 'He's loving it.'

We watch them for a few seconds. Frankie's right; he's clearly enjoying himself, and so is Stacey from the looks of things, gesticulating wildly the way she always does when she's especially into a subject.

'I really like him,' I say. 'Did I mention that?'

'You did,' Frankie says, smiling. 'Multiple times.'

'OK, good.'

'Stacey seems on good form.'

'Yeah, I know. She and Mum are meeting with a potential surrogate next week.'

'Really? That's great.'

'It may come to nothing. I mean, it's such a complicated process, but this one sounds really promising. She's done it twice before so she knows what's involved, and Mum and Stacey reckon they're getting good vibes from her.'

'So you might end up with a little brother or sister after all?'

I smile. 'If all goes well, yeah.'

The garden is packed with friends and family. My mum is now holding Albie, while Ram helps Frankie's mum with the cake, transferring slices onto paper plates and distributing them amongst the other guests. My dad is busy chatting to Ram's mum, Cheryl, and Mum's sister, my auntie Jen. Maxwell is entertaining Laleh and Roxy with his surprisingly good hula-hooping skills while Bex films the entire thing on her phone. A few metres away, Luca is attempting (unsuccessfully from the looks of things) to chat up Ella. I thought about inviting a few of my Arts Academy friends but eventually decided against it. They all know about Albie and have been overwhelmingly cool about it, but, if I'm honest, I like the fact that at college I'm not defined by my motherhood. It's a bit like leading a double life sometimes, but I'm OK with that. It's been a relief to discover Frankie was right. With a bit of help, I *can* do both.

My eyes drift upwards, settling on the frosted glass of the bathroom window. A year ago today, I was up there giving birth to a baby I didn't even know existed. And now, as that same baby is happily passed from parent to parent to grand-parent, I can't imagine my life any other way. Not that it's been easy. That first conversation with Mum and Stacey was horrendous: painful and emotional and sad and exhausting. They tried not to show it, but their hearts were breaking, and no matter how many times I tried to tell myself that I wasn't responsible for their happiness, the guilt was overwhelming. And yet, I went to bed that night feeling lighter than I had done since Albie had been born.

In the days that followed, more difficult conversations followed. We had to tell Dad, and Ram's mum, and come clean to Grandma and Auntie Jen, and Stacey's family and all the other people we'd told. We had to register the birth and decide on a surname (in the end we kept things simple and went for Albie Bright-Jandu). Plus there were logistics to sort. So many logistics.

Piece by piece, we cobbled together a plan of sorts. Tuesday to Thursday, Cheryl would look after Albie while I was at college, with Ram taking over when he got home from school. He would then drop Albie back at mine around 6 p.m., by which point I'd hopefully be home from college ready to feed and bathe him. If Ram didn't have a shift at the rink, he'd stay and read Albie a bed-time story. Mum managed to negotiate a four-day working week so she could have Albie on Mondays, while Stacey agreed to work from home on Fridays, marking papers and preparing lectures while Albie dozed in his Moses basket at her side. At the weekend, Ram and I were in charge. We spent our days taking it in turns to nap (we were both permanently knackered), or pushing Albie's pram around the park.

As Albie slept, we talked. We talked about Ram's university applications and my jam-packed days at the Arts Academy. We exchanged childhood memories and reminisced over the games and TV shows and toys we've outgrown. We debated stuff in the news, putting the world to rights as we racked up circuit after circuit of the park. But most of all, we talked about Albie.

Although things had changed dramatically at home, I was still conscious of rubbing Mum and Stacey's noses in it somehow. With Ram, I was free to be as besotted as I liked. We regularly stopped the pram and just stared down at him, still in shock as to how we managed to create such a perfect little human being, fascinated by his changing features and evolving personality. We talked about our hopes and dreams for his future and confided our fears about all the things we might get wrong.

We talked about pretty much everything but our relationship, tiptoeing around the subject, trying to ignore the sparks of electricity we felt following every accidental hand brush or shoulder nudge.

Everything changed one damp Saturday in early May. Instead of our usual stomp around the park, we holed up at Ram's house, playing with Albie on the living-room floor. As we tickled his belly and played peek-a-boo and pushed toy cars across the rug, music played in the background. Not records this time (records and crawling babies don't really mix), but a playlist on Ram's Spotify. The song took us both by surprise, stunning us into silence.

'First Day of My Life,' I said softly. 'From New Year's Eve.'

'Yeah,' Ram murmured.

We listened for a moment, the lyrics just as potent as they were all those months ago.

'I listened to it,' I said.

'When?'

'New Year's Day. When I got home.'

'So did I.'

'Really?'

'About five times.'

'Try more like eleven.'

Ram raised an eyebrow.

'You're surprised,' I said.

'Kind of, yeah.'

'How come?'

'I don't know. I guess I assumed it hadn't affected you the same way it affected me.'

'Well, it did,' I said. 'Affect me, I mean. I just . . . things were difficult.'

353

Ram nodded. 'We've never really talked about what happened,' he said.

'No.'

'Should we, do you think?'

'We could try.'

And so we did; we finally let ourselves revisit that night, unpicking it together.

And when we kissed for the first time in over sixteen months, Albie let out a gurgle of appreciation we chose to take as a good omen.

It hasn't been smooth sailing. Although the transition from co-parents to couple has in many ways felt natural and inevitable, it's also been scary and loaded with invisible pressures. The fact is, raising a kid is hard. And maintaining a relationship on top of that is even harder. But every time I get overwhelmed, I figure I'd much rather give things a go with Ram and fail, rather than never even try and spend my entire life wondering what I'd missed out on; what we'd both missed out on.

I'm realistic. I'm seventeen, Ram is eighteen; we have our whole lives in front of us and have no idea what obstacles we might face. But right now, I think I'm OK with that. The most important thing is that Albie is happy, and looking at his face right now as he stuffs it with chocolate cake, his big brown eyes shining with delight, I suspect he might possibly be candidate for the happiest one-year-old on the planet.

'Ooh, cake,' Frankie says, grabbing two paper plates from Ram as he whisks past, blowing me a kiss. 'Here,' she says, passing me one.

'Thanks.'

She lifts up her slice. 'Cheers,' she says.

'Cheers.'

I take a bite. 'Oh my God,' I say. 'Your mum has excelled herself, Frankie. No wonder Albie's so thrilled.'

Frankie grins a chocolaty grin.

We munch in silence for a bit.

'Thank you,' I say.

'What for?' Frankie replies with her mouth full.

'For making me braver than I ever thought I could be.'

She puts her arm around my shoulder and pulls me in close. 'Just doing my job.'

I rest my head on her shoulder and take in the scene in front of me. A garden packed with people who I love and who love me in return. And the cherry on top of the cake – my best friend at my side.

I put down my empty plate and wrap my arms around her waist. 'I love you, Frankie Ricci,' I say,

She drops a kiss on the top of my head. 'Not as much as I love you, Jojo Bright.'

Acknowledgements

Thanks to the entire team at David Fickling Books. I've said it at least a hundred times but I'm going to say it again anyway – I feel ridiculously proud and lucky to be a DFB author.

Special thanks to Rosie Fickling for her passion, enthusiasm, imagination and breathtaking efficiency, David Fickling for his never-ending warmth and encouragement, Phil Earle for almost superhuman levels of energy and dedication and Carolyn McGlone for her calm and kindness (you will be sorely missed!).

Thanks to my agent Catherine Clarke (truly the best), and the glorious team at Felicity Bryan Associates. Goodness, I'm in capable hands.

Thanks to Bella Pearson for her ongoing support and friendship.

Thanks to Beth Ferguson for advising me on police procedure. Any errors are entirely my own.

Thanks to Juno Dawson for making an offhand comment

over dinner in February 2016 that inadvertently planted the seed that grew into this book, and to Non Pratt for always being the ultimate writing date.

Thanks to my writing group buddies: Fiona Perrin, Christina Pishiris, Maria Realf and Sara-Mae Tuson. Their continued support and friendship means the world.

Thanks to all the wonderful schools who have invited me through their doors over the past year. Getting to meet the very people I am writing for is both a privilege and a joy.

As always, thanks to my wonderful friends and family for everything they do.

Finally, thanks to Dylan for always being on hand to brainstorm ideas, introducing me to Bright Eyes, and for gently pointing out the perfect title was right in front of me all along.